I0760447

FANTASY & FAIRYTALES

BOOK TWO

GOLDEN CHAINS

M. LYNN

Edited by Melissa A. Craven
Proofread by Patrick Hodges
Cover design by Covers by Combs
Interior design by Bookly Style

ISBN : 978-1-970052-69-5 (Hardcover)

Also by M. Lynn

The Fantasy and Fairytales series

The True Story of Rapunzel

Golden Curse
Golden Chains
Golden Crown

The True Story of Cinderella

Glass Kingdom
Glass Princess

The True Story of Robin Hood

Noble Thief

The True Story of Sleeping Beauty

Cursed Beauty

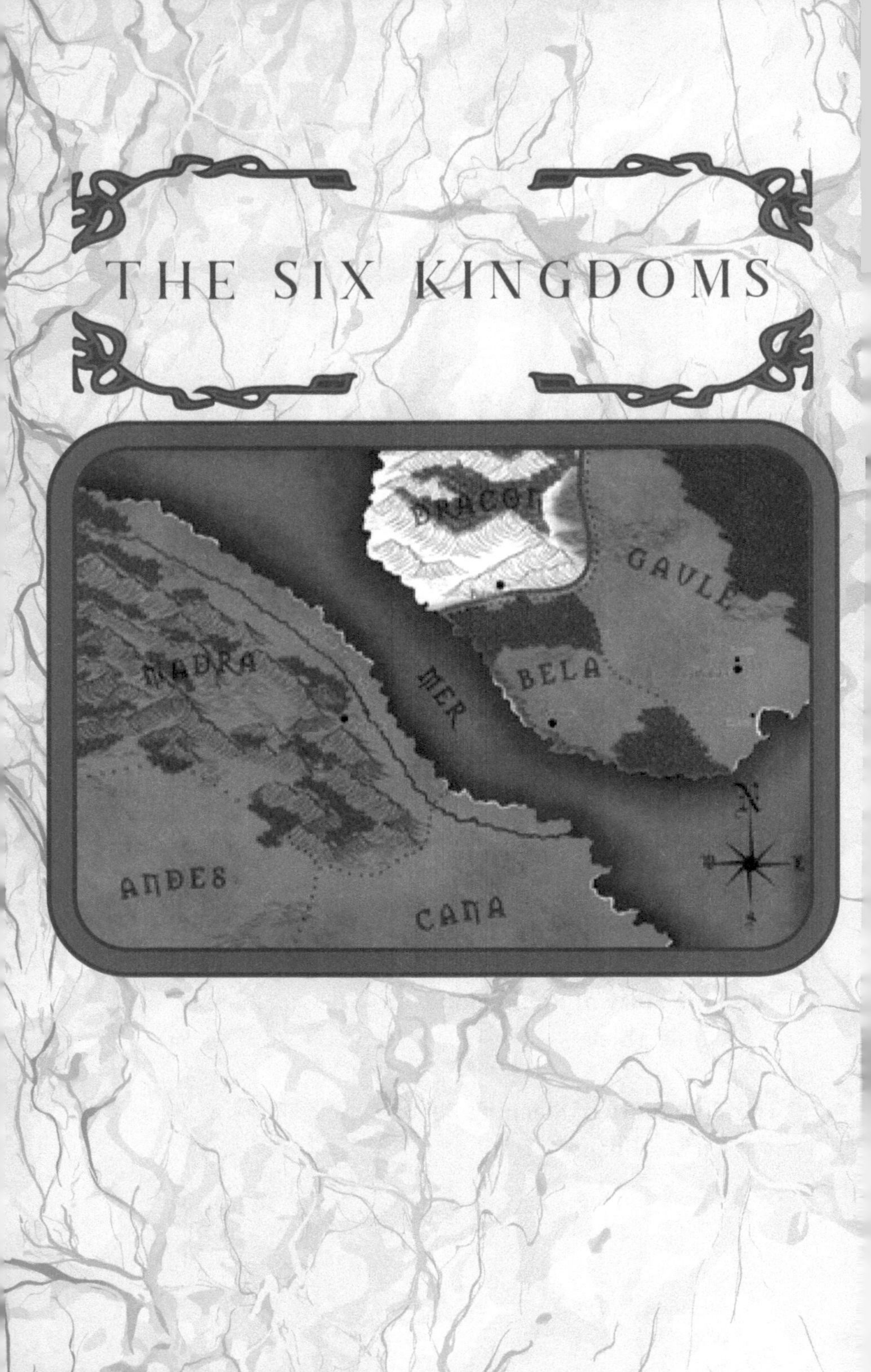
THE SIX KINGDOMS
GAULE
MADRA
MER
BELA
ANDES
CANA

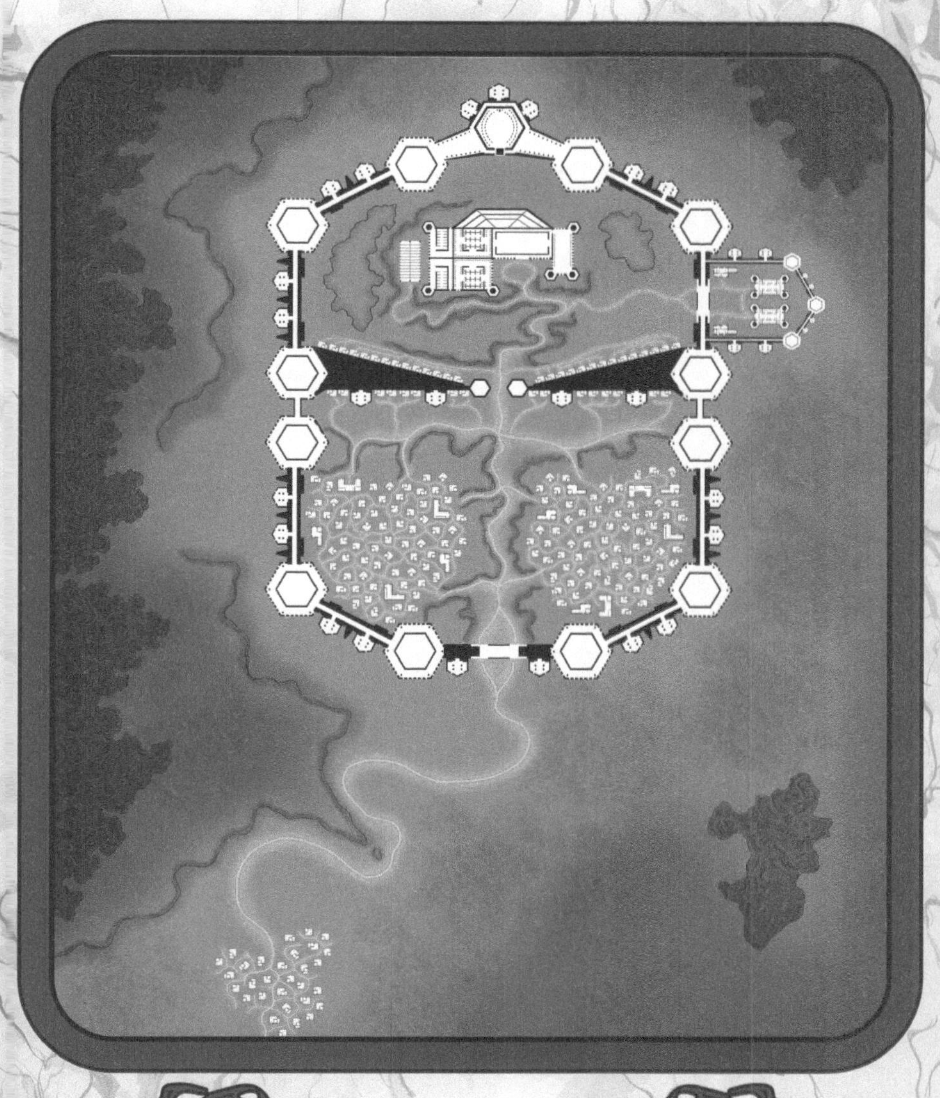

PALACE OF GAULE

To all those having to battle for their own freedom.
Not all chains are seen..

PROLOGUE

Freedom was a dream from a far-off place that no longer existed. It was a concept that made no sense to Matteo Basile. What was choice? He'd never had any. His life was a series of orders, unspoken but wholly felt.

His queen stared down at him with unforgiving eyes. What were they doing past the border? It was his first time setting foot in the kingdom that once belonged to his family, in Bela, but he couldn't fight the warmth that spread through him. He was home.

"Madame." He bowed low as he'd been doing his entire life. For he served La Dame of Dracon and would no doubt serve her until the end of his days.

"Matty, my boy." Warmth filled her voice and when he finally rose to stare into her dazzling emerald eyes, he was transfixed.

Was it her magic? Or simply her beauty?

"How does it feel to be home?" she asked.

What was she expecting from him? His eyes flicked to his father who stood at her side. He gave his son a pleading look.

Warren Basile had been in La Dame's household since Matteo was a child. He served as an advisor, consort, even a lover. He was known to sit calmly on his seat by the throne as his son was beaten before his eyes. Not with fists. No, nothing in Dracon was ever done without magic.

Matteo inclined his head. "Bela is not my home, your Majesty."

A smirk spread across her face and she nodded. "It is now." Raising a hand at her side, she snapped her fingers and her horse was brought forward. They'd camped on the border spanning Dracon and Bela for the night and now stood overlooking a grassy plane.

La Dame leaped into her saddle with a grace that gave no indication of her age. No one in Dracon knew how old their mistress was, but Bela was destroyed centuries ago and the stories claimed she was the one who finally bested the Basiles.

His ancestors.

He climbed into his saddle slowly, his bruised ribs screaming in protest. He'd tried to fight her, escape her magic as it pounded into him the previous night and it only ended in bruises.

As he rode down into his ancestral homeland, he didn't feel like a Basile. He never had. They were said to be powerful, but his magic sputtered and died every time he tried to call it forth.

La Dame pushed her long, shining black hair over her shoulder and regarded him once again. Her kindness was a lie.

"Soon, Matty, all will be explained."

"Why are we in Bela?" he asked.

She raised a brow at his audacity in speaking without permission. Her magic whipped over him, slamming him forward against his horse.

"How would you like to meet your family?"

"My..." He didn't have any family other than his father. They were the last of the Basiles. It was why La Dame kept them close. The legends spoke of power he should have as the first in his generation of the Basiles. Where was that power? Each night, he lay awake praying for it to come. To set him free.

"Your family, yes. You see, there is something your father never told you." She scrutinized him. His expression must have satisfied her for she nodded. "Your father had an older brother."

Matteo pulled up on the reins and his horse jolted to a stop. "I have an uncle?"

The familiar pull of her power forced his horse to begin moving again.

"Had. Your uncle is dead."

The hope that'd risen up in Matteo shattered in his chest. For a moment, he'd thought maybe there was someone to save him from this life.

La Dame continued. "Viktor evaded me his entire life, but his daughter won't be able to stay away."

His daughter?

La Dame laughed, all kindness gone, replaced by the wickedness he knew too well. "Yes, my boy. You are not the oldest of your generation. Persinette was born two weeks before you. But, don't you worry. You will reunite with her soon. I am going to bring Persinette Basile home."

Home? If the girl had any sense, she'd stay away. Why didn't La Dame send someone to force her to come?

As if sensing his question, La Dame sighed. "I don't know what Phillip did, Matteo. When I first issued the curse, he managed to twist it somehow. I cannot bring the cursed one to me against their will. She must choose to come."

La Dame kicked her horse to speed up, throwing a few final words over her shoulder. "I'm counting on you to show her how to grovel. You're good at that."

Matteo raised his face to the bright morning sky. This Persinette must have the power he'd never had. He didn't know where she was or how La Dame would get her to come, but he hoped more than anything she was stronger than he'd ever been.

CHAPTER 1

The overwhelming reek of urine swirled in the damp air. Etta sat in the same cell she'd helped Edmund escape from. How was that for fate?

How long ago had that been? Days? Weeks? Day bled into night in the underground dungeons.

Heavy footsteps sounded against the stone as they neared. Her first instinct was to press herself against the wall, letting the dark hide her cowering frame.

She squeezed her eyes shut. She was Persinette Basile. She didn't fear anything.

If only that were true.

Since her capture, the guards tried their best to break her, and they nearly succeeded. She wasn't the same girl who'd left with Tyson and Edmund in tow.

Her mind drifted to them, trying to block out the guard who'd stopped outside her cell.

Were they okay? Alex might hate her, but at least he hadn't ordered their capture.

A key rattled in the lock and Etta kept her gaze firmly planted on the ground. She pulled in her knees and hugged them to her chest to protect herself.

The guard laughed. She recognized the cruel sound. He'd been there often.

A tear slipped down her cheek. She didn't cry for her bruised skin or aching limbs, but for the king who ordered it. He wasn't the man she'd thought he was.

She knew the pain was coming before the guard's boot slammed into her. "That'll teach you to use magic against us."

She cried out and clamped her teeth down on her lower lip, tasting blood. She'd never used her magic against any of them. Her greatest crime was being born.

He kicked her again, and all strength left her as she fell back. A meaty hand wrapped around her arm, wrenching her off the ground. She struggled to get her feet beneath her as a fist pounded into her stomach.

She'd taken beatings before, mostly when fighting her father, but she hadn't been helpless then. At the thought of her father, a sob racked her body.

"Lance," a voice cut through the dark. One she recognized as well.

Lance released her and her legs shook, but she remained upright. He turned to Geoff.

"You're relieved for the night," Geoff said. "Go get some sleep."

Lance grunted and left the way he'd come.

Etta refused to be grateful to Geoff because she wasn't any better off with him than Lance. He stepped toward her in a flash and she pressed her back to the wall.

One side of his mouth curved up, and he cocked his head. "The king's protector is scared."

She tried to shake her head but it wouldn't move.

"Fitting. You should fear me, girl. Your father killed my king. You betrayed yours." He slammed his palm against the wall next to her head and pressed himself up against her. His sour breath was hot on her face as he leaned in. "It's my turn to be at the king's side now." His hand skimmed down her arm, inching over the front of her filthy shirt. "I can see why he liked you though."

She stood stock still as he continued to explore her. His touch sent a shiver down her spine and her breath lodged in her throat.

"Don't touch me," she spat.

He laughed and pushed away from her. "You aren't worth it. Even the king agrees."

Her lip quivered, but she held in her tears.

"He hasn't come to see you, has he?" Geoff asked, spreading his hands wide. "I'm all you've got."

Another guard appeared and dropped a wooden bowl of grainy mush at her feet. It spattered her legs, and she stared down into it until her cell was locked once more.

When she was alone again, she sank back to the floor and curled around herself. In her state, she couldn't even feel her magic. The only thing that broke through the numbness was the tug of the curse connecting her to a man she hoped she'd never see again.

She wished he wasn't the same man she dreamed of every time she closed her eyes.

Strip back the layers of lies she'd lived her life by, take away the persona she'd crafted, and all that was left was a shattered girl with nothing left to give.

The inner gates of the palace remained closed, cutting them off from the people living beyond. King Alexandre knew it was a matter of security, but it didn't seem right. He nodded to the guards in the tower to open the gate before marching through.

Geoff walked at his side as he'd been doing for weeks. He wasn't officially the new protector. Alex couldn't yet bear to name him that, but he'd taken on the role.

"How is the prisoner?" He didn't need to voice her name to be understood.

Geoff shrugged. "She's a hard one, your Majesty."

"Geoff, for weeks we've been offering to move her from the dungeons and for weeks she's refused. I'm at the end of my patience." Unable to face her himself, he'd set Geoff to make a deal with her and he'd failed. Just the thought of Etta sitting in that cell was enough to steal his breath. "What more can we do?"

"Do, sire? Her crimes are grave. You'd be better served by letting her rot."

Alex suppressed his growl. Geoff voiced what many of the people thought. But she was Etta. He stopped walking and stood at the crest of the grassy incline. A narrow road meandered along the hillside connecting the palace with the ruined village beyond. He closed his eyes and saw her as she'd been that day in the forest. Her rare smile. Her golden hair. How was he supposed to reconcile that girl with the one he now kept as prisoner?

Anders joined Alex and Geoff as Alex surveyed the land beyond the castle, reminding himself what it was he was protecting.

"We must command the nobles near the western border to gather their forces."

Anders shook his head with a scowl. "The village is already lost to us."

They'd received a messenger that morning who informed them of an attack on one of the villages near the western edge of Gaule, near the border of Bela.

"There are still people there and they need aid." Alex turned back to look up at the great walls of his castle. How long would they remain intact once the magic folk came for them?

"Sire." Anders put a hand on Alex's arm to stop him. "Let Duchess Moreau deal with the people. No need for others to call their men from the fields quite yet." He paused. "There's more. The attackers seem to have taken up Persinette's name as some sort of rallying cry. They know you have her and to them, she is a symbol. It's best to distance yourself from it. Once it is dealt with and the crops are in, you can have your army. Your nobles will see to it."

Alex shielded his eyes against the sun and regarded his two guards. Were they right? Waiting could cost them dearly.

"He's right, your Majesty," Geoff said. "There are more pressing matters than attacks on the border. Our reports indicate activity in Bela."

"Bela is a desolate land. No people reside there."

"That used to be true, but we now know La Dame has moved her court to that so-called desolate land."

Alex breathed out slowly, reminding himself he was king. It didn't matter if he was prepared for it. War was coming. A war they couldn't win.

"Why the devil would she be in Bela?"

"Recruitment?" Anders asked. "Maybe she's hoping the magic folk flood from Gaule to her forces."

Alex considered that. The histories claimed La Dame was an even bigger foe of Bela than Gaule. It didn't make sense.

"We need eyes across the border. Send someone."

"Yes, sire," Geoff said. "I think Lance will suit."

Alex turned to walk back through the gates and pressed a hand to his side. It still ached with phantom pains. For weeks, he'd been sleeping fitfully and then waking in agony. Part of him thought it was guilt. Another part knew it was magic.

"Are you well, sire?" Anders asked.

Alex ignored his question. "Have Duke Renoir send a small force to aid Duchess Moreau in the villages that have been attacked. Make it known that he must also provide healers. Then I'd like one-hundred royal guardsmen prepared to march." He met his captain's gaze. "You will lead them."

"But you need me here," Anders argued.

Alex shook his head. Getting the captain away from his scheming sister would do both of them good.

"I gave you a command, Captain."

Anders scowled as he issued a short bow and walked back the way they'd come.

"I tend to agree with the captain." Geoff didn't bother with the respect Alex deserved. "The people near the border have long harbored magic folk. We should leave them to their fates."

Alex's eyes blazed as he rounded on his guard. "Get out of my sight."

"But, sire, I'm your protector." His words cut through Alex.

He took a step toward Geoff and placed a hand on the hilt of the sword at his waist. "Say that again and I'll run this straight through your heart."

Geoff's jaw dropped open. He stood still for a stunned moment before turning and walking away with quickened steps.

Alex scrubbed a hand across his face. Protector. Only one person could hold that title and she'd betrayed him.

He didn't understand how the Etta who'd been at his side was actually Persinette. His oldest friend. The girl who had grown up with him only to be exiled and hunted. But she wasn't a girl any longer, and she'd come for her revenge. Only, he still didn't know what that revenge was. She had appeared loyal. She saved Edmund and Tyson. How did that fit into the monster he wanted to believe she was?

Alex's stormy face made servants scurry away as his feet took him to the stables. They seemed empty now without the two horses that should have been there. Tyson's was a prince's horse, beautiful and strong. Verité was a shit.

Weeks had passed since they left and he still couldn't adjust to a palace that now seemed devoid of love.

He hadn't visited his mother, but she remained confined to her rooms for hiding Persinette's true identity and sending Tyson away from the palace under the traitor's care. Yet, she wasn't the one who plagued his thoughts day and night.

It was the girl who sat in his dungeons. The one he'd thought he loved. The one he didn't know at all.

He stood beside the horse pen, gripping the metal fence so hard his knuckles turned white. "Dammit," he breathed, hanging his head. "Etta." He needed to see her, but he couldn't. Not yet. Not when he was still so angry. He hated himself for leaving her there for weeks. Alex wanted to move her back into her palace rooms to continue her confinement there, but he hadn't issued the plea directly to her himself.

"Your Majesty," a small voice sounded behind him.

He sighed and turned to take in his betrothed. Amalie held such a delicate beauty it was as if she might blow away in the wind.

"Lady Amalie." His voice softened. "I've told you before to call me Alex."

Her forehead scrunched, but she nodded. "My father told me to seek you out."

"Of course he did." Alex rubbed his chin. Lord Leroy had been pushing them together since Amalie came for the ball more than a month before. Her sister had been sent back to her husband, but the younger girl was forced to stay. Leroy probably thought Alex was going to back out of the betrothal.

He had to admit, it'd crossed his mind. He'd even planned the words he'd use. But that was when he thought he wanted to be with Etta. Now he didn't know what he wanted, but the kingdom needed a queen.

"Would you like me to leave, si—Alex?"

Guilt warred inside of him as he watched her guarded expression. He'd never treated her poorly, but he hadn't exactly been kind either. And she was still young. Like his brother.

That thought kicked him in the gut and he leaned forward with his hands on his knees. His brother was wholly unprepared to be out in the world, magic or no. Part of Alex knew he'd never see Tyson again. Another part told him to do anything he could to change that.

But he was king and must rule a kingdom that harbored an extreme hate for magic. Weeks ago, he'd hated it as well. Then he learned three of the people he loved most in the world had a power he couldn't have even imagined.

"Are you okay?" Amalie asked tentatively.

He straightened and closed his eyes for a brief moment, breathing deeply. "No."

"Oh." Her lips pursed. "Okay then."

"Would you walk with me, Amalie?" He told himself it was because he'd feel bad about sending her away, but in that moment, the truth was he couldn't bear to be alone.

She nodded and looped her arm through his when he held it out to her. Her loose fitting, yellow dress blew in the wind as it whipped through the streets. Their steps took them through the outer castle grounds.

Neither of them spoke as Alex led them to his favorite spot. Near the abandoned North tower, there were steps leading up to a section of the wall. In war, archers lined the top. In peace, there was nothing but ghosts.

Alex helped Amalie up the steps. Her breath caught as she took in the view of Gaule.

"Stunning, isn't it?" Alex asked.

"Sometimes I forget about the Gaule that exists beyond the walls of the castle or my father's estate."

He dropped her arm and sat atop the wall. She lowered herself beside him and took off her shoes to place them next to her.

"I don't spend much time out there either," he admitted.

"But you're the king. Surely you could if you wanted to."

He laughed harshly. "You'd be surprised how little freedom I have."

She smiled sadly and raised her eyes to the horizon where the sun was beginning to set. The Black Forrest stretched toward the edge of their view and memories assaulted Alex. He couldn't escape them.

"I went into the Black Forrest," he said. "Even spent the night in there."

Amalie's eyes widened and her tiny mouth fell open. "That must have been terrifying."

Alex shook his head as images flashed in his mind. Etta standing before him, vulnerable. Her blond hair shining as slivers of moonlight illuminated the night. They'd just escaped the attack on the village and yet, he couldn't remember a night so insanely perfect.

"There's this part of the woods where bright flowers decorate the ground as far as the eye can see. I've never seen anything as magnificent as I did that night."

"Is everything we've been told a lie?" she asked.

His eyebrows knitted together. "What do you mean?"

"The Black Forrest is not a place of nightmares. The people we've trusted are not what they seem. Magic… it's not really evil, is it?" Tears shone in her eyes and she wiped them away quickly. "I'm sorry. I shouldn't be saying this to the king."

Something in her eyes told him to trust her and he was desperate for anyone to trust. He put his hand over hers. "I don't know."

"I know some people with magic are bad, horrible people. La Dame is evil. But Tyson… Do you miss him?"

"Every day."

"I was there when he found out about his magic."

Alex turned to her. "How? You didn't come until the ball."

She smiled sadly. "No, your Majesty. The ball was the first time you noticed I was here. I'd been living at my father's palace residence for months." She studied her hands. "I may have been avoiding you."

"Why?" When she continued to look down, he hooked his fingers beneath her chin and tilted her head up. "Why?"

Truth warred in her eyes before it finally broke free. "I don't want to marry you."

He took his hand away and released a low chuckle. "Is that all?"

"Sire... Alex, we are betrothed. We don't have a choice in that. The ceremony was done when we were children. It is binding in the laws of Gaule."

"I know."

They were quiet for a long moment before her voice broke through again. "Do you think Tyson is okay?"

"I have to believe he is. And don't forget, Edmund is with him."

She blew out a heavy breath. "I wish Etta still was." Her eyes widened at her own words. "I'm sorry. I didn't mean that. I know she's the daughter of Viktor Basile. Like I said before, some magic is evil."

Her words didn't sit well with him. He'd never even seen Etta's magic. She'd never used it on him or anyone in the castle. Was it evil?

The words were out before he could stop them. "I loved her."

She slid closer and tucked her arm into his. "I know."

"You do?"

"Everyone in the palace knew. I'm so sorry, Alex."

"As my betrothed, aren't you supposed to be jealous?" He laughed at the ridiculousness of it all.

"I loved Tyson." She sighed. "I do love him, present tense. You should have seen him when he first used his power. He was so happy. I pretend he still is, and that smile haunts my dreams." She peered up at him. "Do you still love her?"

Words caught in his throat, thickening his voice. He shook his head. "I can't."

"Loving someone is something you can always do. It's the hate that takes effort."

"You're not nearly as shy as you seem to be."

She smiled. "And you're not as frightening. Can I give you a piece of advice?"

He nodded.

"Release the queen mother from her confinement. I've been spending time with her in her rooms and I think you could both use each other."

"You're right. She's all I have now."

Amalie squeezed his arm. "Not all. Whatever the future holds for our marriage, right now we can be friends."

He wrapped an arm around her shoulders and squeezed. "I could use a friend."

CHAPTER 2

"Persinette," a tiny voice whispered from the cell next to hers. "Are you awake?"

Etta crawled toward the far wall. She couldn't see those on the other side, but it helped to feel close to the other magic folk being held in the cells.

Henry and Analise shared a cell next to hers and at times, they were the ones who kept her going.

They were her people.

They knew who she was and the hope they'd spoken of in those first days still burned in her mind.

"Henry." She placed a palm against the stone. "Are you okay?"

"Yea, I just wanted to hear your voice." A beat of silence stretched between them. "I'm scared."

Her breath shook as she blew it out. "You listen to me," she said. "We're going to be okay."

In the weeks since her arrest, Etta had learned a lot about the people held in the dungeons.

Footsteps echoed through the cavernous halls and Etta scurried back into the corner of her cell.

"No," Henry yelled before they could see the visitor. "Leave her alone."

"Henry, don't," Etta called. She couldn't have Geoff or Lance's wrath fall on the boy.

Henry tried to yell again, but his words were cut off as Analise quieted him. Geoff hadn't been there in over a day and he was due. But these steps were off; they weren't made by heavy boots. Etta listened closer and when the queen mother rounded the corner, she leaped to her feet, regretting it instantly.

Nausea overwhelmed her, and she doubled over as a wave of dizziness threatened to drag her under its current.

"Persinette." Her name was a whisper on Queen Catrine's lips.

Etta collapsed onto her knees and raised her eyes to take in the familiar woman, relief surging through her. She'd been prepared for another beating.

"Your Majesty," Etta croaked. "You'll have to forgive me if I don't bow."

The breath hissed from the queen mother's lips as she stepped closer. The orange glow from the lantern in her hand struck Etta, illuminating the discolored skin where old bruises faded and new ones stood dark.

"Alex promised me he'd ordered you to be made comfortable."

Hearing his name sent a chill over Etta. "Don't I look comfortable?" She waved a hand around her bare cell. "Your son would like nothing more than to see me sent to the hangman."

"That isn't true."

"I'm surprised to see you. It's been weeks since I was put here."

"Oh, Etta." Catrine sighed. "You must feel so abandoned. I hadn't forgotten about you. Alex has had me confined to my rooms for concealing your identity and your magic from him. He released me tonight."

Etta collapsed back onto her heels. "I should have known. The curse exists for a reason. The Durands and Basiles have always been enemies. How could I let myself trust a Durand?"

"My son is not like his ancestors."

"Your son has kept me locked in here. He's had me beaten again and again." She scooted toward the cell bars to look into the queen mother's face. "If he ever lets me out of here, I'll kill him."

A smile tilted one corner of Catrine's mouth. "I'm glad to see this place hasn't broken you, Etta."

"No matter what you people do to me, you won't break me." She raised an arm to point one finger to her head as she struggled to stand. "Bela exists in here. It goes beyond physical pain. It's who we are." Anger rushed through her and she sucked in a breath. "Bela is everywhere. In your villages. In your armies. We're hidden and we're ready. We're tired of persecution. Bela is coming for you and you don't stand a chance."

Catrine seemed unaffected by the words. "You should take the king's deal."

"I know nothing of any deal." Confusion tempered her anger.

"He's been offering it to you for weeks—since the day after you were brought here. He wants you moved to your rooms in the palace and you have been refusing. He only asks for your cooperation in the war that's coming."

Etta stared at the queen mother in blank accusation. She stepped toward the bars. "You Durands might have shifting loyalties, but I'm a Basile and I won't leave my people in these cells. I will suffer what they suffer. You can't take that from me."

Catrine lifted her chin and scanned Etta's cage with a shake of her head. "We could be great allies, Persinette. I know the stories. A fully powered Basile can defeat La Dame."

Etta's stomach clenched. She'd thought of little else since her imprisonment, but she was not who they wanted her to be. She gestured to her surroundings. "Do I look fully powered?"

"No." Catrine's dark eyes bore into Etta's. "But your words are that of a queen." She turned and left, her steps echoing through the stone prison long after she was gone.

Etta laid back against the cool floor and looked up to the pitch-black ceiling. Catrine's plea had been desperate but Etta wasn't ready to give in.

"Etta?" Henry asked after a while.

"Yeah?"

"Are you our queen?"

If it hadn't been for the curse, she'd have been born in the palace of Bela and raised to rule. Instead, all she could do for her people was stay in that cell in solidarity with them. Her one act of loyalty was to be a symbol. But she wanted to do more, give them something to fight for. Something to believe in. Whether the Belaen people ever had true freedom or not, it could never be taken from them.

She rolled over. "Yes, Henry. I am your queen."

Maybe she wasn't born to serve the curse. If she made it out of the dungeons, she'd lead her people against those who would oppress them.

But she'd practically declared war on Gaule, so who was she kidding?

She'd never make it out.

Alex enjoyed spending time with Amalie. She reminded him of his brother. Amalie began accompanying him to many of his meetings and helping with kingly duties. She was especially good with the people, a skill he sometimes lacked. She was going to make a good queen, and that thought sent his head spinning.

Her arrow flew wide of the target, yet again, as he attempted to instruct her.

"Brother," Camille said, joining them. She gave Amalie a harsh look that was then turned on Alex.

"What is it, Camille?" he asked.

"Why did you send Anders to the border?"

"I don't have to explain myself to you."

She huffed. "He's the captain of your guard."

"And he'll serve me well at the border."

She stepped closer and leaned in, dropping her voice. "You're going to regret this."

"Watch yourself, sister." He stepped back. "Dine with me this evening. I think it's time we discuss an advantageous marriage."

"Excuse me?"

"You're eighteen years old. It is time."

"What about your marriage?" She eyed Amalie.

Alex sighed. "Amalie has a few more years before she is of age."

"I'm not leaving the palace. I'm next in line to your throne."

"And you can be next in line from your husband's estate. The matter is decided, Camille."

She narrowed her eyes and used her cane to push Amalie aside so she could hobble across the training yard in a rush of fury.

A piercing pain shot through Alex's skull and he cried out. His guards came running as he doubled over and the pain traveled down through his abdomen.

"Your Majesty," one of his guards said, gripping his arm. "Is everything okay?"

Alex shook his head. "I need the healer."

"The royal healer went with the troops."

"Then take me to the outer castle." He gritted his teeth as his head throbbed like he'd smacked it against a wall.

His legs were suddenly too weak to support him, so his guards lifted him and rushed out of the inner palace and through the streets. Amalie followed close behind.

By the time they arrived at the healer's shop, Alex could barely lift his head. They barged through the door and a dark-skinned man jumped to his feet.

"What is this?" he asked, eying the guard's uniforms. He stepped closer. "Your Majesty? Put him there." He pointed to a bed along one wall.

The guards set Alex down and pain shot through him. His breath came out in short pants as he grit his teeth to keep a scream at bay.

The healer shooed the others out. "You can remain, my dear," he said to Amalie. "Tell me what happened."

She wrung her hands together. "We were practicing archery and then suddenly he was overtaken with pain."

Cool fingers pressed against his forehead and the healer spoke. "No fever. Good. We can begin to rule out illness as the cause of your pain." He leaned in toward Alex's face and seemed to be examining one spot.

"Why is it red?" Amalie asked.

The healer straightened and stepped back to run a hand through his hair. Alex watched him with glazed eyes. What did he know? There was fear in his voice.

Another presence entered the room.

"Father," the girl snapped. "What is he doing here?"

Alex recognized that voice, but he couldn't place it. All his mind could focus on was the pain.

"I couldn't turn the king away," the healer whispered to his daughter.

"You should have."

"No," he said. "Don't you see what this is?"

The next time the healer spoke, it was to Alex. "Sire, can you describe what has happened."

Alex groaned. "I get these sudden bouts of pain and weakness. I've never experienced anything so horrid as these last few weeks."

"This is not the first time this has happened?" the healer asked.

"No. Sometimes I wake up in pain, other times it hits randomly."

"No," the familiar girl sobbed. "What are they doing to her?"

Her words made no sense.

The healer shook his head. "This is why you should have left me there, Maiya. That girl is too important."

"Father, I couldn't."

"You betrayed your people. I won't say you didn't."

Maiya hiccupped back another sob.

"What's wrong with him?" Amalie asked.

Both father and daughter flinched as if forgetting they weren't alone. The healer thought for a moment. "I have a tonic that will help for the time being but it won't prevent it from happening again."

He went to a table laden with bottles and began to mix them. "It will also put you to sleep so you'll be spending the night here."

He turned to Amalie. "Dear, you can return to your residence. We have him from here."

Amalie hesitated before nodding. She brushed a hand over the top of Alex's head. "Feel better."

When she was gone, the healer helped Alex sit up, and he was face to face with the healer's daughter. It was her. The girl from the village. The one who'd turned Etta in. If he'd had any energy, he'd despise her for taking his Etta away, even if that girl never existed.

But she'd also helped him during the village attack. "It seems you save me once again."

Maiya smiled sadly, tears still hanging in her lashes.

The healer held a cup to Alex's lips and the most delicious liquid slid down his throat. It tasted of honey. Drowsiness overtook him immediately, and he laid back. Hands pressed into the bare skin underneath the collar of his shirt and the pain began to ebb away as warmth filled him. He'd never felt so at peace as he drifted off.

Two people spoke in hushed tones as Alex woke and everything came rushing back to him.

"Do you think she's okay?" the girl asked.

"I think the extent of his injuries last night gives us the answer to that," her father answered.

"We have to get her out of there."

"We must be patient. Our queen will not forgive us if we act in haste."

Queen? Were they speaking of his mother? In his half-awake state, none of their words registered. He shifted on the bed and the voices stopped immediately.

The healer rushed toward him. "You're awake, your Majesty. Good."

"What time is it?" Alex asked.

"Nearly noon."

"What?" Alex shot up, marveling at being pain free for the first morning in weeks. He'd missed dinner the previous night with his mother and sister, not to mention a full morning of meetings.

"The girl who came with you last night returned earlier, but you needed your sleep. That tonic is strong."

"I have to go." Alex jumped from the bed and pulled on his boots.

"When it happens again," the healer began, "return to us."

Alex stopped at the door and turned, finally taking in the healer and his daughter with a lucid mind. They had magic. They were breaking the law with every breath.

The healer met his eye, not in challenge but in question. Pierre. Alex remembered him now. Maiya revealed Etta's identity to him to save her father Pierre.

What was Alex going to do? They'd risked everything in helping him.

Alex shifted his eyes away and shook his head as he ducked out of the doorway and hoped he was doing the right thing.

His father would be ashamed of him. First, he'd let Edmund go. Then he didn't chase down his brother. Now these two. It seemed everyone he was protecting went against the laws of Gaule and the will of his father.

But his father was no longer there. Alex was king and he wouldn't condemn the innocent to die.

It was for those reasons he'd instructed his guards to remove Etta from the cells. She had magic. She was the daughter of his father's killer. But he wouldn't leave her to rot.

If only she hadn't refused his mercy.

He waved to the guards manning the inner gate as he strode by and crossed the courtyard to the front steps. Once inside the great entryway, his duties beckoned for his attention. Geoff was speaking to two of the servants when Alex spotted him. He took his leave of the girls and ran toward his king.

"Sire, we had no idea where you were." He bowed.

"Amalie didn't tell you I was with the healer in the outer castle?"

"We questioned her, your Majesty, and she swore she didn't know. She was quite adamant."

Alex suppressed a smile. He'd have to thank her later.

"A few of the nobles have been looking for you. Lord Leroy has been yelling at all the servants to find you."

Alex adjusted his sleep-wrinkled clothing and began walking. "They can wait. I must see my mother."

Geoff motioned to two other guards and the three of them escorted him to his mother's door. Her personal guard stood outside of it. He was a young man, no older than Alex, and the queen mother trusted him. But Alex had learned not to trust anyone. Including his mother.

The guard opened the door to her rooms and Alex shut it behind him, keeping Geoff from following him.

His mother sat on her velvet couch with her needlework in her lap. She looked up as the door shut and her needle fell from her grasp. She pushed the material off her lap and stood.

"Alexandre," she breathed. "You missed dinner last night and I wasn't sure I'd see you."

Alex walked toward her and some of the cracks that'd formed over the last few weeks began to fill. He hadn't visited her in her confinement. He'd been too angry. All remnants of that anger faded away as he watched her.

"I released you days ago and I'm told you still haven't left your rooms."

She lowered her gaze. "That isn't exactly true. I went to the dungeons last night."

Alex froze, his heart pounding in his ears. She'd seen Etta. He sank down into a chair across from her. She sat back down slowly.

"You went to see her."

"I did."

He rubbed a hand across his eyes. "What did she say?"

A flash of fear crossed her face, but she shook it away. "I'm not going to tell you what you've done is right, Alexandre. You want me to say she revealed some evil plan, that she truly is our enemy. She was angry; I won't deny that. She said some things I won't repeat to the king. I'm afraid, son."

"You're scared? Of Etta?"

"Aren't you? That's why you had her brought back here and locked up. We all know the stories of the Basiles."

His eyes snapped to hers, remembering what he'd been told after Viktor's death. "You're saying it's true? You're telling me they're those Basiles? It's a common enough Belaen name."

She reached out to place her hand on his. "That's exactly what I'm telling you. Persinette and Viktor Basile are the last descendants of the legendary line."

"The line that has been true to Gaule for generations... before the magic purge."

"Not by choice. The legends are true. The Basiles have been cursed to protect the Durands for generations. Etta is tied to you."

He jumped to his feet and stumbled away from the chair to pace the length of the room. "How is any of this possible?"

His mother's somber eyes bore into him. "Our world is one where impossibilities rule the land. Nothing is sacred. Nothing is forbidden. There is no true good or wholly evil. Everything we think we know is about to be challenged, my dear boy. Gaule is no longer protected. Now all we can do is survive."

She got to her feet and walked toward him. "Persinette Basile could have been our greatest ally. Now I'm not so sure."

"I have to see her."

"Be warned, she has not been treated well. That was the main reason I wanted to see you. Please, Alexandre, tell me you did not order such rough treatment."

"What are you talking about?" he snapped.

His mother sighed. "You will see. Go. Make it right."

CHAPTER 3

Etta woke feeling better than she had in weeks. Warmth flooded her body throughout the night, putting her into a deep slumber. Her limbs no longer ached as if she'd been run over by a herd of horses.

She sat up slowly, expecting the pain to come. Scanning her pale skin, her eyes widened at the sight of unmarked skin. The bruises were gone. Her fingers probed her face gently and found it healed as well.

Even the weakness that constantly plagued her was gone. She felt like the old Etta. Her hands itched for a sword or a staff to train with. Not there. When she was free, she'd have all the time to practice.

Her thoughts were interrupted by footsteps hurrying her way. Crouching in the shadows of her cell, she waited.

The guard who appeared was not the one she expected. He was an older man with a kind, weathered face. His armor spoke of his high rank in the Gaule forces. He peered through the bars, his eyes finally finding her.

"Persinette," he said quietly.

"Who are you?" she asked.

"A friend."

"I don't have any friends in the palace."

He laughed, a sound that was foreign in the dungeons. "You'd be surprised. Come here."

She straightened out of her crouch and walked tentatively toward the bars.

He reached his arm through and flipped his hand to open his palm, revealing a meager yellow flower.

A sob broke past her lips as she hesitantly took it. Her magic had been quiet for so long and now it buzzed in her veins. A tear fell from her lashes, tracking down her cheek.

"That's from another friend of yours," the old man said. "She said it would give you hope."

"Maiya," Etta whispered, holding the flower to her chest. Maiya was the reason she'd been caught, but she'd given Etta up to save her father. As hard as she might try, she couldn't fault her friend for that. It felt good to know she wasn't alone, wasn't forgotten in that dreadful place.

The world continued on outside those stone walls and she was no longer part of it, but she would be.

The old guard leaned in and dropped his voice. "I am Simon of the king's own guard. Don't lose faith, Persinette Basile. Descendants of Bela are woven into the very fabric of Gaule. We're everywhere and we have not forgotten our queen."

She thought about the words she'd said to Henry, but he was just a boy. She shook her head. "I'm no queen."

"You're right." He winked. "First, we have to regain our kingdom and then we can have a queen. Your family has our allegiance and we will get you out of here."

Her voice was barely audible as she said, "Thank you."

He inclined his head and left.

Etta stared at the flower in her hands and let her magic flow into it as if it had never stopped. The yellow brightened to a vibrant shade as it began to grow. The wilted petals strengthened and smoothed. Her body hummed with contentment.

She spent hours shrinking it and growing it and crafting the flower to perfection. Her mind was so lost in her magic, she didn't realize she wasn't alone anymore until a throat cleared.

The flower fell from her grasp as her eyes locked onto Alex's. How long had he been there?

He looked the same as he had weeks ago, but what had she expected? Her heart squeezed traitorously, and the curse pulled her toward the bars. She wrapped her hands around them.

Neither of them broke their silent standoff until he stepped closer. "My mother led me to believe you'd been mistreated."

She snorted. "Because being locked in here is treating me well."

"That's not what I meant." He ran a hand over the top of his head nervously. "I thought my guards had been hurting you, but you look... well."

She tightened her grip on the bars. "I look well? Don't let my lack of bruises fool you into thinking you aren't an evil bastard."

He growled. "I have been trying to save you from this fate for weeks."

"Liar."

"You're the reason you're still here. You've been refusing the offer from Geoff."

She narrowed her eyes. "I don't know what you're talking about."

He stepped back. "You don't, do you?" His jaw tightened. "I want you moved into the palace."

"Oh, your mother mentioned that." She leaned forward with an icy smile. "I refused." Pushing away from the bars, she stepped farther back into the cell.

"Be reasonable. You don't belong here."

"I'd still be a prisoner in your household, correct?"

He winced. "I can't release you."

She hummed deep in her throat as she studied him. "I belong down here with my people more than I do with you."

He swallowed hard. "Etta." His voice hardened. "Tell me. Was it all fake? Was it just the curse?"

Her momentary shock at his knowledge of the curse faded quickly, and she averted her gaze. "I don't know."

"You don't know?" he growled.

"Why did you come here, Alex? Was it to finally look into the eyes of your old friend, Persinette? Was it to see if your lover was still here? Do you even know who I am?"

"Persinette Basile."

"You can't even begin to understand who I am. La Dame was our enemy before yours. She destroyed my kingdom and my family. She tied us to you. Only a true born Basile heir can challenge her."

"How am I supposed to believe a legend that has never been proven true?"

She turned her back on him. "When we were children, I knew one day I'd have to serve you. I've known my entire life you were meant to be my enemy, but I was a naïve girl, thinking it was your family name and not you I'd have to hate. I thought you were different from your father." She twisted to face him once again. "But then you continued jailing magic folk, and I told myself it was because you couldn't change a kingdom's laws all at once. Next you imprisoned your best friend, a man who still loves you for reasons none of us can fathom. I forgave you because you also helped him escape—as long as no one knew you did it. You allowed the Black Forest to be raided. Then your own mother sent your brother away for fear of what the king—you—would do if you learned of his magic." She crossed her arms over her chest.

"I no longer see you with Persinette's childish hope, but with Etta's more experienced perspective. I loved you, Alex. I don't know if it was because of the blasted curse but it blinded me. Now I finally see. You will always be an enemy of Bela, an enemy of mine."

He sagged back against the wall, breathing heavily. His eyes latched onto the flower on the ground behind her and then rose to her face. "You created the meadow of flowers in the forest."

She sighed and bent to lift the flower, holding it to her nose. She inhaled and closed her eyes.

"Etta," Alex pleaded.

"My name is Persinette." Her cracked lips pinched together. "The Etta you knew does not exist."

"Persinette, my mother claims we could be allies."

"We could have been."

"Let me take you to more comfortable quarters. Please."

"Will the rest of my people you've imprisoned be given those same 'comfortable quarters?'"

The expression that crossed his face was answer enough.

"Then I will stand by what I said. A gilded cage is still a cage, is it not?"

"Please, Et-Persinette. Work with me."

"No. You no longer have my trust, your Majesty. I have said all I'm going to say. You may go."

She lowered herself to the center of her cell and crossed her legs as she focused on the flower once again. He hesitated for a moment before storming away.

She wanted to get out of her cell, but her people would come for her and she believed in them more than she did the king.

As his footsteps faded away, she folded in on herself, her back shaking with sobs. The curse pulled and strained, wanting to go after him. She wanted more than anything to be able to hate him, but Alexandre Durand had embedded himself in her tattered soul.

Hollowness threatened to overwhelm Alex, and it was his own damn fault. He stormed into his room and slammed the door shut in his guard's face. He deserved everything she'd said to him. What kind of king was he? He couldn't protect his people. He couldn't uphold laws he wasn't sure he even believed in anymore.

He collapsed onto the couch in front of the barren fireplace. The days grew colder and soon it would be roaring with life. He longed to feel its heat. As boys, he and Edmund played games with the fire, daring each other to touch the flames in a bold show of strength. He'd never been burned, but he'd been filled with joy as he sat in that very room vibrating with laughter. Everything had been simple back then.

Even when he was missing his friend Persinette, Edmund had been there. He'd thought of her often, hoping she was alive. He'd never had to doubt wherever she was, she was a survivor. It had killed him to wonder if she hated him for everything his family had done.

Now he knew she did, and it hurt worse than any pain he'd ever felt.

His torn sketchbook taunted him from the table and he ripped his eyes away, remembering the night he'd flung it, vowing he was done with the useless trade. A king didn't have time for pretty drawings, especially when they reminded him of everything he'd lost.

Unable to sit in that room any longer, he sprang to his feet and strode purposefully toward the door.

It was nearing evening, and the palace was buzzing with activity. His guards kept their distance, but others were not so courteous. A servant in the royal livery rushed toward him. "Sire, Lord Leroy has been looking for you all day."

"He can keep looking."

No such luck. As he descended into the practice yard, Lord Leroy was waiting at the bottom of the steps with Camille.

"Where have you been, your Majesty?" he asked sternly.

Alex bristled at his tone. "That is none of your concern."

"It is when there are important matters you have been neglecting."

Alex continued walking toward the swords leaning against a wooden table. He shrugged off his jacket and unbuttoned his collar. Rolling up his sleeves, he turned back to the serpents behind him.

"Brother," Camille began. "We must discuss the prisoners."

"Yes," Lord Leroy agreed. "We must have a show of strength to prove Gaule isn't so easily attacked."

Alex barely heard them as he turned back around to pick out a practice sword.

"Your Majesty," Lord Leroy snapped.

Alex kept his back to the upstart as he spoke. "Tell you what, my lord, why don't you and my dear sister do something for a change. Before my father, the kings didn't rule alone. Their councils actually did things to help the realm. You're my council. You can begin forming a plan without me and I will join you. Now go."

"Alexandre," Camille chastised.

"My entire life, all you people have tried to get me to take my training seriously. Now that I finally have enough anger to stab something, you won't leave me alone." He gripped the hilt of a sword and swung it once to test its weight.

Lord Leroy grumbled as he walked away. Camille followed him and the air became much less suffocating.

The soldiers in the training yard were so wrapped up in their workouts they barely noticed him. His reputation preceded him and they didn't expect their king to be there with a sword in his hand.

The steady drumming of knives and arrows hitting targets rang in his ears. Wooden swords crashed together with constant thuds.

Stepping up to the straw dummy, he shifted his feet and brought the sword down on its neck. He repeated the gesture with more strength than before and his chest squeezed. He went to work beating the dummy as hard as he could, releasing every bit of pent-up frustration. The dummy couldn't fight back. It couldn't look at him with accusing eyes. It couldn't break him.

He swung his sword again and again, but it didn't make him feel any better, any stronger.

"Sire," a gruff voice called through his haze.

He stopped abruptly and turned to see the crowd he'd drawn. How long had he been at it?

The man who'd spoken was a member of Alex's guard but he didn't know him well. Simon. Yes, that was his name. He was an older fellow who barely spoke.

"What?" he asked more harshly than he'd intended. The onlookers didn't bow to him as decorum demanded. He got a few nods, but for the first time in months, he didn't feel like the king. He didn't feel like he was above them. On the battlefield, everyone was an equal and in the training yard, it was the same.

Respect there wasn't given based on the nature of one's birth. It was earned with the sword in your hand.

Simon stepped forward. "Your Majesty—"

Alex cut him off. "Not here. Please don't call me that here. I'm just Alex."

A smile split the older man's face, and he nodded, accepting the plea easily. "Well, Alex, would you prefer to continue bloodying that dummy or do you want a partner?"

"It's a dummy, there's no blood."

Simon's grin widened. "Come on." He led Alex to a clear space in the yard and took his stance. When Alex did the same, Simon laughed. "You're really as terrible as everyone says, aren't you?"

Alex couldn't remember the last time someone had been so honest with him. Other than the words Etta flung at him, it was… new. He shrugged as Simon walked toward him.

"First, you need to relax," Simon said. "Shift your feet farther apart and bend your knees slightly." He scanned Alex's form. "You hold the sword quite well. But you need to be aware of your feet at all times. They will allow your opponent to predict your next move, but they're also the quickest part of you that can move away from an attack."

Simon nodded once and backed away. "Come at me."

Alex shifted his weight and lunged. Simon evaded the attack easily. "Come on, Alex. When your attack misses, don't back off. Attack again quickly."

All light was gone by the time they slowed their sparring. For the last blessed hour, Alex hadn't thought of anything but his next move, the arc of his sword. His arm ached from holding the heavy wooden sword and sweat dripped down his face, but he couldn't remember the last time he'd felt so good.

Simon was faring better as he grinned at Alex. "I dare say we'll make a master swordsman of you yet."

"I'd settle for adequate."

Simon laughed. "I guess in the fight to come, you're of more use as an archer. Though, as king you'll be kept from the worst of it."

"You think it will come to war?"

Simon set his sword down and scratched his jaw. "You're the king. You know better than I."

"I'm not so sure about that."

The old guard studied him for a moment. "When I was younger, magic wasn't outlawed in Gaule, so we had descendants of Bela living right out in the open." His voice was wistful. "They had a saying. Do you want to hear it?"

Alex nodded.

"Good men aren't meant to be king."

Alex's lungs refused to expand. He'd heard that before. He'd thought it was a dream, but Etta whispered it to him before she left to rescue Edmund.

"What does that even mean?" he hissed.

Sadness washed over Simon's face, pulling down the corners of his lips. "Phillip was said to be a good man, and he began the destruction of his kingdom when he went over the wall of Dracon, risking himself to protect the woman he loved."

"That's a fairytale. Bela was destroyed by La Dame, not King Phillip."

"Some call it a fairytale. Others name it history. But the same lesson can be learned. Being king is much harder when the heart in your chest beats true."

"How do you know mine does?"

"I've worked in this palace since you were born." He smiled softly. "But we do not choose our roles in life. You were born to be king, good man or no. It only makes your path forward more difficult."

"Good men aren't meant to be king, huh?" Alex laughed at the absurdity of the statement.

Simon clapped him on the shoulder in a camaraderie Alex hadn't felt since Edmund's departure. His guards weren't friends, but he was grateful Simon broke free of that thinking.

He was about to say something else, but the rumbling of a considerable crowd on the move sounded outside the inner gates.

Alex dropped his sword and didn't bother grabbing his jacket as he jogged across the now empty training yard. Simon picked up his real sword and followed him. Once at the inner gate, he watched the torch-bearing mob march through the streets.

What the hell was going on?

He traveled past the gate and pushed himself into the crowd, getting lost among the faces. No one recognized him in the dark. They followed a cart that bumped over the stone road. It had a covered bed concealing its contents.

People stepped outside their doors as the mob passed, some joining them and others running back inside and slamming doors.

The cart blew past the open outer gate, the driver not bothering to acknowledge the guards on duty. Simon stepped up beside him and stayed close.

Alex knew where they were headed now and fear twisted in his gut as the newly built gallows loomed before them. He hadn't had the chance to have them torn down yet. Anders and Camille had them built in secret. It was their way of dealing with the magic problem.

Two people stood on the platform with nooses around their necks.

When his eyes found his sister standing with Lord Leroy, he bulled his way through the crowd. Amalie stood with them, tears streaming down her face.

"You must see this," her father was saying to her. "I will not allow you to turn a blind eye to the magic pestilence. Amalie, next time you'll obey me."

Alex grabbed Amalie roughly and forced her behind him to protect her from the man he now saw truly for the first time. "What is the meaning of this?"

"Your Majesty," Leroy said smoothly. "You told me to take care of the problem of people from the Black Forrest."

His face reddened, and he clenched his jaw. "And this is what you decided? This isn't right. I told you to begin forming a plan." He didn't notice Camille stepping away from them.

"The punishment for magic is death. That is the plan."

A blast of air blew straight for them, knocking them away from each other. It was all Alex could do to stay on his feet. He looked up at the gallows in time for the air to be cut off when the floor beneath the prisoner's feet dropped away. Camille stood by the lever.

"No," Alex screamed. The two unlucky souls struggled, their bodies jerking and flailing. Their faces changed color as they began to still.

Amalie's sobs rang through the night, but Alex couldn't look away. One of them was a girl who couldn't have been much older than Amalie.

He reached back and pulled her forward to tuck her into his side. Her body shook. Lord Leroy moved toward the back of the wagon they'd followed and opened it to reveal three more wretched people.

"They're too weak," Amalie whispered. "Dany told me they can't call their magic when they're so weak. They can't get themselves out of this."

"Dany?" he asked.

Amalie began to cry again, pointing to the young girl still hanging from the rope. "She was my maid. Father caught us playing a game with her magic."

Alex squeezed her tighter before releasing her. He strode up to the gallows and stepped onto the platform. The crowd quieted as soon as they realized their king had arrived.

He clenched his fists at his sides but forced his voice to remain calm. "This is not how we do things in Gaule."

A cry rose up from the crowd as they threw accusations at him.

He didn't stop. "There will be no more death here today."

"You're weak, brother," Camille yelled. "Father would have had them all executed."

"Father is dead. I am king. You will obey me."

Leroy narrowed his eyes before taking off back toward the castle.

"Sympathizer," someone in the crowd yelled. Others echoed the statement.

"And we wonder why the magic folk hate us?" Alex's voice boomed over the shrinking crowd. "Why they attack us? Maybe we deserve it."

Those were the wrong words to say, and he knew it as soon as they left his mouth. Too many of his people had died. There was an anger in his kingdom that threatened to tear it apart. The crowd shouted insults and tried to push forward, but Simon appeared, holding his sword at the ready. That seemed to deter them. Eventually, they dispersed, leaving Alex, Simon, and Amalie with two dead bodies and three prisoners.

Alex surveyed the prisoners. Clean them up and feed them and they'd look like any of his people.

He made a quick decision. "Go."

They stared at him, stunned and disbelieving. Simon reached into his pocket and procured a few coins, pressing them into their hands. He nodded, and they began to half run, half stumble down the hill that led away from the palace.

"Simon, I need you to go back into the castle for a few guards, a horse, and supplies. We need to bury them."

"I don't think it's a good idea to leave you."

"I'll be fine here. Give me the knife on your belt. Will you take Amalie back?"

"I'm staying with you," Amalie cut in.

He wouldn't argue with her so he nodded to Simon. When the guard was gone, Alex balanced on the platform and began to saw at the first rope with his knife. They'd used fraying ropes, so it didn't take long before both bodies were sprawled on the ground. Amalie held her friend's lifeless hand.

The crowd dissipated as a handful of palace guards rode towards them. Simon returned a few minutes later.

It was quick work to drape the bodies over the back of the horse. Alex's mind immediately went to the meadow in the Black Forrest where Etta's father was buried. He now knew that meant he'd been at Viktor Basile's grave. These two deserved to be buried there as well, but it was too far.

Instead, they buried them at the edge of the woods.

A heaviness settled on Alex's heart as they re-entered the castle. The streets were deserted, but he felt his people's condemnation, anyway.

"I can't go back to my father's palace rooms," Amalie said.

Alex felt for her. She'd been a good friend and had a good heart. Lord Leroy didn't deserve her. Instead of taking her to her father, he led her into the family wing of the palace and stopped at his mother's door.

The queen mother greeted them, her eyes showing her surprise at their dirt covered clothing. "You two smell like death."

Amalie burst into tears.

"Oh dear, I didn't mean that literally. Come in." She placed an arm over Amalie's shoulders. "They've drawn up a bath for me, why don't you take advantage of it?"

Amalie sniffled and nodded, letting one of the maids take her away.

When she was gone, Alex ran a hand through his filthy hair and fixed her with a broken stare. "Mother." His voice shook.

"Tell me what has happened."

So he did, not sparing any detail. Pain flashed in the queen mother's eyes when Camille's role in the day was revealed, but her only other reaction was to wrap her arms around his shoulders, no longer caring about the smell.

He sank into her embrace. Even after he'd kept her confined in her rooms, she'd forgiven him easily. She always did. She was the one person in his life he could count on.

"Amalie can stay in Tyson's room while you decide what to do with Lord Leroy."

He nodded against her shoulder. "Thank you."

"Always, my boy."

He let himself relax for a moment longer before standing. "I'm going to seek my own bath and then fall asleep. Maybe when I wake, all of this will have been a bad dream."

CHAPTER 4

When had his sister grown so cold? Alex sat on his throne in a perfectly fitted leather tunic. Silver rings were sewn along the collar and his crown sat nestled in his hair. He looked like a king. Good men might not be meant for ruling, but that didn't mean he wouldn't do his duty. He didn't consider himself a good man. Etta didn't think him true.

He shook his head. Today was not about Persinette Basile. It was about Gaule and the kind of kingdom he wanted to create.

He gave his sister a hard look, and she stared back unblinkingly.

"Kneel." His voice reverberated around the room. There was always a crowd when he handed out judgments. Their curiosity irritated him, but he had no eyes for anyone but his sister. She was the last sibling he had in Gaule, but that wouldn't save her from his wrath.

When she didn't move, he cleared his throat. "Get on your knees, sister, before I make you."

She pushed her dark waves of hair away from her face to reveal hard lines. His sister was considered a great beauty, but an untouchable one. She gripped her cane tighter and forced her knees to bend. Watching her sink down was painful. She moved slowly, but she hid the discomfort from her face.

Her knees hit the velvet carpet in front of the throne and she fixed her gaze on his face, challenging him. When she spoke, it was so low only he could hear. "You should not be the one sitting on that throne. You shame father. You shame our family."

He lurched to his feet to stare down at her. "I am not the one tearing us apart."

"If you're bent on siding with the magic folk, why is your dear Etta still locked away?"

He refused to tell her Etta chose to stay in the dungeons. He wouldn't give her the satisfaction of knowing how wrong that had gone. Instead, he crossed his arms and scowled. "I am not siding with anyone."

She spat on his boots. "You should be siding with the people of Gaule."

Enough. He didn't want to stare at her face any longer. He'd never gotten along with his harsh sister, but she was family. He'd spare her the dungeons not for herself, but for their mother.

He sat down with a rigid spine and flattened the wrinkles in his trousers. "Camille Durand, I hereby rescind your place in the order of succession."

She gasped. The king had the power to reorder the line of succession but it hadn't been done in a hundred years.

He continued. "A marriage contract has been drawn up. I've been quite generous with your bride price."

She shook her head violently. "Who?"

Alex smiled. Even in punishment, he couldn't be cruel to his sister. He'd chosen a nobleman twice her age, but one who was known to be kind and not a frequenter of court. His estate was in the far northern corner of Gaule where his sister would no longer be a problem to anyone. He wanted her to be happy, but he also needed her gone before he was forced to imprison her.

"Duke Caron," he said finally.

"Caron? But he's old enough to be my father!"

Alex sighed. "It's a good match, Camille, and better than you deserve. He has already begun his journey here and should arrive within days. You will marry and then accompany him to his estate in the North." He broke their locked gazes. "You may go."

She shot him a final stricken look and stormed from the room as fast as someone with a lame leg could.

Alex resisted the urge to sag back against his throne in relief. Instead, he gestured for Simon to bring Lord Leroy to the front. Simon jerked the hefty man down onto his knees. Alex had no kindness for Leroy as he had for his sister.

Leroy hung his head and kept his eyes firmly focused on the ground.

Alex was out of patience. "Lord Leroy, I hereby condemn you for carrying out executions without the crown's consent. You circumvented me. We do not practice cruelty here in Gaule. Do you deny this?"

Lord Leroy lifted his eyes pleadingly. "I was doing what was necessary to protect my kingdom, sire."

A sigh pushed past Alex's lips and his voice softened. "I know you believe that." He tapped his fingers on the arm of his throne and looked out at the nobles who'd come for this. Amalie stood at the back, her face scrunched with nervousness.

He looked back to Lord Leroy. "You will return to your estate. Focus on the running of your lands and the people under your care. You are no longer welcome at court. If you return, you will be arrested. If I hear of you perpetrating cruelty on your lands, you will be arrested." He paused. "There is an ancient codicil in the laws of a betrothal. If one family falls into disgrace, the other need not honor it and disgrace their name as well." He hoped Amalie would understand. "This betrothal is broken. The Leroy family and the Durands will not be tied by this bond."

He grew silent and Lord Leroy fell forward, his hands curling in the carpet. "Sire," he croaked. "This will ruin us."

Alex stood and walked down the steps to stand over the man. He bent and put a hand on his shoulder. "I'm sorry, my lord, but there is more. You were a great friend to my father, and your time here must be finished, but not your family's. I hereby take the guardianship of Amalie Leroy. She will always be your daughter, but she is no longer bound to you, nor you to her. Her financial well-being, including her future bride price, is now the direct responsibility of the queen mother. Amalie will stay here at court, separate from your own disgrace."

Tears broke free of Lord Leroy's eyes. "You would take my daughter as well?"

Alex squeezed his shoulder again. "I am not taking anything, my lord. This was her request."

With a final pat to the man's shaking shoulder, Alex strode down the carpet. The doors were opened for him and Simon stood at his side as he stepped through. Geoff and a few other guards joined them.

Alex knew the people of Bela were wrong. A good man could be a great king as long as he stood by what he believed in and made sacrifices. That was where King Phillip of the stories turned dark. He made the wrong choice. He sacrificed his people and his future descendants for one woman.

Alex would do anything to keep his people safe. Gaule wasn't only made up of non-magical folk. If they were all going to survive La Dame's forces, they had to do it together.

He wished he'd figured that out sooner before the people he cared about were hurt or driven away.

There'd been no assaults for days and Etta didn't want to get used to it. In fact, she hoped someone tried to come at her if only so she could have someone to punch. She'd been weak each of the other times, but since her magical healing night, her body felt whole.

The food had increased since the king's visit, but she wouldn't be grateful. His offer to move her to a more comfortable prison had been insulting. If he wanted to keep her under lock and key, then he'd have to face her in this wretched place. He didn't get to soothe his conscience. Especially not when the other poor people in that place didn't have the option of luxury. He'd done this and she wouldn't let him forget.

She straightened her arms, pushing herself up from the ground before lowering herself and doing it all over again. She had to remain strong and ready.

"What are you doing, Etta?" Henry asked.

She grunted through another push-up. "Preparing."

"For what?"

"For whatever comes next."

A bowl rattled as it was slid through the bars and a chunk of stale bread was thrown unceremoniously into the cell. Too hungry to care, she dipped the bread into the chunky stew she'd grown used to. It softened it enough so she could take a bite but it still scratched her throat on the way down.

She didn't want to know what was in the stew to throw off such a wretched smell, but she wolfed it down like the animal they thought she was. Throwing the bowl to the ground, she swallowed the last bit of bread and sat in the corner of her cell. It was the farthest spot from her chamber pot. There was no lid to keep the stench at bay.

Every time she'd thought she was growing used to it over the weeks, some new inconvenience would bring her back to reality.

She wiped her face on her filthy sleeve, dreaming of a nice bath. Even a dip in the freezing river in the forest would do. She closed her eyes, letting her mind wander to images of her with Verité at the river.

A throat clearing tore through her distraction. She opened her eyes to find Duchess Moreau standing on the other side of the bars.

"Hello, Persinette," she said kindly.

Etta scooted away from her shadowed corner, confusion drawing her brow. She hadn't expected a visit from one of the king's advisers. Then she remembered Tyson. Queen Catrine told her to take Tyson to the Duchess.

"Tyson?" Her scratchy voice couldn't get much else out.

The duchess passed a cup of water through the bars and Etta gulped it down greedily.

"Tyson is safe," she said. "As is Edmund and that petulant horse he arrived on."

A laugh burst out of Etta and she clapped a hand over her mouth. It'd been ages since she'd laughed. "Verité has been good to me throughout the years."

"Yes, I suspected he was yours." She pressed her lips together. "You two seem made for each other."

Etta nodded.

"I can't stay long, child, but Catrine tells me you've refused to be moved."

Etta's eyebrows knitted together. "I can't leave them." She pointed to the hall where her people were caged just as she was.

Respect shone in Duchess Moreau's eyes. "You and our king seem just as suited as you and that blasted horse."

Etta scowled. "I think I'm tired. You should go."

The duchess didn't move. "Alexandre has had a busy few days. He sent both his sister and Lord Leroy away from court as the punishment for their treatment of magic folk. He broke his betrothal. Many in Gaule are angry with him."

Etta's mind whirled faster the more she thought of him. He was protecting her people? Why? And he'd broken his betrothal to that sweet, shy girl. Would his kingdom turn against him?

No, she couldn't allow herself to care. Not when he continued to keep her from her own people.

Etta shrank back into the shadows of her cell. "The king is no concern of mine."

The duchess nodded in understanding, but a sadness entered her gaze. "When I met you before, I thought you loved him. I saw it in your eyes. But love does not end, and it does not give up."

"It also doesn't forgive."

"That's where you're wrong, child. The most important thing love does is forgive."

"I can't love someone who would imprison me for my magic."

"I was under the impression it was because of your betrayal and that the reason you're still here is your own stubbornness." She ran a hand down her dress. "Edmund sent me with a message. I am to tell you La Dame has taken control of Bela."

"Bela no longer exists."

"But the land is still there. She has seized it and if you want to get it back, then you will need Gaule. You will need to make peace with Alexandre Durand."

With that final thought, the duchess left. Etta folded in on herself. How had Edmund done it? He'd forgiven Alex for his own imprisonment, loved him still. Now La Dame had her ancestral home and she couldn't be allowed to keep it.

Edmund was right. A sob shook her body. How could she forget these awful weeks? She felt the curse strong in that moment. It wrapped around her heart like a clamp, squeezing until she couldn't breathe.

Her tears hit the stone beneath her and she watched their trail, numbing herself to the war raging inside of her.

Alex couldn't stand the sight of her in that cell, but he had a plan. He needed to start releasing some of the prisoners who'd been locked up since his father was king.

He hurried toward the one person in the palace he knew he could trust. The late hour allowed him to slip away from his room without any guards. His mother's guard barely glanced at him as he knocked on her door.

He hadn't expected her to be sleeping, night owl that she was, but he'd at least thought she'd be alone. When Duchess Moreau answered the door, he stepped back in surprise.

"Your Majesty." She smiled. "Just the man we need."

He followed her into the sitting room where his mother sat with her fingers curled around a mug of tea.

"Alexandre," she said. "Good news. Your brother is well."

Relief flooded through him as he walked toward the pot of tea and poured some for himself before turning to the duchess. "I didn't know you were back at court."

"I just arrived. I've had a few people to see tonight and was planning to present myself in the throne room tomorrow."

He sipped his tea and nodded, considering her. "How many magic folk have you been hiding?"

She reeled back, her jaw dropping.

"Alexandre," his mother warned.

Duchess Moreau recovered quickly, busying her hands with the wrinkles in her skirt. "I am a loyal subject of Gaule."

"I wasn't accusing you of anything less," he said as he took a seat across from her. "You're protecting Tyson and I assume Edmund as well."

She nodded hesitantly.

"Then it isn't a far leap for me to guess you are a sympathizer."

"Sounds like an accusation to me."

He flicked his eyes to his mother and back. He'd learned he couldn't trust his other adviser. Was the duchess different? His mother gave him an almost imperceptible nod, and he took a deep breath.

"I want to be a good king."

"You are, son," his mother said.

"Bela has an expression."

"Good men aren't meant to be king," the duchess finished for him.

"It's time I begin proving them wrong."

The duchess frowned. "Sire, that saying refers to a specific king—Phillip. It isn't a phrase to take to heart."

"My father wasn't a good king." He turned to his mother. "After his death, you said one good man died that day and one monster. Viktor Basile was not the monster in your mind, was he?"

Tears sprang to her eyes, and she shook them away. It was all the confirmation he needed. He set his cup down and reached for his mother's free hand. "I don't want to be like father."

"You could never," she gasped.

"That's a nice thing to say, but nothing has changed since he died. We are still persecuting those with magic. Our dungeons are full."

Duchess Moreau studied him carefully, tilting her head to the side. "What do you plan to do?"

He swallowed. "I can't free Etta. I want to… but she's now a rallying point. The attackers in the border village claimed they were doing it in her name. She won't allow me to move her somewhere more comfortable."

"That's what she told me." There was pride in the Duchess' eyes.

"You've seen her?"

"That was the first place I went."

"How was she?"

She sighed. "Angry. Prideful. Stubborn." Her lips curved up. "She was a Basile."

The queen mother laughed. "Sounds like her."

"I need to begin releasing people," Alex said.

His mother leaned forward. "Son, that's noble of you. But it's best done with caution. Gaule is ready to go up in flames. Any action that can be perceived as aiding the magic folk will threaten your rule."

"Maybe my rule isn't the most important thing."

She gave him a disapproving look. "Of course it is. You can only help this kingdom while you sit on that throne."

"Before father consolidated the crown's power, the king did not rule alone. Grandfather had a council of citizens to help him lead. So, no mother, my rule is not everything. Not even close. Gaule can survive without me. The question remains—can it survive me, my rule. Because, right now, my people want to tear me apart." He set his cup down and began to pace in front of them, clasping and unclasping his hands.

He kept moving as the words spilled out. "I have a plan. It may make the people hate me more and I don't want the entire kingdom sinking into rebellion if they think I am aiding their enemies, but we may need allies in the time to come. Keeping them caged like animals will not turn them into such. It's a balancing act. I need to free the magic folk, but I don't want word of our activities reaching the villages of Gaule. Not yet. We must only use trusted allies. If we can get the prisoners to Duchess Moreau's lands, they'll be as safe as they can be in Gaule."

His mother got to her feet and set her cup down before stepping into Alex's path and wrapping her arms around him. "I'm worried for you, son."

"I never wanted to be king, but we do not get a choice in all things. Just like I don't have a choice now."

She leaned back and patted his cheek. "You're a good boy. I'm also thankful you chose a kind man for Camille. She is difficult, but she is my daughter."

Duchess Moreau stepped forward. "Duke Caron was a wise choice."

Alex nodded. "Caron will be quite different than she expects. Rumor is his sympathies lay across the border as well and I will have need of him in the future."

Leaving the two of them with vague details of his plan, Alex ducked out into the darkened palace. As a child, he'd never been allowed near the dungeons. Now it seemed as if they were a staple in his life.

The guards on duty bowed as he passed. It was damper than usual due to the heavy rains that'd begun earlier in the day.

He stopped outside Etta's cell expecting to find her intense stare burning into him. Instead, she was curled up in the corner farthest from the waste bucket that sent putrid smells dancing in the air.

Her elegant golden mane was tangled and covered in so much filth it appeared almost brown. Her face was hidden from him, but her tiny body was skinnier than before. Her hipbones jutted out harshly under her torn clothing.

But her chest rose and fell, giving him some sense of comfort. She was still alive and that meant there was hope.

He gripped the bars separating them, wanting to be close, knowing he'd never be close again. He'd seen it in her eyes the last time she'd glowered at him.

Despite the fact she'd been the one who lied and betrayed her king, he'd been the one to break them. To break her.

Turning away, he vowed to himself he'd make it right and walked back to his room where sleep was elusive, but memories ran rampant.

GOLDEN CHAINS

The charcoal scratched along the paper, leaving delicate lines in its place. Alex moved his hand rhythmically as the trees took shape. He blew away the excess charcoal and studied his drawing. He couldn't get it right. The edge of the Black Forest held a darkness he couldn't draw no matter how many times he tried.

"That's a pretty picture." Edmund dropped down beside him in the grass past the outer wall of the palace.

"Are you mocking me?" Alex raised his eyes to study the trees, barely paying his friend any mind.

"I would never, your Highness."

"Edmund, if you insist on bothering me, can you at least be quiet while you do?"

Edmund grinned and shook his head. "Why are you so fascinated with that forest, anyway?"

Alex sighed in exasperation and pushed his sketchbook aside. "Guess I'm done for today." He glanced back longingly at the trees.

"Come on, Alex. I know something is going on. You've been moody lately."

He needed to say it. Needed to get it out. But something stopped him. He thought he could trust Edmund, but what if he was wrong? He looked into his friend's eyes. They'd been inseparable since Edmund came to the palace a few years before.

"I think I saw Persinette in town last week."

Edmund whistled a long note. "That's..."

"Crazy? I know."

"Alex, in the three years since she left, there has been no word. No one can find them. Why would they remain so close

to the palace? From what you've told me, her father is smarter than that."

Alex lowered his chin to his chest. "I tried to reach her, but she turned into an alley and came out on the back of a horse. I watched her ride toward the forest."

"No one lives in the forest."

Alex's fingers traced the lines of the drawing. "Wouldn't it be the perfect place to hide if the king is hunting you?"

Edmund gripped Alex's shoulder and squeezed. "You know as well as I your father has scoured the kingdom for them. They couldn't have gotten out past the wards. They're probably— "

"Dead?" He brushed off Edmund's hand and stood. "Yeah, that's what everyone keeps saying. I know you won't believe me, but I feel like I'd know. If she died, I mean. Edmund, before you, she was the only person..." He wiped his hand across his eyes to hide the sudden moisture. Teenage boys weren't supposed to cry, much less princes.

Edmund nodded like he knew what he meant, but he couldn't. Being a prince was lonely especially as a young boy. But it hadn't been when she was there. He'd always felt connected to her, like she was the person who mattered most.

A horn blew from the front gate as a line of soldiers on horseback crested the hill. They rode two abreast and were followed by a wagon. Edmund jumped to his feet.

Alex started to walk forward, but Edmund held him back as they got a better glimpse of the wagon. It was sizable with metal bars creating a cage in back.

His stomach churned as he saw the people crammed into the cage with barely any room to move. He'd seen it before. For three years, the purge brought magic folk to their dungeons in droves.

"Come on," Edmund said. "Let's go into the palace another way."

The two boys were silent as they added that sight to the list of scenes they'd never forget.

CHAPTER 5

Light flashed through the night moments before a crack of thunder shook the walls. Alex startled from his sleep. He pressed the heel of his hand to his eyes and sat up. Getting to his feet, he walked to his window. Rain pounded furiously against the glass.

Another crash of thunder made him jump.

Gaule was no stranger to storms, but they'd had a calm summer. It was only a matter of time.

There was no way he was getting back to sleep. When Tyson was younger, sometimes he'd make his way to Alex's room when a storm raged. He hadn't wanted to seem like a baby and go to his mother.

Alex smiled at the memory. Ty always tried to act bravely.

Alex missed his brother. It didn't feel the same without him down the hall, without him causing trouble.

He crossed the room and poured himself a glass of wine to soothe his frayed nerves.

A knock sounded on his door and he was surprised to open it and find Amalie standing there in her nightgown. Simon was the guard on duty and he raised an eyebrow.

"My lady," Alex said, inclining his head.

She bowed. "Your Majesty, may I come in?"

He stepped aside to let her by and gave Simon a tiny shrug before closing the door.

Amalie dropped all formality and turned to him. "I'm sorry, Alex. I know I shouldn't be here. People will talk and—"

"Simon won't tell anyone you came."

"Oh." Color rose in her cheeks. "Well, that's good. Your mother put me in a room down the hall and I couldn't sleep because..." She hesitated, casting her eyes on the floor. "I hate storms."

His smile spread from one side of his face to the other. She was young, like Ty. He poured her some wine and she took it gratefully.

"Is it okay that I'm here? I worried you might be sleeping."

"I'm glad for the company." He sat and gestured for her to do the same.

"Oh." She sat as directed and crossed her legs. "Then I guess that's good."

Thunder struck and she jumped to her feet and walked the length of the room before turning to come back again. After a few moments, he set his glass down and stood to still her pacing. He grabbed her shoulders and forced her to stop. "Amalie, it's just a storm. You're safe inside the palace."

Tears shone in her eyes and he pulled her into a hug. She buried her face in his chest as he rubbed circles on her back. When he spoke, his words were muffled by her hair. "You remind me of Ty."

A laugh shook her. "Ty is more terrified than I am of storms. One time, we were in the tunnels when one struck. It lasted into the night and all through to the morning. He tried to put on a brave face, but we ended up clinging together in fear for hours."

He matched her laugh but stopped abruptly when something slammed against the window and it cracked. He turned his head just in time for the glass to shatter.

He threw Amalie to the ground, covering her body with his as the howling wind roared through the room. It sounded like a vortex, ready to suck them through the now fragmented window. Glass flew through the air and he covered both their faces.

The door banged open as Simon barreled through. "Alex!"

Neither Alex nor Amalie could move.

More guards would have heard the window break, and they'd be there to help soon, but all Alex could focus on was the wind ripping through his belongings. Papers flew past them as rain streamed in through the window, soaking everything. A puddle began to form around them.

Simon rushed forward, but before he could get to them, a sharp pain slammed into Alex's abdomen. His body jerked away from Amalie as his head felt like it smacked into something invisible. Something hard. Simon pulled Amalie into the hall and came back yelling for Alex to get to his feet.

He couldn't. It was like a knife slicing through his leg. He searched frantically for the source of his pain, knowing he wouldn't find it in that room.

Simon reached him and pulled him to his feet as he rammed his shoulder under Alex's arm. He all but carried the king into the hall. He used all of his weight but still couldn't shut the door against the wind. Giving up, he turned to the king.

"Are you okay?" he yelled.

Alex jerked back against the wall as another wave of pain hit him. Amalie's eyes widened as she reached toward his face.

"Did you get hit with something?" Simon asked. "You have a strange mark on your face."

Alex couldn't answer him as he doubled over. "Healer," he croaked.

"I'll wake the new palace healer." Simon started to walk, but Amalie ran after him.

"No," she called. "He needs to go to the healer in the outer castle."

"Are you mad, my lady? The sky is breaking apart out there."

She tugged on his arm. "We don't have a choice."

Simon rubbed his forehead. "If anyone learns I took the king out into this, it'll be on me."

"Simon," Alex wheezed. "Do you trust me?"

"Of course."

"Then just get me there."

Simon slung one of Alex's arms over his shoulders and Amalie went ahead of them. Guards appeared behind them at the king's door and they ducked into another hallway. The palace was deserted as people hunkered down for the storm. The alarm would be raised soon because the king was missing and his room was trashed. They'd have to make it out before then.

Alex breathed through the pain as they pushed into the courtyard. A gust of wind blasted into their faces and battered them at an angle.

Simon's graying hair clung to his forehead. He shifted Alex and unfastened his cloak, reaching it toward Amalie. "Take this, my lady."

She wrapped it around her shoulders gratefully and charged ahead of them.

The streets were eerily empty and the guards at the inner gate didn't step out into the rain to see who passed by. Walking was a chore as each new step brought pain. It was everywhere, straining Alex's every movement. He thought he must now know what it felt like to be trampled by a horse.

Why was it happening to him?

Desperation clung to him, shielding him from the worst fears of the storm. Amalie jumped with every bolt of thunder. Even Simon was on edge.

Amalie stopped in front of the healer's door and banged her fist against the solid wood. As Simon and Alex caught up, the door cracked open.

"Please," Amalie begged. "He needs the healer."

The door opened wider and Maiya stood there in shock. Her father appeared behind her. "Maiya, move." He pulled her aside. "Come in. The storm is wicked out there."

They practically fell into the room.

Maiya snapped out of her daze and pointed to the empty bed. "Put him there. I'll make the potion."

"No," Alex said through clenched teeth as he was helped onto the bed. "Just heal me. No sleeping."

"I don't … what?" She looked to her father and then to Simon and Amalie. "I don't know what you think is going on here, but we brew healing potions."

A scream escaped Alex's mouth as a new pain broke free.

"Please," Amalie said. "Just help him. We don't care if you have magic. None of us will say anything."

"You have our word," Simon said.

Alex groaned. "I knew it before. That's why I came back to you."

"Father." Maiya shook her head. "You know what his pain means for her?"

"Who?" Alex writhed, remembering the conversation he'd overheard last time. "Persinette?"

"Maiya," her father said. "Go ahead."

She swallowed heavily and moved to the head of the bed. Closing her eyes, she set her hands on his shoulders and pressed down. Warmth flooded through him and the pain receded. He sighed in relief.

"Thank you," he whispered.

The skin of his neck began to tug and then tighten. His muscles contracted. "Maiya," he cried.

"What's happening?" Amalie jumped toward him frantically.

Alex pulled at his neck as an invisible hand tightened around it. His lungs cried out for breath.

Maiya's father was the first to act. "It's Persinette." He yanked his door open. "We need to get to her." When no one moved, he yelled, "Now!"

Alex scrambled from the bed and darted out into the rain. It became harder to breathe, but his pace picked up and he ran through the night. Amalie, Simon, Maiya, and her father followed him. He stumbled as he became lightheaded when he reached the inner wall. He tried to gulp air and managed insufficient gasps. His head swam, and it was all he could do to keep from falling as he crossed the courtyard. Simon was ahead of him now, but he kept looking back. When Alex reached the interior of the palace, he braced himself against the wall.

"Simon," Alex tried to yell, his voice failing him. Somehow, his guard heard him and turned. "Get to her. Please." He fell to his knees.

"I'm not leaving you." Simon lifted him like he had before without even straining. Amalie, Maiya, and her father had been stopped by a guard, but Alex didn't have time to go back for them. He didn't know what was happening, but he had to get to Persinette.

The stairwell to the dungeons stretched down into the darkness and with the thunder still shaking the world outside, they went down, not knowing what they'd find.

They heard it before rounding the corner. Geoff's voice.

"I'm going to make you beg, you little magic whore."

Simon practically dropped Alex and ran ahead to where the door to the cell stood open.

Geoff had Etta pressed against the wall with one hand wrapped around her throat and the other down the front of her shirt.

He didn't see Simon before the mammoth guard yanked him away. The pressure on Alex's throat eased immediately, leaving a slight ache behind.

Persinette slumped to the ground, unmoving.

Simon knocked Geoff unconscious with two swings of his heavy fist.

Alex crawled across the floor, weakness flowing through him. He hovered over Persinette.

"We need to get her out of here."

Simon nodded. "Think you can walk on your own?"

"Yes."

Simon lifted Persinette into his arms and Alex used the bars to pull himself to his feet.

She had to be okay. He couldn't live in a world where Persinette Basile was not okay.

As he passed Geoff, he hung his head. It was his fault, his guard.

At the top of the stairs, Persinette coughed weakly.

"Get her to my mother's rooms," Alex ordered. "I need to find Maiya."

Simon began to run, the girl bouncing in his arms.

Finding Maiya was easy. She sat with her father and Amalie inside the front door of the palace.

"What is going on here?" Alex asked as he strode forward, trying to keep the weakness he still felt from his voice.

The guard did a double take. "Your Majesty, we've been searching for you."

"That doesn't answer my question." His voice was cold. "I don't have time for this. They come with me. You, go to the dungeons. There's an unconscious guard, and he is to be arrested."

When they were free of the guards, Alex turned to Maiya. "We have to hurry." She nodded and the four of them began to run.

They pushed through the door and into the queen mother's rooms without knocking. His mother sat on the bed next to a still unconscious Persinette.

"How is she?" he asked, rushing to her side.

"Not well."

Maiya ran forward. "Let me see her."

No one questioned her as she set her palms on Persinette's chest. Etta coughed and shifted, but the red line around her neck faded and disappeared.

Alex felt his own lingering pain drift away. Amalie's eyes widened. "Your neck was red as well and now... it's gone." Her eyes flicked between him and Etta. "What is happening?"

"I don't know." He scrubbed a hand across his face.

It was a never-ending night, but he wasn't tired. As he watched Etta, all he felt was relief. She was going to be okay.

Simon stepped up beside him. "If it's okay, your Majesty, I'm going to go alert the guard you're safe."

"Good idea. Also, see what's being done with Geoff. I want him to pay for this."

"I'll see to it, sire." With a smooth bow, he left.

Maiya backed away from Etta. "She should be okay now. She needs to rest."

Her father put a hand on her shoulder. "We will return in the morning."

Maiya's face scrunched in consternation. "Look, your Majesty, Persinette is important to us. I betrayed her once, but for the one person in this world I love more than her. She is everything, so you better—"

Her father cut her off. "Maiya."

Alex's mother moved off the bed and Alex took her spot. He stared down at Etta and cupped her cheek before meeting Maiya's stare. "I promise. I won't let anything happen to her."

"I don't trust you."

"Maiya," her father warned. "He is the king."

"I don't care. I know I played my part in all of this. I gave her up." She stepped forward and pointed one finger at him. "But you put her there. It was your guards that hurt her. Do you even know who she is? This is Persinette Basile, and she is my queen more than you will ever be my king."

Her father dragged her toward the door. "I apologize for my daughter, sire. She doesn't know what she says."

"She won't forgive you," Maiya said as she was pulled from the room and the door slammed behind her.

The queen mother guided Amalie to the door. "We will give you some time, son. Amalie and I will sleep in the guest rooms."

Alex barely heard them leave. He was too focused on the girl next to him. Even in this state, she was exquisite. It wasn't the delicate beauty Amalie had or even the classic looks of his mother. It was as if the fierceness in her heart shone through.

The people rising up in the villages were calling her name. Even those doing so without violence were demanding her freedom. How did she instill such loyalty in people who'd never laid eyes on her? Did legends hold that much power? Or had stories of her traveled wide?

He could see it now. The honor. The nobility. She was meant to lead her people.

She shifted and curled closer to him in her sleep. "Alex," she whispered.

His heart pounded as her hand reached for his. He entwined their fingers together.

"Don't leave me," she pleaded.

He leaned down to kiss her forehead, wishing her words weren't a product of sleep. He put his lips to her ear. "I'm not going anywhere."

She sighed and all he could do was watch her sleep, his heart tearing itself to shreds at what he'd done to her.

Etta jerked awake, her eyes snapping open as she felt the comfort of the bed beneath her. She wasn't in the dungeons anymore. Her gaze darted around the room, recognizing it immediately. The queen mother's rooms.

She squeezed her eyes shut, hoping when she opened them again she'd be back in her dusky prison cell. No such luck. She couldn't be there. The palace was no place for her. Not when the dungeons were full of other magic folk.

She sat up, kicking off the covers, and that was when she saw him. Alex. The King of Gaule was asleep in a chair next to her. He had his feet propped up on the corner of the bed and his chin rested against his chest. His dark hair fell forward to cover his eyes. She had the sudden urge to brush it out of his face and that only angered her. She set her feet into the plush carpet and stood before crossing to the door as swiftly as she could. It was unlocked. She heaved a relieved breath and pulled the door open before slipping into the lit hall. The guard at the door didn't move to stop her as she padded by on bare feet.

Farther along, the door to Alex's rooms stood open and workmen came and went. She peered in noticing the mess immediately. With a minute shrug, she kept moving. She had to get as far as she could before they came after her.

What happened last night? She couldn't remember how she got to the queen mother's rooms. Had they drugged her?

None of the maids scurrying around stopped her. They stared and gave her a wide berth. She didn't know what they knew or how she appeared to them, but she didn't care. The only way she was going to get her people out of the dungeons was to get back there, preferably with help. She'd storm the place if need be.

Maiya and Pierre were somewhere in the outer castle. Would they help her after giving her up? She couldn't trust them, but she didn't trust anyone. Not anymore.

For a while, she'd trusted Alex. The boy she'd known. The king she'd served. But like father like son. Betrayal came easily to the Durands.

The thought raced through her mind. Not all of them. Tyson. She wished he and Edmund were there to help her. She reached the doors to the courtyard that stood open, the sun bathing her face in warmth. She sucked the fresh air into her lungs and her magic tingled in her fingertips. She wanted more than anything to get outside where she could unleash her power and feel whole again.

As she stepped out, a hand clamped down on her shoulder. She spun, ready to fight, and came face to face with Simon. Her body relaxed.

"I thought you were going to drag me back there."

His grip on her tightened.

"Simon," she said slowly. "I have to get out of here."

"How far do you think you could get?" His eyes bounced around wildly.

"Let me go." She yanked her shoulder from his grip.

"Persinette, you look like you haven't eaten in weeks. Your magic is out of practice. You're alone. And..."

"What?"

His lip curved up. "You have no shoes."

She eyed her feet and dropped her shoulders. "I have to help them." Her sorry eyes locked on the man who was supposed to be her ally. "You didn't have to sit there night after night listening to their moans... their screams. I thought I'd go mad."

He put a hand on her back and guided her away from the door where a steady stream of soldiers could hear them. He dropped his voice. "The king is going to help them."

"Let me tell you something about the Durands. They're liars. They want nothing more than the destruction of magic. We're descendants of Bela. They'd murder every one of us if they could."

"You don't know what has been happening around here while you were—"

"A prisoner?"

He scowled. "Not everything is simple."

She sighed. "You're right. I wouldn't get far tonight." Not with the blasted curse holding her back. "But tell me this. When the time comes, will you choose Alex or does your loyalty lay with me?"

He dipped his head to meet her eyes. "You are the last remaining Basile. You are meant to save us. My allegiance is forever with you, my queen."

She nodded and squeezed his arm as she walked back the way she'd come.

Alex was no longer in his mother's rooms, but two maids awaited her there. They smiled hesitantly.

"Queen Catrine thought you might enjoy a bath," the one on the right said.

"The tub is full," the other chimed in. "The queen mother's own lye is in there for your use."

Simon dipped his head before following the two maids out.

Etta removed her crusty clothing and examined every inch of skin. Not a single mark. As she sank into the tub, it all began to come back to her in flashes.

Geoff, the guard who'd been brutalizing her for weeks, with his hands on her. She scrubbed as hard as she could. She could feel his touch and no amount of healing took that away. Her skin turned red as she continued to rub it raw.

He'd closed his hands around her neck with such a look of pleasure on his face. She brought her hands up to her neck, finding it hard to breathe. Her chest heaved. She sucked in a long breath before sinking beneath the water. All sound ceased almost as if Edmund was there using his magic.

Bubbles floated in front of her face as her lungs began to ache. But she didn't want to rise, to face the world. Not when she still felt him. Her attacker.

Then she'd been saved. Before her world went black, Alex had been there. He'd come. He'd been choking as well, their curse giving him her pain. It had all disappeared after that.

She broke the surface of the water, gasping for breath. Tears stung her eyes, and she wiped them away angrily.

She wanted to go back to minutes before when she didn't remember. She wanted to forget. She stood, letting the water run from her skin. Grabbing a bath sheet, she wrapped it around herself and stepped out. She barely dried herself before crawling into bed, not bothering to dress before doing so. She wrapped her arms around her chest as she tried to keep herself from falling apart.

A curse rolled off Alex's tongue as he stepped into his mother's rooms. Etta hadn't answered his knock, so he'd let himself in. It was freezing. After the storm, the entire palace was cold, but most of the rooms had fires roaring. No one had thought to start one in here. He'd have a word with his mother's maids.

He went to the fire and began poking around. In all honesty, he couldn't remember the last time he'd started a fire himself.

"Dammit," he snapped, his own uselessness stinging him. Could he do anything for himself? Apparently not. He was every bit the spoiled king people thought he was. Giving up, he walked to the bed to make sure Etta had enough blankets. She was curled up in the velvet covers, but her entire body shook.

"Etta," he whispered. "Are you cold?"

"No," she whimpered. "Please... go away."

He didn't listen to her, instead taking a seat next to the bed. She rolled over to glare at him, keeping the covers tucked under her chin. Her golden hair was slightly damp and drying wildly around her face.

When her scowl deepened, he realized he'd been smiling.

"You look like you're feeling better," he said.

"I was feeling just fine in your dungeons."

"I tried to bring you here ages ago."

"You still don't get it." Her eyes rolled toward the ceiling. There was no anger in her voice this time, only resignation.

He leaned forward with his elbows on his knees. "Etta, I do. I want to help the rest of the people down there."

"What's changed? Some of them were put there by you."

"Me. Everything. I don't..." He rubbed a hand across his face. "If I can trust one person with magic, why can't I trust more?"

"You trust me?"

"Well... yeah."

"I lied to you," she argued.

"I've heard." He winked.

"My father killed yours."

"We are not our parents."

She paused for a moment. "I don't trust you."

His smile dropped. "Etta, so much of what you've gone through is my fault and I will never forgive myself for that. I can't even imagine what I've put you through."

She closed her eyes for a brief moment and when she spoke, her voice was no more than a whisper. "But you can, can't you?"

"Can what?"

"Feel it. Feel me."

He released a puff of air. "I feel everything."

"Your father hunted us for years—"

"Etta—"

"Let me finish. He was cruel and ruthless. But I once asked my father if he hated him. You know what he told me?" She stopped, struggling to get the words out.

Staring into her eyes was like looking into his own soul, tarnished and bruised and when she continued, her voice had lost its strength. "He said your father was still like a brother to him. It would have broken his heart to have to kill him. He did it to save me. But do you see the point? This curse of ours makes me care for you whether I want to or not."

"That's why you told me it wasn't real that first time."

"Because it's not."

He moved to sit on the edge of the bed and looked down into her face. "It sure feels real."

"Alex." Her voice broke on his name. "You held me in your dungeon for weeks. Last night, your guard almost … had me. I should despise you. When you aren't around me, that's easy. In my cell, I planned what I would say to you if I ever got free. But now you're here, now that I'm looking into the eyes of the boy I've known since I was little, all I want is for you to kiss me."

He stretched his arm out to brush the hair from her face but she flinched away from his touch.

"I'm sorry, your Majesty." Her formality was like a punch to the gut. "You should go."

Dark anger flashed across his face and she scrambled back away from him. "I want to kill him. Geoff is lucky he still has his head. He's lucky I didn't gouge his eyes out just for looking at you. Etta." He swallowed hard and closed his eyes. "If he'd …"

"I know," she whispered. "I know it wasn't you. But I can't separate it."

"You blame me." He got to his feet, not taking his eyes from hers. "You should. It's my fault. All of it. But hear me in this—if anyone ever touches you again, I'll gut them myself."

She looked away as he crossed the room. He shut the door behind himself and leaned his head against it. He had duties to attend to, but he set off to find Simon. He needed something to hit.

As soon as Alex left, Etta wanted to call him back and tell him to kiss her until she could forget, until the memories no longer broke them apart. But that was not how her story could play out.

What had she been thinking trying to escape? The curse wouldn't have let her get far from him without the pains. Sometimes she failed to remember who she was. Persinette Basile. The girl with nothing to her name but a curse. She didn't even have a horse anymore. No family. Just an empty kingdom that La Dame had taken from her and her people.

The door opened again and her traitorous heart leaped at the thought of Alex returning. But it wasn't him. His mother walked in carrying a tray. Her maid scurried in behind her trying to take the burden, but the queen mother shooed her away.

Another young girl entered and Etta recognized her immediately. They'd met at the ball.

She released the edge of the blankets no longer caring what these people thought of her. Alex was the one the curse tied her to.

She climbed out of bed and the girl's mouth dropped open at Etta's brazen nakedness. Etta smirked. "Amalie, right?" She didn't need to ask. She knew. This was the girl betrothed to Alex.

Etta stretched her half-starved body as Amalie's head bobbed. God, she was young. It was almost too easy. Looking around the room, her eyes latched onto the vase of flowers on the table next to the bed. Her lips curved into a smile and she reached it. Power surged through her, warming her chilled limbs. It writhed just underneath her skin as she held her hand over the selection of flowers. Her index finger rotated of its own accord and her body relaxed into the flow of power as the flowers grew. And grew. She stepped back as they shot up past her head. The vase cracked and broke apart around the stems. They didn't stop until they reached the ceiling. Etta pulled her magic back, leashing it once again. Using it on the flowers was not the same as being outside, but it sated her for the moment.

And if it freaked these people out, that was a bonus. They already knew who she was so she might as well show them what they were dealing with.

When she turned again, Amalie was so pale guilt worked its way in. She didn't run though. Something blazed in her eyes. Curiosity?

She seemed to forget about Etta's bare state as she hurried toward her to examine the flowers. "You did this with your magic?"

"Yes." Etta narrowed her eyes.

Amalie touched the overgrown flowers in awe. "That was…"

Etta knew what she would say. An abomination. Frightening. Illegal.

"Beautiful."

She opened her mouth to respond, but no words came out.

"Etta," Catrine snapped as she walked toward them. "Put some clothes on."

Etta turned to the queen mother with cold eyes. She hadn't put her in that dungeon, but she was still a Durand and not to be trusted. Not anymore. "If I make you uncomfortable, release me."

Catrine huffed. "Why? You have to stay near Alex, regardless."

"I could live in the outer castle instead of as a prisoner."

She shook her head. "You don't even know what's been happening. It isn't as simple as releasing you."

Etta sat in one of the chairs and took an apple from the tray Catrine had brought in. It crunched as she took a bite. Wiping juice from her chin, she pinned the queen mother with a stare. "Tell me."

Two short raps sounded from the door. Catrine answered and spoke in low tones to Simon. His eyes widened slightly when he glanced past her to see the naked Etta.

Embarrassment bloomed in Etta's cheeks. Catrine said nothing to them as she left to follow Simon.

Etta rubbed the goosebumps on her arms, trying to keep the cold away as the maid started the fire.

"Persinette." Amalie's voice was shy.

"Call me Etta."

"Alex told me you said everything about Etta was a lie."

She bit into her apple again to give her time to think. Did Alex tell his betrothed everything? No. She shouldn't care. They would live happily ever after and she'd... she'd break the curse. She set her apple down and pushed away from the table. Clothes had been laid out for her on a chair in the corner. Loose fitting pants and a warm, suede shirt. She dressed and turned back to Amalie.

The girl's face was so honest, Etta couldn't help her sigh. She'd lose that, eventually. Etta didn't know if she'd ever had it herself.

There was no use for lies anymore. "I have been preparing to be Etta since I was eleven years old." She dragged her hands through her hair so she could twist it into a braid. "I guess you could say that Persinette is the part of me that no longer exists."

Amalie stepped closer, excitement in her eyes. "But they call for you. It's Persinette they want."

"Who are you talking about?"

"The people. There have been attacks in the border villages. The attackers call for you, but I hear the rumors. The other magic folk call for you too. Why?"

Etta tied the end of her braid. "I don't know why any of them would think I can do a damn thing."

"Is it true? Are you their queen?"

Etta's eyes sharpened. "That's dangerous talk, girl." She scanned the room for the maid but she was gone.

Amalie cast her eyes to the ground. "You helped Tyson. I think that means I can trust you."

"One thing you'll learn if you survive long enough is the only person you can trust is yourself."

When Amalie lifted her gaze again, her eyes no longer betrayed her age. They were hardened beyond her years. "It sounds to me like you don't even trust yourself."

Amalie sat and busied herself with putting food on each of their plates. Was she right? Etta lowered herself into the chair and leaned back. The truth was Etta felt like a past she couldn't shake, but Persinette was a future she wasn't yet prepared for. Where did that leave her? Sitting across the table from the woman who was betrothed to the man Etta didn't want to love. Separated from her people. Unable and unwilling to lead.

They called for her release based on her name alone.

She had to prove herself a worthy Basile.

CHAPTER 6

A hand clamped over Etta's mouth, jolting her from sleep. She struggled against the restraint and Geoff's face swam in her vision. Her body thrashed as panic clawed at her chest and she lashed out with her teeth, catching the fleshy part of the hand holding her down.

"Ow, dammit, Etta."

The voice wasn't Geoff's. Her vision cleared and Alex peered down at her. He removed his hand and held it to his own lips.

"You drew blood."

She shrugged and scooted up in the bed so she was sitting. The blanket fell from around her shoulders, revealing bare arms and the low cut of her sleeping gown. She watched Alex's eyes skim her chest. His breath hitched before his heated gaze connected with hers. She quirked an eyebrow.

"You shouldn't be here," she hissed.

He grinned. "You won't be saying that in a moment."

"I'm not going to sleep with you."

He laughed, and she wanted to strangle him. "Is your mind constantly on sex?"

She scowled. "You're the one breaking in here in the middle of the night and staring at my chest."

"I wasn't staring."

"I guess you didn't look any longer than your betrothed did when I was walking around naked."

"She's not... you were just walking around without any clothes?" He smirked. "Why?"

Etta shrugged. "She blushes easily, and I was in a mood."

"You're always in a mood."

"Tell me why you're here or leave me be."

His eyes lit up. "I have everything planned. Tonight, I don't have to be king."

"What do you mean?"

"Put these on and I'll prove I'm not your enemy."

He set the clothing on the bed and shut the door to wait for her. Curious, she scrambled to her feet. He'd left her tight black pants and a black linen shirt. There was even a pair of shiny black boots. It was her kind of outfit. She finished tying the laces and pulled on a black cloak, using the hood to cover her golden hair.

When she met him in the hall, he eyed her and nodded in approval. He was dressed similarly. Simon joined them and the three walked through the empty palace. Outside the main corridor, a familiar face greeted them.

"Maiya," Etta gasped. She knew Maiya must have been the one to heal her, but hadn't spoken to her.

"Etta," Maiya cried, rushing into her arms. "I'm so sorry."

"Shhh, I understand. You had to save your dad."

"This is great and all," Alex cut in. "But we don't have time."

"What are we doing?" Etta asked.

"Fulfilling a promise," Alex answered vaguely.

Maiya looped their arms together. "We're setting our people free."

Alex explained. "I had a friend in the kitchens put a sleeping drought into the guard's food. I know personally that it works like a charm." He looked to Maiya who shrugged.

Shaking his head, he went on. "It's easy, really. When you're the king, at least. All we have to do is let them out. Maiya is here to heal any that need it. I have the list of crimes to differentiate between dangerous criminals and magic folk. We'll get them into the outer town where they'll disperse and hide out until morning when they can get past the outer wall. There's a wagon laden with packs of food waiting on the other side. After that, they're to be on their own."

Etta looked from Maiya to Simon. He nodded with a smile on his face. When she turned to Alex, there were tears in her eyes. She gripped his arm and stretched up on her toes to press her lips against his cheek. "Thank you."

He took a knife from the sheath on his belt and stretched it toward her. "You may need this."

Since becoming a prisoner, she'd felt naked without her weapons. Her entire worth had been tied up in her ability to handle them. As she curled her fingers around the hilt, a small smiled spread across her face. She nodded once, and they headed down into the dark.

Memories assaulted Alex as he walked farther into the musty dungeons that sat beneath his palace. Only days ago, he'd stumbled down those same stairs choking and gasping for breath. That wasn't what haunted him, however. It was the image of Geoff holding Etta against the wall.

She'd stopped fighting and the girl he knew had more fight in her than any man in his guard. He thought he'd been too late. Regret washed over him as he covered his nose against the smell of filth.

They walked around the sleeping form of the guard and made their way down the long hall toward the back. Etta gripped the bars at the end of the hall and spotted an older woman who was huddled in the corner.

"Analise," she whispered. "It's me."

"Persinette?" The woman clambered to her feet, swaying slightly. She moved closer and looked into Etta's face. "I told them you'd come back."

Etta smiled. "There's no way I'd leave you down here." She turned to Alex expectantly.

He tossed the keys, and she caught them mid-air before spinning and jamming them in the lock. The iron door opened on rusted hinges and Etta rushed in. She didn't go to Analise, but to the other corner that had been hidden in shadow. Alex hadn't seen the man curled on his side. No, not man. He was only a boy.

"Henry," Etta cooed, brushing damp hair back from his face. She knelt and pulled him into her lap. He went like a rag doll, his chest rising and falling rapidly. "He's burning up." She turned pleading eyes on Maiya.

Maiya knelt beside her and placed her palms against his cheeks. She closed her eyes. In moments, the boy's breathing evened, and he opened his eyes slowly.

Etta let out a sound that was half sob, half laugh. "I wasn't too late."

"We saw them take you," Henry said, looking up at her. "We thought you were dead."

She hugged him. "I promised you I'd get us all out of here."

Alex finally understood why she refused to come with him when he'd tried to save her from this place. These people. She'd told him and he hadn't listened. They were hers and she was theirs. He got it because he was a king and he belonged to the people of Gaule.

"Sire," Simon said, stepping forward. "I don't think we want to linger."

He took the keys from where Etta had left them in the lock and walked to a nearby cell. After unlocking it, he handed them to Simon. "You and Maiya start releasing the prisoners on the list. I have something else I need to do."

Simon scrutinized the list in his hands and nodded before disappearing around the corner with Maiya.

Geoff hadn't yet woken, but he mumbled in his sleep. A perverse sense of pleasure warmed Alex as he studied the filthy form of the once guard before him. If he woke, he'd see his king and be able to tell anyone who would listen of how the king freed the prisoners.

Alex clenched his fists at his sides. He wanted more than anything to just kill the man. Etta appeared at his side.

She didn't speak as she walked forward and knelt down to look into his face.

Finally, she spoke. "You need to get out of here. He can't see you."

"Or you."

Her shoulders slumped in disappointment as she saw the truth in his words.

Geoff began to stir and Alex pulled her back. "A time will come for you and him. We can't just kill him."

He released her and stood over the stirring cretin. With one swift kick to the head, Geoff went still. Alex bent to feel his pulse. "Good. Just knocked him out."

"You and I have different definitions of good." Etta turned to leave the cell and Alex followed.

Joining the group, he turned to Analise. "Do you need healing?"

"No." Her voice was frigid as she stared at him. "I just want to get my grandson out of here." She pushed past him weakly and focused on the boy. "Henry."

"I'm okay, grand-mere." He got to his feet as if he'd never been sick at all. Alex had seen Maiya's healing enough to not be surprised by it, but there was still something otherworldly about it.

Analise crushed him to her and Etta jumped to her feet. She went to where Simon and Maiya were helping the others.

Alex hung back as Maiya healed those who needed it, providing much-needed strength. Etta spoke to her people in quiet tones, reassuring them. Simon stood silently by her side.

Alex glanced at Geoff's cell once more before moving toward the stairs. His father would be ashamed of him for choosing magic folk over those he'd call "his people." But his father hadn't taught him how to rule. He'd taught him how to avoid his mistakes.

There was no possible way to silently move a crowd of this size. Alex found himself wishing for Edmund and his magic. His friend would be by his side if Alex hadn't betrayed him as well. The power that had frightened him once would have helped them now.

Etta met his gaze and he would've guessed she was thinking the same thing. "Henry," she said.

The boy came toward her and she regarded him, putting a hand on each shoulder.

"I need you to be brave for me, Henry. Let your magic free."

His eyes, round as saucers, flicked to the king in fear. Something tightened in Alex's chest.

Etta shook her head. "It's okay. Pretend he isn't here."

Henry gave a bob of his head and closed his eyes. A weight settled around the group and all outside noise was snuffed out in an instant.

"Does he share Edmund's power?" Alex whispered.

"No. Edmund controls the wind… to an extent. His magic is quite weak, but he can push sounds away. Henry's is more like a cloak settling around an area, a cloak of silence. Magic is specific to each person. No two people will have identical powers."

She threw an arm around Henry's shoulders and kept walking. Alex hadn't seen her like this since she returned to the palace. A smile lit her face, replacing the intensity he knew her for. Even though they were far from safe, the tension drained from her posture as she talked to the people she'd been locked up with.

It reminded him of when they were young and she was carefree, stealing from the market, climbing roofs, and running along the tops of the walls. He'd been mesmerized by her then and couldn't take his eyes off her now.

She said it was the curse, but he refused to believe in that cruel reality. Maybe he'd believed it at first, but then he'd seen Etta locked in a cell and he knew. His feelings went much deeper than a string of magic tying them together. She may not see it yet, but he wasn't ready to give up.

At the top of the stairs, Simon made sure the coast was clear. At the late hour, only the night guards roamed the palace grounds. Alex had made sure specific guards were on duty to avoid any unforeseen problems.

They only had to get past the inner wall.

Etta removed her knife and flipped it once in her hand before pulling up her hood and nodding to Alex.

The first group began to run.

"Remember, if we get caught helping magic folk, they'll rise up and demand my crown," he whispered.

She gave him a blank stare and mimicked his tone. "Remember, if we get caught, they'll demand my *life*."

She took off and the corner of his mouth curled up as he followed her. Out in the courtyard, the moon shone bright, lighting their path as they made it to the far wall. Footsteps sounded in the night.

A young man in the group of free prisoners stepped forward and held out a hand. "Hold still," he hissed.

A guard he hadn't assigned to the night watch walked through the courtyard and Alex held his breath, waiting to be seen. Why was he roaming the grounds? Was someone looking for him? The guard kept moving, turned, and returned to the palace.

Alex released a breath.

Etta leaned close. "Torrence saved our asses there, making us blend into the wall." She pushed away from him. "How does it feel to be at the mercy of magic, King?"

She took off again, and he followed. They wound their way through the streets and he began to recognize where she was leading them. He grabbed her arm and jerked her to a halt.

"We can't use your old house, guards live there now."

She ripped her arm from his grasp. "I've used it before."

She picked up her pace and before long, the group was standing beside the old crates that once held Viktor Basile's chickens.

So many of Alex's childhood memories were attached to that house. He'd avoided it since Viktor and Persinette were run off. A long breath escaped him. She was back. Standing right next to him. But none of it was how he'd imagined it would be.

The small two room house stood pushed up against the inner wall as if it wasn't meant to be there. Ragged wooden walls tilted back, getting support from the stone structure behind them. Thin wooden boards has replaced the old thatched roof.

Henry's cloak of silence descended on them once again and people started to climb from the crates onto the roof before leaping onto the wall. It wasn't an easy climb, and many struggled. An older gentleman was dangled from the wall when Simon stepped forward to help. The man Alex trusted more than any other guard, pulled himself onto the roof with ease. Alex watched in fascination as he did the same on a high stone wall that rose next to the roof. His eyes widened when Simon bent and grabbed the man by the back of the shirt before hauling him up. He didn't even strain. Alex closed his eyes.

"Of course," he said to himself. There were even magic folk in his guard. He pushed the initial anger down. That wasn't him anymore. Simon lifted his head and pierced Alex with a sympathetic look. Was that pity? Alex's gut churned. Did they all pity him? The idiot king who imprisoned friends and betrayed allies. He shook his head. Now was not the time for doubt.

Simon pulled each person over the wall before helping them climb down the roof on the other side.

When it was Etta's turn, she jumped with a grace he'd forgotten she had. Her fingers caught the edge of the roof and she climbed over. Before she could make a jump for the wall, a door opened and out walked a young girl.

Alex stepped forward, his mind spinning for an explanation of their presence. Before he could give it, Etta leaned over the edge. "Hi there," she said. "It seems like you catch me in this situation a lot."

The girl jutted out her chin, taking no notice of Alex. "Did you save them?"

Etta nodded. "I'll keep saving them."

"Good. You can't let the king destroy magic."

The words hit Alex with the force of a bludgeon.

Etta winked and then kicked off the roof, landing smoothly on the wall.

"Hey," an angry voice yelled as a sizable man stepped out the door. "You."

Alex scrambled from the roof to the top of the wall. "Go," he hissed to Etta. She disappeared down the other side as bells began to clang. "The alarm."

"Stop," the guard yelled as his wife joined him.

Alex didn't hesitate before dropping onto the roof on the other side. He leaped to the ground and landed in a roll before popping back up. He tried to catch his breath as his eyes found Etta. "They must've found the empty cells."

"And soon they'll know you're missing." She walked hurriedly away from the wall. The rest of their group had already dispersed through the town as planned. There were people in place who would help them and give them fresh clothes and supplies.

Etta sped up and led him around the corner. "Would they believe you were just out for a midnight stroll?" She pressed herself into the shadows at the side of the building but he could still see her smirk. "You could go back to the palace as if none of this ever happened."

He shook his head and peered around the corner. Light spilled onto the street as the door to the tavern opened. A group of men exited, their drunken voices carrying on the night air.

"Come on," he said after they'd passed. "We need to find a place to hide out for the night."

She gave him a curious look, but he didn't have time for explanations. When he'd decided to help the people in the dungeons, he'd made a promise to himself.

It was time to let her go.

Even after everything, the thought of not having her near broke something inside of him. But she was Persinette Basile. She wasn't meant to be a prisoner and if they had any hope against La Dame, she needed to be free.

They crossed the street, careful not to make a sound. Where was the kid with the gift of silence when you needed him? Oh, right, on the run.

Alex shook his head. Etta led them on a winding path through the town that made up the outer castle. They passed the stables, and he saw her eyes flick to them sadly. Would Etta get to reunite with Verité when she left? He hoped so.

He knew where she was taking them and as they neared the northern edge of the castle walls, the tower rose up over them. He smiled at the memories of the girl who'd claimed she could climb the outside of the imposing structure. The smith's shop down below was closed up for the night, but he could still hear Persinette's howl as she fell. She'd refused to cry, but her face showed her pain.

Etta met his eyes as she stood in the entrance and he knew. She was remembering too.

The tower hadn't been in use during his lifetime and a layer of dirt covered the stone floor on the inside. The staircase spiraling toward the upper levels was crumbling and broken.

When Alex spoke, his voice echoed through the tall chamber. "Why did you choose this place?"

She shrugged as if the memories meant nothing to her. It was her way. Brave, fierce, uncaring Etta. Only, he'd seen the other side of her. The one who created a beautiful meadow of flowers. The girl who was kind to children and saved his brother.

His biggest fear in this world was that he'd killed that girl. Locked her up and released her when she'd lost all that was good.

Etta cleared her throat. "This is as good a place as any to hide. No one ever comes here."

He tore his eyes away from hers, unable to bear the coldness any longer. She shivered and rubbed her hands up and down her arms underneath her cloak.

"Are you cold?" he asked.

"I'm fine."

He walked closer. "No, you're not. You're freezing." He began to unfasten his cloak to add it to hers, but she stopped him.

"I don't need your help. I can take care of myself." Her voice lowered, and he wasn't sure her next words were meant to be heard. "I got used to the cold in my prison."

He turned away from her and sat down against the wall, resting his arms on his knees and leaning his head back.

Etta sat against the opposite wall.

After a while, he finally spoke again. "Can't you make a fire or something?"

She leaned forward and drew her finger through the dirt on the ground to reveal a crack in the stone. "That's not how magic works. My power is growth, enhancement. I could turn a twig into firewood, but making it catch fire is beyond me."

"The stories say the Basile's have immense power, and that's why only you can defeat La Dame."

She sighed sadly and held her open palm over the crack. Grasses began to grow through it and a hesitant smile appeared on her face. It was mesmerizing. Her face shifted, and the smile grew. "This is all I can do and I'm fine with that." She snapped her hand shut, and the grass receded immediately. She turned blazing eyes on him. "I know what the stories say. They've been a weight on my shoulders since my father died and I became the heir of the curse. I can't be the only hope. You can't put that on me. If you do, we're all doomed." She crooked an eyebrow. "Unless I can get close enough to strangle her with weeds."

A laugh burst out of Alex. "I'd like to see that."

"Wouldn't we all?"

"Who would've imagined after all these years and everything that has happened, a Durand and a Basile could end up on the same side."

She grew quiet for a moment and hugged her knees to her chest. "I'm not going to forgive you." She rested her chin on her arm. "If that's what tonight was about. I'm glad you helped them, but it doesn't change anything you've done."

She hardened his resolve to release her. As much as he wanted her, if she didn't want him, there was no point.

She shifted so she was lying on her side and turned away from him. "Goodnight, Alex."

He sighed. "Goodnight."

Her breath soon evened, but there'd be no sleep for him. Not when Etta was just feet away. Not when he didn't know if she ever would be again.

The bells from the palace still pierced the night, and he knew the panic that would've ensued upon finding the king missing. They'd turn over the whole damn palace looking for him, assuming he'd been taken by the escaped prisoners. By Etta. She'd be blamed for releasing them. And he'd be blamed for letting her betray him yet again.

Alex's power was slipping through his fingers. His father's power lay in the fear his people had for him. The nobles who didn't fear him were his greatest allies against the magic folk. When blood ran through the streets of Gaule during the purge, he'd solidified his support. No one dared to go against him.

Alex was not his father. He couldn't sit by and watch his people suffer just to keep his nobles happy. His father's voice rang in his head. "The King of Gaule serves at the pleasure of his people." He could be removed. Replaced.

One day, they'd force him to take a side. Publicly. Not in the dark of night. There'd be no more hiding from his choices. It was easy to do the unpopular thing in the shadows.

The ones who'd had their villages destroyed by magic folk wouldn't understand. They wouldn't differentiate between good magic and evil.

He pressed the heel of his hand against his eyes. Was he doing the right thing?

A whimper sounded from Etta's lips and a shiver wracked her slight frame. He blew a puff of temperate air onto his hands to thaw his frozen fingers and crawled across the floor to her. Her entire body shook in her sleep and blue tinged her lips.

"Etta," he whispered, touching her cheek. It was ice cold.

She groaned, and he ran his hand over her long hair. Unclasping his cloak, he draped it over her as a frigid breeze blew in through the door. The chill settled in his bones.

Making a decision she would hate him for in the morning, Alex lay next to Etta and pulled the cloak over them both. He looped his arm over her and dragged her back to rest against him for warmth.

He told himself they were just sharing their heat, but he couldn't deny the way his body reacted to her. She fit perfectly with him and a sense of rightness hung in the air. Resting his chin on her shoulder, he breathed in her scent and closed his eyes.

As he fell asleep, he couldn't help the tightening in his chest. How was he supposed to let her go?

"Alex," she murmured, her lips turning up into a smile. Sleep added a softness to her words. "I missed you."

He kissed her cheek, and she still didn't wake. "I don't care if you say it's fake or if you'll always hate me. I love you Etta and that'll never change."

She hummed in contentment and he knew that come morning, she wouldn't remember his words at all.

Something heavy sat across Etta's chest as she woke on the cold stone floor. Sunlight streamed in through the door, illuminating Alex's sleeping form next to her. She let herself relax into his hold for a moment, remembering the times before he'd found out her true identity. They'd cared about each other, but that wasn't enough.

Slowly, she slid out from under his arm and the cloak that was wrapped around them both. She smoothed her braid as she walked toward the door to look out. It was early enough that the smith wasn't yet in his shop, but they didn't have long.

Rubbing her arms for warmth, she walked back over to Alex and nudged him with her foot. He grumbled and rolled over. She wasn't in the mood for this.

Narrowing her eyes, she considered him. How had they ended up curled together? It didn't matter now. They had to go.

"Come on, you royal ass," she snapped, nudging him harder.

His eyes snapped open, and he jerked up, his gaze bouncing around the room. "Have we been found?"

"No, you idiot, but we have to go."

He climbed to his feet and shook out his cloak before pulling it around his shoulders. She adjusted her hood to cover her hair, and they joined the rest of the castle that was just waking up.

Keeping their heads down and hoods up, they made it past the guards searching houses for any signs of the prisoners. They passed unconscious men lying outside the tavern door and stable lads giving the horses their exercise. No one spoke to them and they were able to slip into the stream of people exiting past the outer gates.

As soon as they were free, Etta pushed back her hood. "That was way too easy."

"Etta," Maiya's voice reached them and she turned to see her friend. Pierre was beside her.

Fear struck her. Maiya had done her part. She shouldn't be risking herself further.

"What are you doing out here?" she asked.

"We feared for you," Pierre answered.

Etta touched Pierre's arm. "You don't know the meaning of the word."

His lips tipped up into a hesitant smile. "We always worry for you, my dear."

Maiya turned to Alex. "They searched our place last night."

Alex nodded. "I'm going to have some explaining to do." He grabbed Etta's arm and pulled her along the outside of the wall. "Past the edge of the forest, there is a wagon laden with food. That is where your people are meeting you."

"Me?" She stopped, glancing from Alex to a surprised Maiya and Pierre. "Alex, what are you talking about? We're supposed to meet them together."

He reached out to cup her cheek and for once, she didn't want to pull away. "I'm setting you free." His other hand came up to hold her face in place. There was nowhere to look but his eyes. "You never should have been a prisoner."

"No—" she breathed.

He stopped her, resting his forehead against hers. Their breath mingled and Etta gulped back a sob. He didn't know. He couldn't. He knew of the curse, but he didn't understand. Freedom was so close. He was handing it to her, but it wasn't his to give.

"I'm so sorry," he whispered. "You say you won't forgive me, but it is I who won't forgive myself for breaking the thing I love most."

"Alex—"

He stopped her words with a kiss. She didn't know if it was the curse or some lingering love for him, but she gave him every ounce of passion she possessed in that one moment. She never wanted it to end. But a kiss couldn't change the past and she broke away.

"I can't go," she said, her breath coming heavily. She pushed away from him for some much-needed distance.

"You have to."

"You don't understand," she yelled as she put her hands on her head. "I-" The words clogged in her throat.

Alex glanced around to make sure the four of them were still alone.

Pierre stepped close to Etta and laid a calming hand on her shoulder. "Help him understand."

How was she supposed to do that? How could she tell him the only reason she'd first wanted to be by his side was because she'd had no choice. There was never another option. And she'd hated him for it. For imprisoning her long before he ever locked her away. It wasn't his fault, yet she blamed him.

When Etta's eyes met Alex's again, they shone with tears. "This curse." She pounded on her chest. "It exists right in here and has more control over me than you know." She wiped her eyes and turned away from him, kicking at the ground. She flicked her hand, and a vine snaked up the wall angrily.

"Etta," Pierre warned.

She pulled her magic back. She'd tried to escape the curse once when she went with Edmund and Tyson. And it had almost torn her up inside.

She turned to face him again, and the tears were replaced with fire. "La Dame knew what she was doing when she cursed my family and tied us to our enemies. You, Alex, are my enemy and this wretched curse won't allow me to leave you. You must have felt it when I left the first time."

His widening eyes told her he had.

She shook her head. "It was the cruelest fate of all. Your father hunted us for years, but we could never go far. We couldn't escape. My father had to leave me for days, sometimes weeks at a time whenever your father left the castle to go into the far reaches of the kingdom. He had no choice and now I don't either." Her voice softened to a whisper. "My freedom was never yours to give."

CHAPTER 7

Many of the prisoners had made it to the forest, but the group before Alex was considerably smaller than the one that left the dungeons. Many likely hadn't made it out of the palace without being caught. There was nothing more he could do for them.

Alex examined the people he'd freed. Some of them were just children. He shook his head. How could he have kept them locked away?

His eyes found Etta. The same way he'd been able to imprison her. He'd learned long ago to separate himself from his feelings. A lasting lesson from his father. But what was a king without feelings? Without loyalty, empathy... without love?

Simon passed food around. It wouldn't be enough, but it was all they could do. It was up to these people now to save themselves.

They'd begun to regain their strength and there in that haunted forest, they were able to use their magic once again.

Analise raised her arms to the sky, and it was almost as if she pulled the rays of light through the tree cover. How was that possible? And more importantly, how could that be evil?

Alex closed his eyes as the warmth of the sun struck his face. A stillness resided over the freed magic folk and that peace was where joy lived. Where it thrived.

He'd never seen anything as astounding as the sight before him. Magic swirled in the air, wrapping them in its wonder. It was a sight to behold. A young girl shot sparks from her fingertips, making Henry jump to miss them. She did it again, and the children laughed. True laughter, not like the polite guffaws of those at court.

Etta walked up beside him. "They trust you, your Majesty."

He tilted his head in question.

"We've been taught to hide our power with every fiber of our beings. You are witnessing what few others in Gaule ever have."

"What is that?"

"True freedom. Not the kind that is forced upon you or given reluctantly. There is no greater force than complete freedom." Her lip curled sadly. "That is what this forest has always represented. Until recently."

He couldn't meet her eye. He might not have given the direct order, but it was his men who raided the forest.

Her last words were so low he almost didn't hear her. "I envy them."

He wanted to call her back as she walked away. To promise he'd devote his life to finding freedom for her. But his feet stayed in place. He glanced down to see roots wrapped around his boots, preventing him from going after her and making promises she knew he couldn't keep.

He crouched down and sawed at the roots with his knife. By the time he was free, the group was beginning to disappear farther into the trees.

"Where are they going?" he asked.

Etta looked up from where she stood with Maiya and called back, "Home."

Her smiled dropped slowly. No one knew what they'd find in Bela. La Dame was said to be there, but was she any more dangerous for magic folk than the people of Gaule? Alex regretted the things his people had done and knew it wasn't over.

Maiya stepped in front of Etta and pulled her into a hug. "We're going with them."

Etta nodded as if she'd been expecting this, but tears shone in her eyes when she followed Maiya back to Alex.

Pierre held out his hand to Alex. The king stared at it, unable to remember the last time he'd shaken someone's hand. He took it tentatively, still expecting a bow from the man.

"It isn't safe for us in Gaule anymore," he said, "but you have done our people a great service."

Alex nodded and released his hand. When Pierre turned to Etta, he bowed low and Alex understood. Etta was his queen even if she'd never worn the crown.

Etta touched his cheek. "Thank you. For everything."

He stood and kissed the top of her head, not as a subject would, but as someone who cared. "Your father would be proud."

A tear dripped down her cheek. "You think so?"

Pierre smiled and nodded. "We will be waiting in Bela for the day you come home."

"Be safe," Alex said. "Stay far from the palace. La Dame controls that territory now."

When they were gone, Alex turned to Simon. "Sure you don't want to go with them?"

He grunted. "My place is by your side."

Alex squeezed his shoulder as he turned and began the trek back to the palace. How was he going to explain his absence? The entire palace was surely searching for him. He sighed, running a hand through his hair, and glanced at Etta. She added another complication.

How were they tied together and he'd never known? The pain he'd felt after she'd left with Edmund and Tyson was unlike any he'd ever felt before. He'd felt as if his heart was being ripped through his body.

If they found a way to free her, he knew what that meant. She'd leave. Even after everything, he didn't think he'd survive that. Would she even remember him once she was with her people again?

Who was he kidding? Breaking La Dame's curse might not even be possible. But what was worse, Etta staying only because she had to or leaving because she could go where she wanted to be – and it wasn't by his side.

She'd never wanted to stand with him.

Everything made so much sense now. The tournament. Her entry. The way she fought. She'd been forced into all of it. His stomach churned. A young girl made to fight experienced warriors against her will.

But she'd won.

And what had her prize been? A chance to obey her family's curse. What kind of cruel fate was that? He glanced sideways at her, but her stern face gave nothing away. What was she feeling? Angry? How could he blame her?

Maybe they'd been broken long before she'd kept her secrets from him. Long before they'd even met.

They returned to the castle where a line of guards stretched through the outer castle's streets. They busted through doors of the shops and homes that kept the palace running, turning people out of their beds.

Had they seen the king? Did they have any information on the escape from the night before? Were they traitors?

Those that answered no weren't believed, but the ones who'd been a part of the escape stayed silent. Both sides were doing it for their king – they thought.

Alex didn't have a plan. No explanation. But he was the king. He didn't need to explain anything.

If only that was the way it worked in Gaule. He was only as powerful as the strength of his noble's support.

Before they passed the gate, he held his hand out to Etta. "You can't walk through the castle with a weapon." She stared at him in open hostility. "You're still a prisoner in their eyes."

She scowled. "Then how am I going to protect you?"

"You aren't my protector any longer. Simon is here, and I have gained some skill with the sword."

She snorted, but hurt flashed in her eyes as she handed over her knife.

Simon stayed close to his side as they walked forward. The guards saw him immediately.

"It's the king," one shouted excitedly. A murmur worked through the rest of the guards at the gate and when Alex passed through, he was peppered with questions.

"I must get to the inner palace," he said, ignoring their inquiries.

He stood tall and pushed the cloak aside to reveal the hilt of his sword as he strode through the outer castle with purpose. Residents gawked at him. Some cheered. Others whispered. Tension and unsaid accusations filled the air. Did they know what he'd done?

His people wouldn't forgive him for freeing magic folk. He'd known that.

They passed the healer's shop that now stood vacant. Someone would claim it soon enough. The stables were busy with activity but it ceased as the grooms stopped to watch the king pass.

"Not the triumphant return you hoped for, is it?" Etta asked.

Alex didn't answer, but Simon edged closer. "They know."

As Etta searched the faces, she knew Simon was right. Did they think their king a traitor?

A familiar face waited for them outside the inner walls and Etta hissed. Camille clung to her cane as she leaned against the wall, her damaged foot curled back. When she saw them, her eyes immediately went to Etta and narrowed before landing on her brother once again. She pushed away from the wall as they neared.

"Camille," Alex snapped, anger swirling in his dark gaze. "What are you doing here? And where are your guards?"

"We need to talk, brother." She turned, and they followed her. To their surprise, she didn't go through the inner gate, but around the corner instead. Camille ducked through a doorway.

When they joined her, her eyes bounced between Etta and Simon.

"They shouldn't be here," she said.

"They stay." Alex crossed his arms and leaned against the door. His sister's shit was not what he needed to deal with.

She bit her lip. "Fine. I obeyed you, brother. In fact, Duke Caron and I decided not to wait for a wedding and said our vows in front of a priest."

"Then why are you here? Shouldn't you be on your way to his estate?"

"I was getting to that. We were prepared to celebrate our marriage and stay away from court as you'd suggested."

"Ordered."

She scowled. "Are you going to keep interrupting me?" When he stayed quiet, she went on. "In the hours after we were wed, my new husband received a correspondence. He was invited to a meeting here at the castle with a group of nobles wanting to remove you from the throne."

Etta sucked in a breath. Simon went impossibly still.

Alex began to pace. Remove him? His father stripped the council of power and they'd been the only ones able to remove a king. The only way to do it now was to… he snapped his head up. "Sister, do they plan to have my head?"

She couldn't get the words out. Alex hadn't seen Camille cry since she was a child, but there was no mistaking the shine on her face.

"Alexandre, I don't want you to die."

He stopped pacing to face her. "Your husband?"

A satisfied smile quirked her lips. "He is loyal."

He nodded. That was good. A plan began to form in his mind. "I can't sit here in the shadows while they plot against the kingdom. I must confront this before we become embroiled in rebellion."

Camille grabbed his arm and jerked him back from the door. "Aren't the shadows what you used last night to empty the dungeons?" Her voice held all the harshness he knew she possessed, but something made him stop. She hated the magic folk more than anyone. Her disapproval of him was evident.

He narrowed his eyes. "Why are you here?"

"I already told you."

Etta stepped in. "I know people like you, Camille. What's in this for you?"

"You don't know anything about me," Camille spat. She turned pleading eyes on her brother. "You have to make them see. This is our family we're talking about."

He finally got it. She wanted to protect the legacy. He turned away from her. For just one moment, he'd thought the sister he'd always protected, always loved had loved him back. Had come for him. His family was broken. Tyson was gone. He didn't know what to think of his mother and her secrets. Hope was a dangerous thing, and it'd risen in him so quickly he hadn't seen it coming. He'd wanted this one part of his family to be put back together.

"Alexandre." Her voice was so soft, he stopped. A sigh escaped him. She reached out and he let her grab his hand. "You have to save yourself."

When he turned back around, his eyes connected to hers and held fast. "What do I do?"

"The magic folk escaped on their own using their powers. They entered the palace and kidnapped you."

Etta growled.

Camille threw her hands up. "Fine, you can say Etta and Simon rescued you if you want to save them the nobles' wrath."

Etta stepped between Alex and his sister. "You think we're worried about ourselves?" She turned to face Alex. "You can't possibly be listening to her. If you tell them you were kidnapped by magic folk, they'll send out the guard to hunt them down."

"That isn't our main concern," Camille said.

Etta whirled so fast no one could have stopped her before her closed fist smashed into Camille's high cheekbone.

Camille fell back. Simon caught her to keep her upright and prevent her from lashing out. Etta started forward again, but Alex wrapped an arm around her waist.

"Let me go," she growled.

He couldn't. Not unless they wanted a brawl right there in that tiny room. Etta might not always see Alex as the enemy, but Camille was different.

And she was his sister. She was a Durand.

"Enough," Simon barked.

All three of them stared in surprise as his stormy eyes zeroed in on them. He shook his head. "All our hopes depend on the young."

Etta and Camille talked over each other as they began to protest, but Alex knew Simon had a point. There were more important matters than old scores. He released Etta, but planted himself between the two women.

Simon stared at each in turn before stepping out the door. Alex followed him, still unsure what he was going to do.

"Alex." Etta ran to catch up to him. "You can't possibly be considering this."

"Of course he is," Camille said. "He's the king and his first responsibility is to Gaule." She thought for a moment. "He could always claim he was out with his mistress."

Alex spun on her with a growl.

"That's not... a horrible plan." Etta's voice was tentative and so unlike her.

"No," he snapped. "You're a magic woman. As my prisoner, you are no threat. As my mistress, there would be a target on your back."

"Just think about it, brother." Camille grabbed his arm. "Don't put your life in danger in order to protect her."

The irony of it all almost made him laugh. Almost. The tournament seemed so long ago. Etta had won it to become his protector and now all he wanted to do was keep her safe.

"Camille, I'm going to need a list of the nobles at that meeting. Can your husband aid me in that?"

She nodded and released his arm. Tears stained her cheeks, and he wrapped his arms around her. Her cane knocked to the ground with a crash, but he didn't let go.

"Stay safe, brother," she whispered. "You may think me false, but I do wish for that."

He let her go, and she picked up her cane and disappeared around the corner.

As they started toward the palace, his eyes darted around. If his own people were coming for him, it could be any one of them. Who was this assassin to be? He drew in a deep breath as Etta stepped up beside him.

"Please." She paused to steel her voice. "Just consider what it is you do."

He issued an abrupt nod and entered the courtyard, suddenly knowing exactly who he was and what he must do.

CHAPTER 8

Chaos was king.

In the absence of the ruler, nothing was as it should be.

Etta stopped walking as a line of guards barred their way.

"No one is to enter the palace," one yelled from high atop the scaffolding behind the gate.

Alex straightened his shoulders, lengthened his spine, and pushed back his hood. The well-trained guards showed no reaction on their faces.

"Let your king pass," Alex demanded.

They finally parted and Etta and Simon followed Alex across the courtyard and up the front steps of the palace.

Nobles and their servants crowded into the halls, bumping and jostling Etta, but she managed to stay on her feet. What was happening? She couldn't remember a time when there'd been so much activity.

Amalie appeared among the fray and when she spotted them, relief flashed across her face. She rushed forward. "Your

Majesty." Her voice carried and the servants in the hall froze and turned toward Alex.

They whispered to each other that their king had returned. It was said with such obvious relief and glee that Etta scowled at them all.

Almost as one, the servants bowed. Alex stared at them. "Rise," he said. "I need baths drawn in each of our rooms and supper delivered." They ran off to fulfill their duties.

Amalie considered him. "Sire, don't you think it best you address the nobles first?"

He smiled. "Glad to see you were worried about me, Amalie."

She flushed and mumbled, "I had a good guess as to where you were."

"Making nobles wait is good for them." He put a hand on her shoulder. "I am king and will address them when I am ready."

He started walking again and Amalie kept pace. "You should know many of the nobles of the realm are here, more than usual. I don't know how they arrived so quickly. Word hadn't gotten out about your missing status."

"They were already in town for a meeting of their own."

She nodded as if this wasn't surprising at all.

It worried Etta. Alex might act as if everything was under control, but he was in danger of losing it all. After all that had transpired between them, she was surprised she could still care. But she did. More than anything. If something happened to him, it would kill her—literally—but she was more afraid for him than for herself. She knew how the kingdom worked. Her father taught her well.

The nobles supplied the palace with everything it needed from food to gold, even armies. The palace guard was under the king's command, but the greater forces were the ones amassed by nobles from the people living on their lands. If they revolted, the kingdom would fall into war.

They stopped outside Etta's old room and she was snapped from her own thoughts. "You'll be staying here again," Alex said. "Now that you are recovered, my mother would like her rooms."

Etta opened the door and nodded.

"I will be in the throne room at sundown," he said before leaving her.

Before long, a handful of servants showed up with food and water for the bath. After living on prisoner's rations, her stomach flipped and roiled when she even thought of the aromatic meats on the sparkling platter, but she uncorked the wine and poured herself a glass.

It warmed her throat as it slid down and began to calm her nerves. Alexandre Durand was a mystery. His next actions would define him and she hadn't been able to read what he was thinking. The prince she knew thrived on being well-liked. He was comely and charming. He loved opulence. The prince became the king and now she felt as though she didn't know anything about him.

He'd hated magic. He'd spoken out against it many times. He'd arrested her people.

Then he'd saved them.

He imprisoned her, said she betrayed him, and then claimed to love her.

She drained her wine and refilled the cup as she walked into the washroom. Setting it on the floor next to the tub, she removed her filthy clothing and sank into the lukewarm water with a sigh.

She lifted her wineglass to her lips and let it dribble down her chin as she drained it once again before sliding under the water.

Was tonight going to be the end of her? Would the people they'd set free be hunted? Would Alex be the friend she loved or the enemy she hated? He couldn't be both.

She broke free of the water with a gasp, splashing it over the sides onto the stone floor. Stone. Everything in that damned palace was cold and hard and she shouldn't be there. She kicked the water in frustration.

After scrubbing her skin raw, she stood and dried herself before dressing in the clothing she found in the wardrobe. Catrine must have prepared for her return.

She walked to the familiar window. When she'd first arrived in that room, she'd stared longingly out of the window, wishing to be anywhere but there, knowing she had no future but the one within those walls.

A knock on her door made her step back and turn. "Enter."

Simon appeared with a gentle smile on his face. He held a long wrapped parcel in front of him.

"Persinette." He inclined his head. "The king sent me." He set the parcel on the table.

"Care for some wine?" she asked.

He arched a brow. "How much have you had?"

"Only a little." She swayed on her feet.

He shook his head and grabbed her elbow to guide her to the table. "Let's get some food into you."

She didn't argue because he was right. She needed something to soak up the wine. It calmed her so she hadn't stopped.

"In my defense," she said slowly. "I deserve it."

He laughed softly as he set a slice of bread and hunk of cheese on her plate. "More than most."

She collapsed into a chair. "I am a queen with no kingdom."

"To be fair, you weren't raised to be queen, so that was never taken from you."

"I am a prisoner and this curse will keep me chained here for the rest of my days." She slouched as the room spun around her.

"Ahhh, well that you were raised for."

A hiccup punctuated her scowl. "Fine then, I'm a warrior with no weapons."

"A true warrior doesn't need weapons."

"Are you trying to vex me?" She shot him a glare.

He stared back. "Are you trying to make me pity you?"

She bit into the bread and chewed. "No."

"When you were in the dungeons, I promised to free you." His smile fell as he glanced away. "I did not know the true meaning of the curse. I didn't know you couldn't leave."

"Simon." She stopped eating for a moment. "Don't think for one moment you failed me. You've done more for our people than even I have. I heard what you did at the gallows."

"That was the king's doing."

She nodded. "He's changed his position on magic and it could cost him his throne."

Simon scratched the back of his head. "I truly don't know what he will do at the meeting tonight."

She closed her eyes for a brief moment. "Just promise me you'll protect him. He needs you."

When she glanced at Simon again, he was smiling. "I'll have help." He stood and began to unwind the fabric wrapping his parcel.

A gasp escaped her as a blade was revealed. She recognized it immediately. "My sword," she whispered. "How?"

"He's kept it since you were arrested." He held the hilt towards her. "Maybe even then he had faith you would use it in his service once again."

Her fingers closed over the golden hilt. It fit her hand like it was meant to be there. The blade was light but strong as any other. Her father always told her it wasn't a blade that won the fight, but how one used it. Even so, he'd had this one made specially for her. It was part of her.

She walked to the open area of her rooms and cut an arc through the air. Her movements were sure, confident. It was what she was meant to be doing. She spun on one leg and flung her arm out as she stumbled forward, the wine stealing her balance.

Simon chuckled and when she faced him once again, he bowed.

A smile lit her face. "So, I was told you began training Alex with a blade."

Simon chuckled. "I don't know how a prince survives so long without the skill."

"I tried to goad him into dueling with me when we were young, but he was always lost in his sketches." She set her blade down with a dramatic sigh. "Maybe it's better to have a king whose first inclination isn't to fight."

"Unless that's the only thing left to do."

"Yes, unless that."

Still feeling the effects of the wine, Etta twisted her damp hair into a braid and left her room behind. The entire palace seemed as if it was waiting for something. The servants were holding their collective breath.

Etta took notice of every face and each action as she made her way to the throne room. She brushed her hand over the sword hanging at her waist as dread filled her. It was her first time roaming the palace on her own since she was protector and she couldn't help but feel something important was about to happen.

The doors to the throne room were shut, but upon seeing her, one of the guards opened them and let her through. The room was crowded with nobles. Some lived near and had been able to make the journey immediately. Others must have been in town for the meeting Camille mentioned.

Alex hadn't yet arrived, but Amalie found Etta and beckoned to her.

"Do you know what he's going to say to them?" Amalie whispered. She'd come in a gown cut perfectly for her. Yellow lace trailed the curves of her torso over the sky blue high-waisted dress.

Etta wore her usual black pants with a tight black top. If she ended up having to use the sword at her side, she'd need the mobility a dress lacked.

Plus, she hated the things.

"I wish I did." Etta finally answered with a shrug as she leaned against the wall to wait. She made her sword as visible as possible as she watched the nobles congregate amongst themselves. They wore an array of clothing ranging from bright silks to plain muslins. Etta was the lone woman present not to wear a dress.

The women stared, and the men kept their distance. Did they recognize her? Did they see the sword at her side? Was this the first time most of them had been around a magic woman?

The gawking woman pointed, her angry words floating on the thick air. "It's one of the prisoners."

Etta clenched her fingers over the hilt of her sword.

A sudden yearning to be outside hit Etta. Then she'd show them what she could do. Their reactions would almost be worth having to hide it for so long. None of them understood because they didn't try to understand.

They'd call her dangerous, but they didn't know how truly dangerous she could be.

Their ignorance blinded them. La Dame wasn't only coming for the people of Bela. Gaule would need allies – those with magic – or would find themselves very much alone.

Maybe if they stopped persecuting those with magic in their blood, they'd see how much they needed Etta and her people.

Instead, they were going to find themselves very much alone.

"Has Alex told you of the border?" Amalie asked.

"I haven't seen him since he dropped me at my rooms."

The young girl glanced around to make sure they wouldn't be overheard and leaned in. "La Dame is still in Bela. Our scouts report she has repaired the old palace there."

Etta sucked in a breath. "Not possible."

"They saw it with their own eyes."

"Amalie, that palace is in ruins." At least that was what she'd been told her entire life. "There is nothing left to repair." She rubbed her eyes. "But the bigger question is why she'd move herself there when her palace at Dracon is supposed to be the grandest there is."

All thoughts of La Dame disappeared when the double doors were thrown open and Alex faced the crowd.

Etta pushed away from the wall and elbowed her way through the bodies blocking her view. They scowled, but she barely noticed. The only thing she was focused on was the king who was walking down the long, carpeted aisle with a hard glint in his eye. He rolled his shoulders back and held his chin high, refusing to look anyone in the eye.

Chain mail rattled with each step he took but it was hidden behind a black surcoat embroidered with a deep green dragon. It was tied at the waist by a heavy sword belt. He'd come to the throne room armed. That alone sucked the air from her lungs. He'd made sure both of them could protect themselves.

A fur-trimmed mantle of velvet sat lightly on his shoulders, puffing out at the sleeves. He shifted his hand to the hilt of his sword, drawing every eye in the room to the jeweled instrument they had no doubt he knew how to use now.

His dark hair stood out beneath his golden crown, but it was his eyes that had the nobles in the room staring in silence. They blazed with a fire Alex wasn't known for. There was a purpose to every step. Etta had never seen Alex like this and she realized what she was seeing.

He was truly becoming the king. He was owning it for the first time. That throne was his. These nobles were his subjects. It was his birthright and now she saw it was truly what he was meant to do.

Catrine followed a step behind her son in an emerald gown of satin and fur. Simon was the only guard to accompany them, his eyes wary. Camille was nowhere to be found, but she'd been banned from court so he couldn't very well allow her before the throne.

Tyson should be up there. Etta sighed. Alex could've used his brother. Edmund too.

Alex reached the steps leading up to the throne and took them slowly. Simon and Catrine stayed on the lower dais. When Alex turned to gaze over the assembled nobles, the group bowed.

Etta followed suit, anticipation working its way into her heart. Alex looked so very much like his father on that throne as his gaze turned to stone. He looked heartless, uncaring. She straightened and pushed back into the crowd to find Amalie. The girl was watching Alex with rapt attention.

"Can you believe I almost had to marry him?" she whispered.

Etta grimaced.

"I mean, the king has been good to me, but look at him."

Etta did. He still hadn't said a word.

Amalie went on. "He has less of Tyson's kindness. Tyson couldn't be king because there's nothing cold in him. He's all heart."

Etta turned away to scan her eyes over Alex. Amalie was wrong. Etta had seen Alex's kindness when he freed her people, when he protected her from the cold. She'd felt it every time he'd kissed her. Alex had broken them. Or she had. She didn't truly know. There'd been many lies and betrayals. Was he about to crush the final piece?

Alex finally spoke. "Bring him in." He flipped his hand to the door.

It opened, and a guard dragged forward a well-dressed man Etta recognized instantly. She'd been in the dungeons for Lord Leroy's disgrace, but she'd never forget his disdainful looks. The man was dragged forward and dropped in front of Simon, near the throne.

A few people in the crowd gasped.

"My king," Lord Leroy said, trying to get to his feet.

"Simon," Alex barked.

Simon placed his hand on the back of Leroy's neck and forced him down.

Alex raised his voice. "This man was banished from court."

Amalie gripped Etta's arm so tightly she feared it would break.

Alex scrutinized Lord Leroy. "Yet, he returned with ideas of rebellion."

"That wasn't me, sire," Leroy cried. "It was Duke Caron."

Alex laughed but there was nothing humorous about it. "I tried to have mercy before, but no longer. I hereby strip you of your title. Your tax income forfeit to the crown. You're to be exiled to your own estate with guards of my choosing." He narrowed his eyes. "You may leave."

Simon hauled him to his feet, but Lord Leroy jerked away from him. "You can't do this."

Alex jumped to his feet and his voice boomed throughout the room. "You are lucky to be leaving here with your life. Don't make me change my mind."

Simon passed Leroy to another guard, and he was dragged from the room screaming obscenities.

Alex sat back on his throne with an eerie stillness. Catrine moved to the side of him and sat in a chair on the level below. Simon shot threatening glances toward the assembled nobles, many who were as traitorous as Leroy.

The public door banged open and a silver-haired man rushed in. He moved with the grace of a trained fighter, but was dressed better than any noble present. He wore a velvet coat with puffed sleeves over a silk shirt and tight-fitting breeches. His face was another matter. Attractive in a rough sort of way, but his eyes were alert and trained on the king.

He reached Alex and handed him a paper.

"That's Duke Caron," Amalie told her.

Camille's husband. Curiosity had Etta watching him. Many of the nobles scowled at him, but the duke grinned as his eyes passed over the room. His gaze met hers and he winked. She ripped her eyes away.

Alex stood and began to read from the paper as his guards rushed in. It was a list of names.

"Robina Garion." A commotion rose across the room as someone screamed. Two guards wrapped their hands around the upper arms of a red-haired woman with thick spectacles. She kicked and yelled obscenities at them as they hauled her through the public entrance.

The crowd of nobles left behind murmured and began yelling at the king. Their voices ran together as Alex called out the next one. "Paulo Deorga and Olivia Deorga." This couple stared at each other as they were taken from the room. Their demeanor spoke of nobility but the actions they were arrested for did not.

Alex was tragically efficient. Not every person accused was present, but the room began to thin as he continued reading names.

The king barely acknowledged the men he was condemning. When the last one had been hauled away, he raised his eyes to the remaining crowd. "The men and women taken from this throne room today stand accused of treason."

That was it. No explanation or words of comfort. Only a cold statement.

Amalie was crying beside her and Etta put an arm around the girl's shoulders as the kingdom came down around them. This was only the beginning.

Alex cleared his throat. "There has been speculation as to what occurred in the castle during the last twenty-four hours." He set his jaw and swept his eyes across the room.

Etta stepped forward so he could see her. Amalie was still attached to her arm, but in that moment, Etta felt very much alone. When Alex's gaze finally met hers, he pressed his lips into a line and huffed out a breath.

Etta's heart beat wildly as if it would jump out of her chest. She needed an indication, a hint of what he was about to do.

"Magic is evil," he said.

Etta couldn't breathe.

Alex continued. "That's what I've been told my entire life. Magic has created every one of our problems. It's why we needed the wards and why we began to fall apart when they were gone." He paused. "I think it's time that as a kingdom we acknowledge that our problems are of our own making. Magic folk are no better or worse than non-magic folk. There is evil in magic, but there is also good."

He stood from his throne and walked down the steps. His mother joined him as a show of support.

"Yesterday eve, I released the magic folk from our dungeons." A rumble erupted from the crowd and he held up a hand. "They did not escape. I was not kidnapped."

His eyes locked onto Etta's. She felt the curse wrapped around her heart. It squeezed and pulled, but it was more than that. She breathed deeply, her lungs aching for more. She felt as if every word he spoke was only to her, for her. This was how he began to put them back together.

Alex finally broke his frosty king demeanor and the corner of his mouth lifted. "The truth is I spent the night—and really the past year—learning even as we fight against it, magic can be our greatest ally. Those that possess it and want to use it for good must be protected. Over the next few days, we will be issuing royal decrees changing some of our oldest laws. I hope it is a start to making things right."

His nobles began calling out questions, some in anger, others in curiosity. Alex didn't answer a single one as he left the room behind.

Etta bent over, trying to catch her breath as the words she'd waited for him to say hung in the room.

Amalie was still crying from watching nobles she'd known her entire life get taken away and her father lose everything, but Etta couldn't focus on anything besides the man who'd just told his entire kingdom everything they believed was wrong.

Alex had done it. He'd taken their mission from the shadows and brought it into the light. She closed her eyes as tears welled underneath the lids.

Nobles began filing out, talking loudly amongst themselves. Etta didn't hear any of it. She clutched at her chest and wiped the tears away.

She didn't care if it was the curse. The past couldn't hold her back. She was no longer the girl who'd deceived the King of Gaule and Alex was no longer the magic-hating king who'd imprisoned her.

It was everything her people needed. Everything they never foresaw.

And all she knew was she had to go to him.

She needed Alex to make it feel real.

She needed him to be on her side.

Alex slammed his door behind him, preventing his mother and Simon from following him. He lifted his crown off his head and set it on the table, relieved to have the weight of it gone. He didn't want to have to be that kind of king. The one who imprisoned his own nobles and frightened his people, but that was what was needed. He didn't have to like it.

He pressed his fingers against his closed eyes and sighed. Gaule couldn't overcome a rebellion. Not now.

He thought of the meeting he'd had before going into the throne room. People were disappearing from along the border. Gaulean people. Gone. The messenger arrived in the early morning carrying a report from Anders. The captain kept it curt. He didn't like Alex, but he was a loyal man. His report could be trusted.

Where could La Dame be taking his people? They were sure she was the culprit. That meant the missing people were in one of two places: Bela or Dracon. Bela was still a mystery, but Dracon was worse. It was impregnable with imposing walls encircling the mountain kingdom. It wasn't a vast realm, but it never had to be, not with the magic in their blood.

Alex's hands shook as he gripped the edge of the table and bowed his head. He needed to regain his sanity. He needed to be able to think.

His heart raced as he thought of what he'd just done. Gaule hated magic. The laws wouldn't change overnight and the people may never accept his words. Had he just put a greater target on himself? Now, instead of magic folk, it was his own people sitting in his dungeons.

A leather-bound book called to him from the bookcase and he stalked toward it. It'd been a long time since he'd allowed his mind to be sucked into his drawings. His fingers ran down the worn spine before flipping over the cover. He sucked in a breath and let it trickle back through his lips as his past stared right back at him. The first few pages had been torn out in a previous fit of rage long ago. Now a more recent picture of Edmund stared back at him.

He traced the lines of his face. "I could use your counsel right about now, my friend." He'd do anything to have Edmund and Tyson back with him. Where were they? He didn't know if they were safe and there was no way to contact them. To tell them how much he wanted them by his side.

He took the sketchbook and moved to the couch. The next image was of Etta as a young girl. His eyes roamed the beauty he'd drawn her with and he knew. Even then, he'd loved her.

His father would be disappointed in him. He'd call him weak to be controlled by a woman, to allow her to change him. But Alex had finally taken the first steps toward becoming the kind of king he wanted to be. It wasn't by some coronation. That happened ages ago. But taking his throne the way he had tonight had been because of that woman and those she fought for. They made him see he couldn't hold himself back for fear of his people. There was power on the throne, but it had to be taken. He understood that now.

He flipped to an image he'd drawn while sitting atop the outer wall, reminding himself what he fought for. Gaule. Its soul was written in the grassy hills that had once been stained with blood. In the villages that only knew peace because others didn't. In the face of a princess who thought cruelty was righteous.

The question remained. Could Gaule be saved from itself?

He stood and slid the sketchbook back onto the bookcase. It hadn't provided the answers as it had when he was younger. There were many holes in his knowledge of Bela and Dracon. He could thank his father for that.

He had to see Etta. She'd know what to do.

When did he start trusting her so fully? The question stopped him in his tracks. The girl who'd lied to him was now the one he needed by his side.

With a shake of his head, he yanked the door open before colliding with someone.

"Alex," Etta yelped as she fell backward.

He grabbed her around the waist to steady her and suddenly didn't remember the questions he'd had. Not when she was so warm in his hands.

"I'm sorry I startled you," she said quietly, tilting her face up to look at him.

"It was my fault." Where were his words?

Her cheeks reddened, and a smile curved her lips. "It really was." She glanced down to where his hands were still clutching her waist. "I don't think I'm in danger of toppling over any longer."

"No?" He grinned.

She bit her lip as she shook her head.

"Would you like to come in?"

Her eyes flicked to the guard who stood silently by the door, a reminder that the king was never alone.

For a moment, he thought she would decline. She chewed on the inside of her cheek and studied him. "Okay."

A wave of relief washed over him as he led her in and shut the door.

"Would you like some wine?" He walked toward the table.

She followed close behind him. "Not really, no."

He went on. "I was coming to see you because we have some troubling reports I thought you may be able to shed some light on."

"Alex," she said.

He poured himself a glass of wine and turned to her. "Are you sure you wouldn't like some?"

She shook her head. He brought the glass to his lips, but her hand on his arm stopped him. He lowered the goblet and met her intense gaze.

"What you did today…" She inhaled deeply. "You became the man I never thought you'd be."

He set his wine down. "Etta—"

"No, I need to get this out. I don't usually say the right things. Everyone tells me I have a destiny. I'm supposed to be their queen, but I don't know how to help them. I don't have the power they need me to have. For years, I've been training to serve, not to lead. I'm the cursed, but I didn't know what that meant." She tilted her head to the side as her eyes shone. "Today I saw you lead. You were amazing. And I thought maybe I could be that for my people too. But I'm still cursed. I'm still tied to you, my enemy."

He stepped forward and hooked his fingers underneath her chin to tilt her face up. "You know it's treason for you to call yourself queen of anyone who still lives in Gaule."

She nodded.

"Yet, all I want to do is tell you how much I believe in you. Is that the curse?"

She hiccupped back a laugh. "I don't think so. I think that's you."

"How much of this is real, Etta?" He leaned his forehead against hers and inhaled.

"Does it matter anymore?" she whispered as she gripped the front of his shirt to hold him there.

He moved his lips to her ear. "No, I don't suppose it does."

She groaned when he sucked her earlobe into his mouth and he pulled her against him. His lips traced the soft skin of her cheek until finally claiming her lips in a searing kiss. They melted together and Etta ran her hands up his chest before taking hold of his collar and pushed the jacket from his shoulders. Alex threw it away as his fingers skimmed the heated skin where her shirt met her pants.

Every emotion of Etta's imprisonment came bubbling to the surface as she pushed his shirt up and over his head.

"Etta," he whispered. "I'm so sorry. I did not order what was done to you, but it was still my fault. It happened under my watch. Geoff was my man." He pulled her into a crushing hug and she buried her face against his bare chest.

"I know. I can't forget it, Alex."

He released her and stepped back. It would always stand between them whether he'd done it to her or not.

She wiped a hand across her face and he cursed himself for causing her tears.

"I can't forget it," she repeated, stepping toward him. "But, Alex, everything inside of me is reaching out to you. My head may be conflicted, but my heart..." She took his hand and pressed it over her heart. "...it only beats for you."

He reached out his free hand and dried the tears on her face with his thumb. "I love you, Etta. I think I've been in love with you since watching you win your first battle."

She smiled. "You were just jealous of my sword skill."

A laugh burst out of him. "You were the most incredible thing I'd ever seen. I don't know what's in store, and I can't promise we'll never be on opposite sides of a war. That's what we were meant for. But right now, I'm so in love with you it hurts and if I don't kiss you again, it could very well kill me."

"If you don't kiss me again, I could very well kill you."

He kissed her softly, smiling against her lips. His fierce Etta. He spun her around and dragged her shirt over her head as she walked backward toward the bed, never releasing her.

Even as he loved her, he knew. Their bliss wouldn't last for long.

Contentment. A feeling she'd never truly known. Was this as close as it got? Etta rested her head against Alex's firm chest as she traced the ridges and valleys with the tips of her fingers.

Alex tangled his hand in her wild hair.

"So soft," he whispered.

She hummed in response, wishing they could stay there forever. Each time she'd been with him before, she hadn't gotten the chance to wonder at the meaning behind it all. Alex was the king of Gaule and she… didn't know what she was. No longer protector. Not yet queen. Lover was too trivial a word.

"You're thinking too hard." Alex cupped her cheek as she shifted to look up at him.

"How do you know I'm thinking anything?"

He touched the space between her eyebrows lightly. "You have a line here." His fingers moved to dance across her lips. "And a frown here."

She sighed. "I don't know where this all leaves us."

"Why does it have to leave us anywhere? It could stay with us." He bent to kiss her lips. She lifted her head to deepen the kiss.

When he pulled back, she sucked in a breath as if she'd never breathe again.

"There was something I needed to talk to you about tonight." He wrapped his arms around her back. "It's crown's business."

Sitting up, she gathered the sheet around her. "What is it?"

"Can you tell me what you know of Bela?"

Her eyes narrowed. "Why?" Whatever they'd shared, he was still the king of Gaule and she couldn't yet trust his intentions for Bela.

He rubbed his chin, considering her. "People are disappearing from the villages along the border."

"I thought those villages suffered recent attacks. Could that be the cause?"

"Our sources tell us the disappearances began before the attacks. We have no way of knowing if they were magic folk or not, but we have our suspicions."

She brushed her hands through her hair absently. "Couldn't they be abandoning Gaule of their own free will now that the wards are gone?"

"We thought of that, but these people left everything behind. Families. Belongings. It's all still there."

"Are you sure they're not in the dungeons of one of your nobles?"

He blanched at that, but kept his measured tone. "I considered that as well. It is unlikely, but still a possibility."

"What's more likely?"

He thought for a moment. "We know La Dame is in Bela. What we don't know is why."

"You think La Dame is abducting the magic folk of Gaule?" she asked. "That's... probable. Why would she need them?"

He shivered. "She likes to play games. My father always said that of her. She has a bit of fun with her enemies before destroying them."

"Oh, I know that all too well," she whispered.

He pulled her back down to him and brushed her hair back from her face. "I know talking about Bela is hard for you."

Etta relaxed into him. "It's not that. I really don't know much, having never been there. I only know what my father told me. It used to be a thriving kingdom stuck between the mountains and the sea with great white cliffs and ports where ships from across the great sea would bring all sorts of trade." She smiled at the memory of her father's stories of Bela. "Everyone who lived there had some sort of power, but most were quite weak... except for the Basiles." She trailed off and buried her face in his neck.

"You don't have to talk about your ancestors," he said, running his palm along the bumps of her spine.

"My father told me Bela is unlike anything you've ever seen. The ruins of the ancient palace sit on a set of cliffs overlooking the sparkling sea." She was quiet for a moment. "I don't know anything that will help you."

"I'm sending some soldiers across the border," he said.

Etta sat up to look at him, but Alex didn't meet her eyes as she scooted from the bed.

"Maybe we should be the ones to go." She stared down at her hands.

"You know we can't risk that."

He was right, but it didn't make her feel any better. She was the one who should be protecting her people. If La Dame was taking them, she needed to find a way to stop her.

Alex started walking toward the table when his foot caught on the rug and he stumbled, unable to catch himself. As he crashed to the ground, a laugh burst from Etta's lips.

"Are you okay?" Her words were muffled by the hand she clapped over her mouth.

A wry smile appeared on Alex's handsome face and he smoothed his hair back before climbing to his feet, giving Etta the perfect view of his firm derriere.

"Stop staring at me," he said as he made his way to the table. "Or I won't give you any wine."

"Too bad I left my sword in my room." She grinned. "I'd fight you for it."

He looked back over his shoulder. "I wouldn't stand a chance, would I?"

She laughed in answer.

"That's what I thought."

As he poured two glasses of wine, she studied his every movement. "I have a confession to make."

He held the glasses by their stems as he walked back over and offered her one. "I'm not used to so much truth from you."

The words stung, but she hid it by sipping her wine. "Someone must have slipped me truth serum because I usually let my sword speak for me."

He smiled over the top of his glass.

"I've been rooting for you." She shifted her eyes away from him as the words warmed her face.

"Rooting for me?" His brow arched.

"To prove me wrong. I came to the palace knowing you were my enemy and wanting to hate you for it."

"So, what changed?" He sat down on the corner of the bed and she scooted over next to him.

"Edmund."

Just the name sent a smile to Alex's face and Etta went on.

"When I realized what you meant to him, I wanted you to be good, to be honorable. I didn't want him to be hurt."

He took her hand in his and squeezed. "How long did Edmund know about you?"

"Since before the tournament. I met him in the village and may have..." She took a sip of wine and the next words spilled out as one. "Tiedhimupwithweeds."

Wine shot from Alex's mouth and his chest heaved as he laughed. "Did you cover his mouth? Please tell me you did."

She shrugged, and he laughed harder.

"That doesn't scare you? That I can do that?"

He stopped laughing abruptly and got to his feet before setting his wine down. He rubbed the back of his neck as the silence continued.

He turned to peer back at her. "It does."

Those were the only words she got before he walked into the other room mumbling about needing something to eat. His confession sat heavy on her chest and she didn't know how to change it. He was still afraid of the one thing that made sense to her and she was terrified of his fear. What if that fear one day made him undo all the good he was doing?

He didn't have the right to say that to her and walk away. Who did he think he was? She didn't care that he was a king. They had a conversation to finish.

She swayed as she got to her feet. Had she had that much wine?

The wine sloshed over the side of her cup as she stumbled through the room. "Alex?" she called, suddenly not feeling well. The wine sat like poison in her stomach. "Alex?" Her feet dragged as she walked into the dining area where a tray of food rested untouched on the table. "Alex, I think something's wrong."

Her mind clouded over as her feet hit something and she fell forward. The wine goblet went flying, sending red spray across the floor. She got to her knees and gaped at what she'd tripped over in shock.

Alex lay sprawled on the ground. She crawled toward him and shook his shoulder.

Her words slurred as she demanded he wake. "Are you okay? Alex. Alex!"

The fog in her mind thickened and control over her limbs slipped away. Her arms gave out and as her head slammed into the chilled stone floor, darkness bore down mercilessly.

CHAPTER 9

It was impossible. Matteo grew up in La Dame's household and never would have imagined the true power she possessed.

When they'd first arrived in Bela, it was to a pile of rubble. The castle was nothing but a set of ancient ruins sitting alone on the cliffs. The land surrounding the castle had been an overgrown jungle.

As Matteo stood on the balcony high up in the folds of the castle, his eyes swept the tall towers of gleaming white marble and the manicured grounds they presided over. How was any of it there when weeks ago, it hadn't been?

"Matteo, darling," a deceptively sweet voice called from inside.

Matteo flinched and turned to walk back through the doors. La Dame sat at the round table in the center of the room. Matteo's father, Warren, stood to her right.

Matteo walked forward and bowed stiffly.

"Hmmm." La Dame tapped a finger against her chin. "It would be much simpler if you weren't a Basile."

He forced a blank expression onto his face to hide the burgeoning smile. La Dame's greatest power had no hold over those with Basile blood in their veins.

"It would, my Queen." Warren inclined his head.

Matteo was past being surprised at the extent of his father's loyalty to the woman who'd kept them prisoner all these years.

La Dame narrowed her eyes at Matteo. "Warren, I'm not sure your son understands the extent of my power."

Matteo's father wouldn't even look at him. "I think not, my lady."

La Dame stood and pushed back her chair. As she walked toward Matteo, she straightened her inky black dress. Her steps were smooth, and she swayed her hips with each one. La Dame saw every move as a seduction of sorts. Matteo clenched his jaw as she reached him and cupped his cheek in her palm.

She traced her fingers down over his skin and gripped his chin roughly. "You have some work to do, my boy, but before that, I have some things to show you."

She waved a hand toward the door, and it swung open of its own accord. Two guards entered dragging a young man in a ratty soldier's uniform. "This is Lance. He is a new arrival."

La Dame turned to the man as the guards dropped him on the ground and moved to stand by the door.

"Get up," La Dame ordered.

Lance didn't move.

"I said, get up."

An invisible force yanked his head back and pulled him to his knees before making him stand. His head lolled forward.

La Dame peered back over her shoulder and grinned. "Isn't it magnificent?"

She wanted him to agree. She thrived on validations. But Matteo's stomach churned. He managed a short nod.

"Dance," La Dame ordered the man.

He began to move slowly.

"Faster."

The man's eyes struggled to stay open as his feet moved quickly and his arms swung out in front of him.

La Dame clapped her hands together. "You're a marvelous dancer, Lance." Her eyes connected with Matteo's as she issued her final order. "I'm going to need you to push this through your heart." She held out a thin dagger and Lance didn't hesitate in taking it.

He pressed it against his chest.

"No," Matteo screamed. "Stop this." He lifted his eyes to the woman who held all the strings. "Please."

Lance jerked and stabbed the dagger deep. He fell back as his blood pooled around him, stark against the white of the marble floor.

Matteo fell to his knees and retched. The soldier wasn't the first person he'd seen die, not by a long shot, but it never got easier.

"Why?" he whispered.

La Dame opened her mouth to answer, but closed it and pushed back her auburn hair. She turned away as a guard rushed toward her.

"My queen, we have an urgent matter."

She nodded and followed him from the room, stepping over Lance's body in the process.

Matteo's father put a hand on his shoulder.

He shrugged it off and stood.

"Son," Warren began. "You must get a better handle on your emotions."

Matteo glowered at him. "Like you, father?"

"She's trying to break you."

"Why? Why am I so important to her?" He sat at the table and buried his face in his hands.

"Because of the blood that runs through your veins. The Basile blood protects you from her control and that frightens her."

"What if we were to escape?" He lifted his eyes to meet his father's. "I know we could."

Warren shook his head. "She would find us, son. She won't let a Basile roam free."

"There already is one who roams free."

He flicked his gaze to the door. "It is only a matter of time before La Dame brings Persinette here. Be prepared. You're going to meet your cousin."

The door slammed open, making father and son jump apart. La Dame charged through with a grin on her face. She rubbed her hands together. "My boys, we have a special guest in the palace."

As if called, the guards from before led a young man through the door. His wrists and ankles were shackled, and the chains clanked with every step.

"Warren, Matteo, I would like you to meet the Prince of Gaule, Tyson Durand."

Matteo jumped to his feet, his breath catching in his throat. A prince of Gaule. La Dame just gained the largest bargaining chip of all.

"Where are your manners?" La Dame demanded. "Bow."

Matteo obeyed mechanically, knowing it was better not to resist. When he rose, he studied the prince's face. An air of defiance lit in his eyes. He held his shoulders high, his back straight, and his direct gaze met each of theirs in turn.

La Dame faced Tyson. "Now, it's your turn. Bow."

The boy didn't move. He didn't look like he was even breathing.

"Bow," La Dame screamed.

Tyson gnashed his teeth together. "You are not my queen."

Her hand flew out and struck him across the cheek. "You will do as I say. Get on your knees."

"No."

Matteo winced as La Dame motioned for a guard to punch Tyson in the stomach. His respect for the prince grew with each passing moment. How was he resisting the magic?

Tyson doubled over.

"On your knees."

He clutched his gut and breathed deeply before straightening up. "I am a prince of Gaule. I don't kneel to anyone."

She nodded to a guard who snatched a chair so quickly, Matteo didn't see it happening until the wooden seat cracked against Tyson's back. He crumpled to the ground, wheezing.

La Dame leaned down. "How are you resisting me?"

Tyson coughed, spitting blood onto the floor, but didn't answer.

"Oh my." La Dame straightened. "It can't be." She covered her mouth with a laugh. "Viktor, you old bastard." She looked down on Tyson once more. "Well, I guess the bastard is you."

Matteo stepped closer and La Dame whirled on him. "Matty, meet your cousin." She laughed again. "I wonder if the old king knew. A Basile as a prince of Gaule. That is the strangest thing I have ever heard."

She was still laughing as she walked from the room. Four new guards marched in and hauled Tyson to his feet. Another guard wrapped his strong grip around Matteo's arm, pulling him along behind the others.

Matteo fell to his hands and knees as he was shoved through an open doorway. Tyson landed in a heap beside him as the door slammed shut with a clang. The click of the lock echoed across the space.

Tyson rolled over and let out a cough.

Matteo crawled toward him. "Are you okay?"

He coughed again. "Where are we? Who are you?"

"My name is Matteo Basile." He climbed to his feet and reached down to help Tyson. "Welcome to Bela."

"Bela," Tyson wheezed. "I know, but where—"

"The palace."

Tyson shook his head. "There's no—"

Matteo gripped Tyson's arm and hauled him up. "The questions will drive you mad. It's better to accept your fate as it unfolds."

Tyson's eyes widened and Matteo felt bad for the young prince. Was it true? The prince of Gaule was a Basile?

Or did he just want it to be true? To have some connection beyond his father.

Any fight Tyson might have had was long gone as he let Matteo sit him down on the bed. His mouth opened repeatedly, but no words spilled out.

"Remove your shirt," Matteo said softly. "I need to make sure she didn't injure you." Not like he could do much if she had. Unlike the people of Dracon, Matteo wasn't a healer.

Tyson winced as he pulled his tunic free and ducked his head to get it off.

Matteo's brows drew together at the sight of the Prince's body riddled with bruises. "These didn't all come today."

"No." He didn't elaborate and Matteo didn't ask him to. They were strangers thrust together and trust was not easy to come by.

Matteo examined Tyson's bruises in silence, thankful there were no open wounds. He scooted behind him and his mouth dropped open. The skin of his back was puckered with burn marks.

Tyson must have recognized his stillness. He dropped his head.

"We cannot control the actions of others." Matteo slid around and handed him back his shirt. "Only the willful deeds of ourselves."

The young prince nodded and pulled on his shirt.

"You should be fine," Matteo said. "I didn't find any broken skin."

A harsh laugh rumbled through Tyson's chest. "How do you define broken?"

"I meant you have no open wounds."

"I know." He laid back on the bed gingerly, wincing from the burns and stared up at the ceiling.

How odd it must feel to the boy. Matteo shook his head. He'd been around La Dame's magic his entire life and it was still strange to him. They were prisoners in a palace that shouldn't exist.

Tyson turned his head to fix Matteo with a stare, his eyes betraying his age. "What did La Dame mean about Viktor Basile?"

"Only those with Basile blood can resist La Dame's magic."

"Viktor ..." Tyson stuttered. "He was my father? No... I... my father was the king of Gaule."

"There's no other way you could have resisted her."

A breath shuddered out of Tyson. "But, how is any of this possible? I'm a prince."

"You are," Matteo agreed. "Just not of Gaule. Our line descends from the last ruling family of Bela and that fact saved your life just now."

"The Basiles are her enemy."

"But she doesn't want to just kill us. She wants to bring us low, make us beg. She wants to take everything from us. No, we can't just die. We have to play her game."

CHAPTER 10

"Etta." The voices were far off and she barely heard them through the pounding in her head. A searing pain ripped through her and she jerked awake. A blanket covered her naked body and for a moment, hope filled her.

"Alex," she wheezed, reaching her hand out in hopes he would take it. But she knew he wouldn't. He was gone. "They're taking him."

"They already took him." Simon crouched by her side and helped her sit up, keeping the blanket tucked around her. She couldn't even muster up embarrassment at how he must have found her.

"They're too far." She bent forward as the ache persisted. "I can't… I can't breathe." A tear rolled down her reddened cheek. "I can't stand it."

For the second time in her life, she felt the curse truly hurt her as she was separated from her charge. She shook her head to rid it of the remaining fog. "What happened?"

She struggled to climb to her feet and Simon steadied her. The brightness of the day blinded her and she shielded her eyes.

The door banged open, making Etta jump as Catrine rushed in with Amalie on her heels. "Where is my son?"

Etta's legs couldn't hold her up any longer, and she collapsed into a chair at the table. "I don't know." She pressed her forehead to the solid wood. "I'm so sorry."

Catrine began to search the room frantically for clues and Amalie crossed to Etta and put a hand on her shoulder. "He's going to be okay."

"We don't even know who has him." Etta clenched her teeth against the pain. "I'm supposed to protect him."

"Not anymore," Amalie said.

Etta closed her eyes. The girl was right. Etta had been more prisoner than protector of late.

"Etta," Simon said softly. "How did they take the king?"

"How?" Catrine spun. "We should be more worried about who." She stopped at the table and her shaky fingers reached for the ewer sitting beside the dinner tray from the night before.

The memories poured in and Etta jumped to her feet to knock the ewer from the queen mother's hands. Red wine flew through the air as the ewer crashed to the floor. Etta glanced at the pool of wine near where she'd woken up.

"What on earth?" Catrine turned and lifted the skirts of her wine-soaked dress. Streaks of red ran down her face.

"Don't let any of it get in your mouth." Etta wrapped the blanket tighter around her and grabbed a napkin from the tray. She held it out.

Catrine took it and dried her face.

"You think it was the wine?" Simon asked.

"It had to be."

Catrine sank into a chair and her dark hair shifted forward to cover her face as she bent at the waist. "My boy."

Simon thought for a moment. "I'll set people to questioning the palace servants. I'll question the guards who were on night duty myself, especially the ones at the gate. We'll send out search parties."

"You won't find him." Etta clutched her stomach. "He's already too far. I can feel it." She raised her eyes to meet his.

"I'm sending them anyway. We have to do everything we can to find our king."

"Have you considered the worst?"

He shook his head. "We can't go there."

"We know he's alive because I'm sitting here right now. But he could be on his way to La Dame. You have to let me go after him."

"We don't know that's who took him, Etta. If she didn't, and we sent you directly into her arms, both you and Alex could be lost, anyway. While he is in danger, we must keep you safe."

Etta sat on the corner of the bed and crossed her arms.

His face softened. "We will find him." He turned on his heel and barely made it to the hall before beginning to bark orders to the guards outside the door. No one had been able to figure out how they'd been put to sleep as their king was stolen.

A sigh pushed from Etta's lips. Catrine left without another word and part of Etta thought the queen mother blamed her. She understood because she blamed herself as well. She was Alex's protector. He might say he had Simon now, but she'd pledged to keep him safe. Even when she'd hated him, she wanted to keep watch over him.

And she'd failed.

Amalie gave her a sympathetic smile before closing the door behind her and leaving Etta alone. Unable to stay in the king's room any longer, she pulled on her clothes and hurried back to her own rooms. Pain clouded her mind once again and a scream sounded. Had that been her?

She barely made it to the bed before she passed out.

The horse leaped forward to avoid a dip in the road and Alex abruptly woke. He opened his eyes to a view of the rough ground. He'd been draped over the back of a saddle.

Pain. All he remembered was pain. It hadn't gone away and as he shifted, it grew worse. The ropes around his wrists tightened as he tried to reach forward to hold onto the saddle he was draped over.

"We need to get him to the palace," a rough voice said. "She'll take care of the rest."

Palace? Was he going home?

Even in his foggy mind, he knew that wasn't right. He'd woken up periodically over the past two days before descending into darkness once again. Each time, they'd been on the move. They must have barely rested. They'd stopped at a village for fresh horses and he'd been hauled onto a new beast before taking off again. No one rode with him, but his horse was tied to the one beside him. There was no getting away in his current state.

He struggled to breathe with the agony tearing through his chest. That wasn't the sleeping drought they continued to force on him. Only one thing could turn him completely inside out. He'd felt it before. The curse.

Etta. He closed his eyes, trying to remember if she'd been okay. There was nothing. At least the burning in his veins told him one thing. She was still alive. How had they gotten into the palace? Magic?

He lifted his head to see his captors. He counted seven other horses, but his blurry vision couldn't quite make out their rider's faces.

His fingers pulled at the shirt they'd dressed him with to loosen the collar around his neck.

They turned to leave the road and take the rougher path over open land with no regard for their horses.

Someone trotted up beside him. "Hallo yer Majesty." He flashed him a gap-toothed grin before turning to the others. "We should stop fer a kip. His royalness looks a might slouched here."

"Louis," a hard feminine voice said. "Since when do you give the orders?"

Louis bowed his head. "Sorry, Madame."

The woman held up a hand to stop their trek and dismounted from her horse. She walked around so she was level with Alex's head. He blinked away the fuzziness and scanned her thin frame. She appeared like she belonged in a sewing room, not on a horse, and certainly not taking part in the capture of a king. Her light brown hair was tied back from her high cheekbones and ebony skin.

"Does the king wish to sit up?" she asked sweetly.

"Yes," Alex managed to get out.

The woman nodded to someone behind her and Alex's ropes were jerked so hard, he tumbled from the horse and lay on the ground, unmoving.

A smattering of laughter surrounded him.

"Gabe," she called. "Paul. You two get him back onto his horse." She turned to glare at Louis. "We do not stop until dark."

Alex was hauled roughly to his feet and lifted into the saddle. He hunched forward, doing all he could to stay on.

They took off at a gallop and Alex's horse was tugged along. He scanned his surroundings, trying to figure out where they were. He didn't know how long he'd been out but the sun overhead told him it'd been through the night at least. He glanced back once, knowing soon he'd no longer be in Gaule.

When night came, they made camp using the various powers they possessed.

Their power frightened him, but Etta's words were embedded in his mind. Most people's magic was quite weak. He saw that weakness in his captors and that more than anything gave him hope that Gaule could defeat them.

They tied him to a tree near the horses and he tried to take comfort in their familiar sounds. But there was no comfort to be had. There was no way out. As soon as they crossed the border into Bela, he'd be out of reach. He leaned his head back against the tree and shut his eyes.

At the sound of footsteps, he snapped them open.

The woman who'd given orders before, stood watching him.

"Need something?" Alex asked.

She held out a crude bowl. "I brought you supper, King."

He took it and stared down into the watery stew. "Why would you feed a dead man?"

A smile curved her lips. "What makes you think you're a dead man?"

"I was drugged and kidnapped." His brow pinched together.

She laughed and the rage inside of him threatened to boil over. He was in too much pain to be rational.

Without thinking, he threw his bowl at her. Surprised arched her brow as the steaming substance struck her. She wiped it away with a grimace.

"You're going to regret that when your belly is aching in the morning." She turned and walked back toward the group.

His shoulders sagged as he clutched at his chest, willing the pain away. His teeth ground against each other.

No, he didn't want the pain to subside. It was the only thing telling him Etta was okay.

It started to rain in the night, the water soaking Alex to the core. A shiver overtook his body, and he whipped his head around to look for his captors. They were huddled under a makeshift shelter. Louis and Paul were laughing as they pointed to him and the rain pounded mercilessly.

A crack of thunder split the sky and Alex hugged his arms across his chest as water dripped from his hair onto his face.

Lightning flashed, and he ducked away from the tree as far as his rope would allow. The horses nearby stomped and neighed as they too were exposed in the downpour. One reared up as the thunder grew louder. It crashed back to the ground and kicked its back legs up.

A soothing murmur came from the direction of the horses and they began to calm.

"Esme," Louis yelled. "Get yer skinny ass back here. It ain't safe."

Esme ignored them as she continued toward the horses. They stomped in agitation, but didn't jump as more lightning tore through the area.

"It's okay," she cooed. "Everything is going to be alright."

Alex began to relax as well. Even as his muscles loosened, he knew it was false. Her magic took hold of him and he no longer noticed the rain or the roar of thunder.

The horses went silent. Esme reached out her hand and the nearest one nuzzled his nose into it before folding his legs under him and laying down.

Esme turned around, a satisfied smile lighting up her face, and her hair slapping against her cheeks in stringy tresses. She gave a short nod of her head and returned to the hastily erected shelter to get out of the rain.

The horses made no more sounds and Alex was finally able to drift off into a dreamless sleep.

He didn't know how long he'd slept before rough hands woke him. They gripped the collar of his soiled shirt and hauled him to his knees.

The shirt tore as he was pulled forward. It was cheap, obviously not made for a king. And on top of that, it itched.

"Up you go, your Majesty," one of the ruffians, he thought it was Paul, growled.

A fist collided with his side, but he barely felt it over the pain that had started anew as soon as he opened his eyes. He didn't make a sound.

Gabe yanked his hair, pulling his head back to look into his face. "La Dame said we gotta bring him alive, but she didn't mention anything about whole." He slammed Alex's head back into the tree.

Still, Alex refused to make a sound.

"Let's make him squeal like the Gaulean pig that he is."

A knee rammed into his shoulder and he fell sideways, unable to break his fall with his hands tied.

A cackle rang through the air.

Alex lay still as they took turns kicking him. It didn't matter. None of it did.

The silver glint of a knife flashed in front of his face and Paul studied it. "Think La Dame would mind if we kept a few pieces for ourselves? He is the Gaulean king after all. We'd be heroes among all magic folk."

Alex squirmed until he was able to roll himself onto his knees once more. He was not the enemy of magic folk. If anyone was, it was La Dame. But they didn't know that. And he wouldn't beg.

He lifted his eyes and his gaze bore down on Paul and Gabe. Uncertainty entered Gabe's eyes, but Paul stepped forward and pressed the flat edge of the blade against Alex's cheek. The metal chilled him, but he didn't look away.

Then it was gone. Paul crumpled to the ground with an arrow in his back.

Alex trembled in relief before peering up at his savior. Esme stepped on Paul's back to pull her arrow free, unconcerned with his groan or the blood dripping from the iron tip.

"Gabe," she snapped. "Go prepare the horses."

Gabe looked like he wanted to protest, but his body jerked and moved away, leaving Alex to bear the full weight of Esme's consideration.

"Thank you," he said.

Her face was bland as she observed him. "That wasn't for you." She glanced at Paul's now lifeless body and then back at him. "La Dame has plans for you."

Days later, they crossed over into Bela and every ounce of hope within him died.

CHAPTER 11

The round chamber once serving as a gathering place for the council that ruled the kingdom was full for the first time since before Etta's father resided in the palace. It had fallen in to disuse when the old king dissolved his council and chose to consolidate the crown's power. It had been a time of peace so his noble's armies weren't needed and as long as the palace continued to pay a fair price, their supply of goods wouldn't be cut off.

Peace couldn't last forever and now they had no king and no wards.

Etta watched the empty seats fill up. These same nobles who'd watched as Alex imprisoned their fellow lords and ladies, now waited to be part of leading the kingdom. Without the king, the council must be reinstated.

A hand landed on Etta's shoulder and she flinched away. A haze of pain clouded her mind and every touch felt like a knife grazing along her skin.

"I never thought I'd see a council sit in this room again." Duchess Moreau's voice held a deep sadness.

"Do you trust them?" Etta asked through clenched teeth.

"Not even a little, but they're all we have now."

"We need our king."

Etta lifted her eyes to the circular room as the duchess gave her a pointed stare and moved toward her seat.

She knew what was expected of her. She had once been protector, and they wanted her to take up that mantle once more. His life was worth more than hers to them, but she had to be careful, to wait for the right moment, to prepare.

Part of that preparation was making sure the kingdom didn't fall apart in Alex's absence. She had a duty to him, but she also needed to prevent further persecution of her people.

Queen Catrine took the highbacked seat normally reserved for the king and Etta moved to stand behind her chair near the wall. Duchess Moreau was to her right and Duke Caron planted himself firmly on her other side. Camille stayed by her husband and refused to look Etta in the eye.

The bruise on her cheek had not faded in its entirety and a jolt of grim pleasure entered Etta's heart as she remembered the way it'd felt to finally give the princess what she deserved.

Simon joined Etta as the queen mother cleared her throat. The chatter in the room persisted despite more of the her attempts to begin.

They didn't have time for this. Etta drew her sword in one movement and slammed it down on the sturdy circular table. The surface shook from the impact and the sound made each of the nobles go silent.

"Queen Catrine wishes to begin," Etta growled, her voice echoing off the domed ceiling. Many of the faces paled and Duchess Moreau's eyes held chastisement in them.

The queen mother's voice shook as she began and then grew strong. "Our kingdom faces great adversity. As many of you know by now, the king was abducted from his rooms."

A round of questions broke out, the nobles speaking over one another. Etta narrowed her eyes, ready to quiet them once again. There was no need because they obeyed when Catrine held up her hand.

"Little is known," she said. "We have been searching the realm for days. You have each been instrumental in providing soldiers for the searches on your lands and I thank you."

For days, the queen mother had been almost inconsolable. How had she found the strength to control this meeting?

She continued, her voice even. "We must decide how to move forward. Alex had no heir."

Camille kept her eyes trained on the table. They'd all heard her lose her place in the line of succession.

"I move to allow Gaule to be temporarily ruled by this council. All those opposed, speak up now."

No one made a sound.

"Okay." Catrine folded her hands on the table. "We are now the governing body of Gaule. Our first order of business must be calling in the armies from your fields."

"During harvest?" A man across the table objected. "That's mad, woman."

The queen mother opened her mouth to speak, but Duchess Moreau beat her to it. "Respect, Lord Trevellais, or we will have you removed. A queen deserves the same obedience as any king."

The man's angular face reddened. "Your Majesty, I meant that we need our people in the fields."

Catrine pinned him with unforgiving eyes. "The harvest is meaningless if there are no people left to feed. Don't underestimate the dangers we face. Gaule could very well be on the brink of destruction."

Her bluntness sent a shock throughout the room.

Catrine drummed her fingers against the polished ebony wood and lifted her eyes to a map of the realm hanging on the far wall. "But you are correct, my lord. The harvest must come in. Those on your land can provide one member of the family to the army and one to the harvest."

He choked. "You expect women to work the fields?"

"Their limbs work as well as any other, correct? I don't see why those without young children can't do the tasks their husbands do. If they'd rather not, they can join the army."

Another noble gasped at that. "You'd have women fight?"

"We have women in the palace guard," she said smoothly.

"But this is war. Women simply don't have the skill."

Etta had heard enough. She slid her knife from its sheath on her leg and flung it. The blade stabbed into the table inches from the nobleman's hand. He jerked his hand away and widened his eyes.

"Do you know who I am?" Etta stepped forward.

"Yes," he stammered.

She smiled. "Good. If you'd like to prove my womanhood prevents me from being a skilled warrior, I'm happy to challenge you."

"Etta," Catrine snapped. "Enough."

Etta shut her mouth with a scowl.

Catrine turned back to the nobles. "You will provide this council with your army or we will all perish."

"What about our peers in the dungeons?" The woman sitting next to Camille asked.

"What about them, Lady Toro?" Duke Caron spoke up. "Traitors, all of them."

Lady Toro shook her head, her elaborate braids barely moving. "We cannot afford to be calling the nobles of this great kingdom traitors when their only crime was attempting to keep us safe."

"By betraying the king?" Caron scowled.

"By standing up against the magic folk. Look at what is happening now. We are preparing to fight a war against the people we should have eradicated."

Etta tensed and Simon gripped her arm. She tried to shake him off, but he didn't let go.

"Lady Toro," Duchess Moreau began patiently. "Our fight is not against the magic folk of Gaule. The discourse is with La Dame and her forces. If we were to ally ourselves with magic in this realm, we may have a chance."

Arguments broke out immediately.

"Like her?" someone yelled above the rest as he pointed to Etta. "The kingslayer's daughter?"

"That is enough," Catrine yelled. "Etta is under my protection and she will be a great asset in this battle."

The nobles continued to shout accusations. Words like "murderer" and "whore" were bandied about.

One assertion rang in her ears louder than the rest. "How do we know she wasn't involved in the king's kidnapping?"

"I have to get out of here," Etta whispered to herself.

Simon released her, and she walked to the other side of the table to yank her knife free. The nobleman's eyes widened, but she paid him no mind as she sheathed it and bolted from the room, their voices following her into the corridor. As the door shut, cutting off their arguments, she leaned against the wall, breathing heavily. Pushing away from the wall, she began to run, stumbling twice as the pain hindered her. Alex was getting farther away. She felt every step between them.

Her legs took her into the outer castle and she didn't stop running until she was through the gates. Turning left, she walked along the grassy hill at the base of the walls. When the agony became too much, she fell to her knees, trapped in a sea of pain and fear. What was happening to Alex?

She leaned her back against the wall and hung her head. Guards and villagers passed through the gates with only curious glances toward her.

Tomorrow, she'd go. There was no other way. Nothing remained at the palace for her. She must trust the queen mother to protect her people. But, how could she?

Her stomach cramped and she doubled over, tears stinging her eyes. The sharp sting sliced through her once again. Lifting her shirt, she felt for the heated spot where he must have been hurt. It felt as though a heavy boot thudded into her stomach and she cried out.

Blurry visions swam before her eyes. Verité? Was she hallucinating? The horse lowered his head to nudge her with his nose.

"Verité," she whispered. "I often dream of you."

He snorted, his breath blowing the hair from her face.

Her smile was weak as she struggled to sit and took in the beast clearly for the first time. It really was him. "How are you here, my friend?" His amber eyes met hers as he lowered his head. Reaching out her hand, she stretched her fingers against his soft neck in disbelief.

He stomped his foot, and she gripped his mane to pull herself to her feet, leaning on Verité for support. She rested her forehead against him and smiled. "I missed you." Tears pricked her eyes. "I can't believe it's you. Where did you come from? Where are Edmund and Tyson?"

Fear gripped her heart. If Verite was there, that meant something could have happened to them.

What was she supposed to do now? When she left to go after Alex, she'd have to search for them as well. If they were… she couldn't even face the thought.

Darkness closed in around them. "Come on, boy." She tugged on his mane, her voice shaking. "We don't want to be out here after they close the gates for the night." She stumbled over her own feet but managed not to fall as she led him through the gates. He followed without question, as always, his trust in her was complete.

By the time she made it to the stables, only lanterns lit the doorways. A stable hand greeted her at the door.

"Shit," he said. "Where'd ye find the bastard biter?"

Etta stepped around him without a word.

"Mademoiselle, I can take 'im from here. It's my job, yeah?"

He tried to step between Etta and Verité but Verité snapped his teeth and the man jumped back with a yelp.

"I'm taking an empty stall." Etta continued walking, forcing her face not to show the twinge of each step. "The only person that comes near this horse is me."

The man gaped at her as she led Verité into a stall at the end of the row and set about obtaining grain from the feedbags and water from the barrels along the wall. Verité set in to his feast hungrily.

Etta slid the door shut and peered over the top. The rotting wood came up to her chest, giving none of the privacy she wanted, but she was too exhausted to care. Sitting down against the wall, she closed her eyes. After a few moments,

Verité lowered himself beside her and she was able to sleep for the first time since Alex was taken.

The crunch of teeth biting into an apple filled the air, but Etta wasn't ready to open her eyes. She laid against Verité's warm side, his broad body a protection against anything that would come—including intruders intent on waking her in the wee hours of the morning.

She slid one eye open, barely registering the lithe blond man sitting atop the half wall of the stall. Relaxing into sleep once again, her thoughts filled with Edmund and how weird it was he'd returned to the palace.

Her eyes sprung open, and she bolted upright. "Edmund."

He bit into his apple again and grinned, letting juice dribble down his handsome face. It was the most precious thing she'd ever seen because he was there. He was alive. He'd come.

"I see my newly made friend abandoned me for you." He gestured to the horse who'd risen to his feet so quickly, he'd almost thrown Etta to the ground.

"He was my friend first."

What did you say first to someone whose very presence allowed you to breathe again?

Edmund swung his legs over the wall and jumped into the stall before tossing the remaining apple to Verité. "Ah, I can't deny the truth in that, but we've come to an understanding, him and I."

She climbed to her feet and crossed her arms over her chest. "Is that so?"

"Yes. I keep him supplied with apples, sometimes carrots, and he leaves all of my digits intact."

"You've been spoiling him, then?" She laughed. "I won't forgive you for fattening my horse."

"Your horse?"

"Yes, what do I have to do to reclaim him? Defeat you in a duel? Again."

He shrugged. "Not this time. Palace life has probably made you soft."

Her lips pressed together to suppress a laugh. The feeling was fleeting and on its heels came guilt. How could she laugh and joke when Alex was in danger?

When her smile fell, Edmund crushed her to him. They clung to each other as if everything around them was falling away.

"We'll get him back," Edmund whispered hoarsely. "I promise you that."

"You came back."

"I had to."

She nodded against his chest, taking comfort in the fact that he was the one person who understood what it felt like to lose the true Alexandre Durand.

Her body tensed up as a new spasm struck her. Edmund stepped back and gripped her arms as he met her gaze. "What is it?"

"They're moving again." Tears hung in her lashes. "I can feel it."

"The curse?"

She nodded, gritting her teeth to keep from calling out. Edmund pulled her back to him. "We must leave as soon as we can."

He released her and turned to the bag he'd left hanging on the door. Pulling out another apple, he glanced back at her. "I thought you might be hungry."

"Edmund, I've been living in the palace. I have access to the kitchens."

He shifted his eyes away sheepishly. "I know some of what has befallen you, Etta. I kind of thought you were still a prisoner, and I'd have to mount a rescue."

"I was imprisoned on the king's order. You would have defied Alex for me?"

"To save him, yes. Even if it was only to save him from himself. You didn't deserve anything you endured. I would have been here sooner if I could."

She accepted the apple he extended her way. "You've missed a lot."

"So have you," he countered.

Biting down slowly, she studied his face. He didn't look changed, but life outside the palace was hard when there was no safe place for their kind.

A breeze blew through the stall, alleviating some of the horse's stink and she smiled.

"Why do you think we'll be able to help him?" she asked.

He paused for a moment, swallowing a bite. "Because I know where he is."

"How could you possibly?"

He brushed a hand through his long blonde locks. "It's a long story. I'll tell you, but first, we must begin our trek. I arrived in the village yesterday." He patted Verité's side. "This beast ran off the minute our backs were turned."

"Our?" Relief rushed through her. "Tyson is with you."

His eyes strained and he shook his head. "I have a young healer traveling with me."

Etta snapped her eyes to his. "Who?"

"We met her during the attack on the village. Her name is Maiya."

The world began to spin. Maiya was supposed to be removed from all of this. "What about her father?"

Edmund thought for a moment. "I came upon a group of magic folk traveling toward the border. After I convinced them not to cross it, I told them where I was headed. Maiya said she needed to help. Something about making up for betraying a friend. Her father tried to stop her, but she's stubborn. He was needed to lead the group to safety so he and Maiya parted ways."

"What about Tyson? Where is he?" Etta's hand shot out to clutch at the wall.

"We need to get you to Maiya." Edmund ignored her question and put a hand on Etta's back and she stepped out of his reach.

"Her healing won't help me. I'm not injured."

"We have to try." He opened the stall and ducked out to get a saddle from the hook on the far wall. Etta struggled to throw a blanket over Verité's back. When Edmund returned, he took it from her and finished saddling the horse before lifting her easily onto it. He climbed on behind her and snapped the reins. The stable hands jumped out of the way as they thundered out onto the street.

Edmund held an arm firmly around her waist and it was the only thing keeping her from falling.

Verité was different from other horses. Even in her weakened state, when Etta rode him, she felt inspired. It was the same connection that existed when magic flowed from her fingers.

Edmund steered Verité out through the gates and onto the road. The last time Etta had been to the village was during the attack. Since then, it had begun to come back to life.

"I thought the village was destroyed," she said, awe filling her voice.

"I had as well." Edmund's chuckle vibrated against her back. "When Maiya and I arrived, we planned to hide out in the ruins of the town, but those had been cleaned up. People were returning and beginning to rebuild."

"I wish Alex could see this."

"Me too."

They turned onto the familiar road where Maiya's healer shop had been located. The building had stood strong during the attack. They tied Verité in the alleyway. The irony of it being the alley where she'd tied Edmund in weeds upon their initial meeting was lost in a cloud of pain.

Edmund slung her arm over his shoulders and half carried her into building where Maiya waited.

Maiya rushed toward them. "Oh my, is she okay?"

"It's the curse," Etta bit out as Edmund helped her onto a bed.

"I don't know if I can heal that." Maiya shifted her uncertain gaze to Edmund.

"Try," he pleaded.

Maiya nodded and stood beside the bed. Her steady hands raised the bottom of Etta's shirt to reveal bruised skin.

"I can heal these." She pressed her palms to the discolored skin and the throbbing in Etta's abdomen began to fade. Pale skin shone brightly under her touch.

Etta breathed out heavily and Maiya moved to the head of the bed. She lifted the collar of Etta's shirt and slid chilly fingers down to place them where her heart beat against her chest bone. She closed her eyes as concentration creased her brow.

The tightening on Etta's heart began to ease, and she peered up at her friend. "Thank you."

Maiya took a step back and wrung her hands together. "I wouldn't thank me yet. You can't possibly believe my magic can defeat even a part of the curse. The pain will return."

Etta sat up, free of pain for the first time in days. "So, when do we leave?"

"Tomorrow." Edmund paced the room, his steps loud in the confined space. "First, I must speak with the queen mother." He stopped moving and sat in a chair, hanging his head. "I must tell her I failed. I didn't protect her son." He raised his tortured eyes, searing his sorrow into her. "La Dame has Tyson as well."

Maiya stayed behind while Etta and Edmund left for the palace. At the gates, Edmund pulled his hood up to cover his hair.

One of the guards stopped them with hard eyes. "Persinette Basile, we've been told to watch for you."

"Well, you see me. Now let me pass."

Another guard joined the first, and she didn't recognize either of them. But they knew who she was, what she could do.

"We can't allow you in the castle unescorted." The first man drew his sword in threat. "Your kind isn't welcome here."

The second guard spit on the ground at Verité's feet. Verité showed his teeth with a growl.

Edmund tapped her thigh, and she nodded. All sound was pushed from the place as Etta slid from Verité's back. Her eyes scanned the surrounding area for signs they weren't alone. A smile curved her lips, and the guards took a step back.

She didn't draw her sword as she walked toward them. "The queen mother will hear of this."

"The council has control now." The first guard gripped his hilt tighter. He was young. A puppy. The second was older, and he'd been smart enough not to draw his weapon.

Edmund chuckled behind her. "If you think Queen Catrine Durand doesn't rule that council as if they were her kingdom, we may have to forgive your insolence on account of your clear stupidity."

"Don't come any closer," the older guard commanded. "Times are changing. We are taking back our kingdom that Alexandre Durand gave away to people like you."

She stopped inches from the tip of the sword. "That's King Alexandre." Knocking the sword aside easily, she lunged for the younger guard as she called her magic forth. Slamming him back against the wall, she forced the sword from his grasp as the vines climbed the stone, wrapping first around his ankles before slithering up over his torso. He screamed, but Edmund's magic made sure no one heard.

She released him and turned to the second guard who had drawn his sword. He charged toward her, blade raised, and she twisted out of the way. He chopped at the air and she evaded each move with ease. He cut at her legs and she jumped.

"Need some help?" Edmund leaned back in the saddle casually.

"Wouldn't want you to tax yourself," she called back, ducking as the blade sailed over her head.

"Just don't get yourself killed by this fool. Wouldn't want Alex to die as well."

"Your concern is touching." She spun again, exhilaration rushing through her. If she drew her sword, the fight would be over instantly, but she needed the fight to take her mind off everything else.

As her lungs began to burn and the guard's heavy swings arced wildly, she ducked and grabbed his arm. She knocked his blade to the ground. He threw a punch, but it missed its mark and she shook her head.

"Edmund," she called, releasing the man's wrist. A forceful wind aimed straight for her opponent, pushing him up against the wall so Etta could tie him there as well. Without another glance, she remounted Verité.

"That looked like fun." Edmund rested his chin on her shoulder.

"We have to figure out what's going on here." She snapped the reins and entered the outer castle. "Why'd they let us through the gates this morning and refuse us entry now?"

"This morning you didn't look like Persinette Basile. You were bundled in my cloak and could barely stay on the horse."

She arranged the hood on her cloak to cover her golden hair and keep her face in shadow. Guards patrolled the streets, and she avoided looking at any of them directly. Why was the royal guard wandering the outer palace?

They bypassed the stables to ride Verité directly toward the inner gate.

"Why is it shut?" Etta scanned the gates for any indication of what had happened in the short time she'd been away. "We've only been gone for a few hours."

"Oi," a gruff female voice called down to them from the top of the inner wall. "Step back from the gates. None are allowed entry."

"We need to speak with the queen mother," Edmund called back.

"We don't allow any traitorous bastards in here."

Etta shielded her eyes to look up at the woman, not recognizing her. She wore a guard's uniform with a chain mail headpiece. Her weathered face regarded them coolly.

Pushing back her hood, Etta narrowed her eyes. "I am no traitor. I am Persinette Basile."

The woman disappeared and a few minutes later, the door at the base of the gates opened and Simon peered out, ushering them in.

"Etta." He helped her dismount. "I'm glad you're safe."

"What's happened?"

"Many things." He nodded toward Edmund in question.

Etta put a hand on his arm. "Simon, do you know Edmund?"

"Of course. We were in the king's guard together." He held out his hand. "Good to have you back."

Edmund shook his hand, and they left Verité in the courtyard without removing his saddle, knowing he'd be okay on his own. The palace was full of people. Some were guards or servants, but others looked like simple townsfolk.

"You look better than you did yesterday," Simon noted, leading them through the halls.

"Maiya's back." She gripped his arm to stop him. "What are we walking into here, Simon?"

"The past few hours have been hectic. After you left the council meeting yesterday, things devolved. They voted to release the nobles we'd been holding. Everything else blew up from there. Nobles are choosing sides. The guard has splintered. They're seeking out suspected magic folk in the outer castle. Some have taken refuge in the palace."

"All of these people are magic folk?" Edmund's eyes bounced from face to face as they continued walking.

"No." Simon turned into the royal family's wing and they left the refugees behind. "Others just came for protection."

"Why should they need protection if they have no magic?" Edmund asked.

They stopped outside Catrine's door and before Simon pushed it open, he turned back to them. "Because this isn't just the purge of years past. It's a rebellion."

Those two words stuck in her mind as they entered the room. Queen Catrine sat in front of the fireplace next to Duchess Moreau and Amalie. Camille stood at the table pouring wine and her husband, Duke Caron, paced nearby. Each face turned to them as the door slammed shut.

Catrine was the first to rise.

"Edmund?" She rushed toward him. "Dear boy, it is good to see you." She cupped his cheek, and he inclined his head.

When he straightened, there were tears in his eyes. "I have failed you."

Etta took his hand in hers. There was much to discuss, but he needed to get the words out.

Catrine waited patiently.

"La Dame has Tyson."

She sucked in a breath and stepped away from him. "How?"

"We were in one of the border villages when it was attacked by La Dame's forces. At first, we thought they were friendly because they were calling out Persinette's name. But then the fighting began. It was magic against magic as many of the villagers were descendants of Bela." He swallowed thickly. "There was a man who could control fire. When I used my magic on him, it increased the flames. Not even Tyson's water could put them out. We were trapped on opposite sides of the flames. I saw his shirt catch fire. A magic man put it out, but then they took him. I couldn't stop them."

Catrine stumbled back to her chair and fell into it, a sob caught in her throat. Amalie moved to put her arms around the queen mother's shaking shoulders.

Edmund wasn't finished. He knelt in front of her. "I'm going to get him back. Him and Alex."

"How do you know the same woman took Alex?" Camille asked, handing her mother a glass of wine. She turned her stony eyes on Edmund.

Edmund didn't look at her, his eyes still trained on the queen mother. "I've been searching for information on where they'd take Tyson. There are taverns known to be frequented by travelers and guards from Dracon. I never found any information on the young prince, but instead I stumbled upon the brother of a man who'd been sent on an important mission. He boasted about it to any who would listen. He didn't know what the mission was, except that it involved journeying to the palace of Gaule."

"That's why you came back." Etta took a seat and rested her elbows on her knees. "You knew he was in danger."

"I was too late."

Catrine reached out to touch his shoulder. "You risk a lot by being here."

"I won't be here long." He got to his feet. "I'm headed to Bela."

Silence echoed across the stunned room.

Etta joined Edmund. "I'm going with him."

Duchess Moreau smiled tightly. "As much as we could use you two here, there are no others I would trust with such a mission. No others who would give their lives for our king."

Amalie loosened her arms around Catrine. "I fear I must go too."

Etta shook her head. "I'm sorry, lady Amalie. This is no mission for a lady of court."

"Alex has been kind to me and Tyson... he's the only true friend I've ever had. Don't I have as much right as you to risk myself for them?"

Duchess Moreau beheld her proudly even as she issued a final order. "No, Amalie. If you were to go into Bela, I fear you would not return to us."

Etta held a grudging respect for the young girl who was willing to risk everything as she was, but she still couldn't have her come. "Amalie, this isn't like us saying farmer's wives can go to war. We won't be among an army or facing unskilled warriors. La Dame is the most powerful magic woman in the world. There's a very real chance we are all going to die."

Amalie crossed her arms, but nodded in understanding and didn't utter another word.

Walking toward the table where the wine sat, Etta tried to loosen some of the tension in her shoulders. She reached for the wine, her hand pausing in mid-air as memories came back to her. What if the wine was drugged again? What would happen to them then?

Nausea churned in her stomach as she stared at the pitcher. It was the cause of all their current misfortune. Without thinking, she knocked it to the ground. The pitcher shattered and burgundy wine splattered onto her legs and spread across the floor.

The chatter in the room stopped abruptly as they stared at her in shock. As if none of it had happened, Etta strode to the couch and plopped down, crossing her legs.

Simon went in search of servants to clean up the mess as Edmund sat beside her. "You okay?" he whispered.

"Of course she's not okay." Camille's voice was grating. "She's insane."

"Camille," her mother warned.

"No, she needs to hear this." She crossed the room to stop in front of Etta. "You can't stand in a council meeting intimidating our nobles. You can't make threats. You can't throw pitchers of wine. Persinette Basile is seen as the enemy. Magic folk are seen as the enemy. I'm still not sure they're not, but I will always choose my family's side. But you, Etta, need to stop making this so much damn harder for us."

"You're out of line, Camille," Edmund growled.

"Says the man who lied to us for years."

"Enough," Catrine snapped.

Duke Caron took his wife's arm and pulled her away.

"We have too much to deal with without you two at each other's throats." Catrine glanced to the wine and back to Etta. "Are you alright?"

"Just tell me what happened in the council meeting after I left." Etta ran a hand over her braid to calm herself.

Catrine sighed. "As soon as we gave the council ruling powers, every decision must be put to a vote and the result would stand. They chose to release the imprisoned nobles and to reinstate penalties for magic. We were helpless to stop the momentum once it began. As soon as the votes were announced, the guard began to fracture. We sent runners into the outer palace to offer protection for magic folk and then closed the inner gates. Part of the guard stayed, but a greater part began following orders of others on the council. They haven't attempted to gain entrance to the inner castle, but it's only a matter of time. We are prisoners, I'm afraid."

"There are other ways out of here." Etta leaned forward.

"There are too many people within these walls. As long as our supplies last, there is no safer place for us."

"How long will supplies last?" Edmund asked.

"Six months at least." Catrine's forehead creased. "More if we cut rations. When the wards came down, Alex began preparing the castle for possible siege." Her voice grew quiet. "We just didn't expect we would need to barricade ourselves against our own forces."

"Why aren't we considering surrender?" Camille planted her hands firmly on her hips. "Surely that's preferable to any sort of fight. We can't outlast them."

To Etta's surprise, it was Camille's new husband who gave her the answer she didn't want to hear. Duke Caron turned his grim face to his young wife. "And what of the people we're protecting here?" He shook his head. "None of us imagined there were so many magic folk living right alongside us in secret. They were our friends, served in our households, and even took up positions guarding the kingdom. We cannot allow the tragedies of the purge to begin anew."

"Send a runner to the border." Duchess Moreau sounded exhausted. "Alexandre sent a sizable part of the guard to the garrison near my lands." She pulled an emerald ring from her middle finger and extended it to Etta. "When you arrive at my estate, make sure this gets to my steward. He will call my people from the fields to take up border patrols as the guard returns here."

Etta slipped the ring into a pouch at her waist and stood. "We shouldn't wait any longer."

Queen Catrine rose to face her. "Persinette Basile, this kingdom has not been good to you or your family. You will never know how much I regret what has happened. We have had our differences, but go now with our sincerest gratitude and all the hope we can muster."

Etta inclined her head and Catrine pulled her into a hug. Etta stiffened, but didn't pull away. Next, Catrine moved to Edmund. "We've never deserved you."

Edmund smiled sadly and Etta envied him. He didn't hold back, didn't retain grudges. He hugged Catrine as if the past had never happened at all, as if he hadn't been imprisoned and run off.

Etta turned away. Would she ever truly be able to forget the past?

Amalie gave her a tearful goodbye and Simon escorted Etta and Edmund back into the hall. A heavy silence hung in the air.

They didn't look at the people they were leaving behind as they walked. Would the palace be able to withstand a siege?

As they reached a familiar door, the curse tugged at her and she breathed deeply, willing Maiya's healing to last longer. On the other side of that door was an unused chapel with the entrance to a short tunnel through a part of the castle where the inner and outer walls connected. It let out on the far side, away from the gates. Etta used it once before—to sneak Alex back into the palace after their trip through the forest.

Etta put a hand on Edmund's shoulder. "This is where I leave you."

His eyes widened and Simon began to protest. "You must leave this way."

Edmund nodded in understanding. "Meet me at the edge of the forest. We'll be able to take a direct path this time so it should only take a few hours to get to the village."

"You can't be serious." Simon scowled at them. "What is more important than getting out of the palace?"

Edmund clapped him on the back. "She has someone else she needs to get out, but only one person can ride him fast enough to get through streets teeming with traitors." He pushed open the door behind the altar and stepped through without another word.

Making sure the door shut securely behind him, Etta headed back the way she'd come with Simon on her heels. There'd be no secret tunnel for her escape. She'd have to flee through the streets of the outer castle.

"When I tell you to," she began. "I'm going to need you to open the gate enough for me to slip through."

"This is suicide, Etta," he growled. "Think of Alexandre."

"I think of little else. If I'm going to save him, I need to do this."

Verité lifted his head when she stepped into the courtyard and Simon grunted.

"This is about the damn horse, isn't it?"

She ran a hand down Verité's neck. "He isn't just a horse. He's a part of me and if I'm going to go up against La Dame, I need to be whole."

She climbed onto the saddle and nudged him around. Jerking her head toward the gate, she looked down on Simon. "You may want to tell your men what to do."

His eyes held all the concern his words lacked. "Persinette, all the hope of Bela goes with you and that of Gaule. If you perish, the king does as well and that can only mean darkness for all of us. Bless you, my queen, and keep you safe."

She reached down and touched the top of his head gently. "I won't let our people down."

He walked briskly to the gatehouse and had words with the guards there. Before the gate opened, he climbed the stairs to the top of the wall with a bow in hand. Three other guards joined him, knocking their arrows, and aiming them onto the street below.

The gate opened slowly, wide enough for Verité to slip through. She held one hand in the air as guards surrounded her and the gate closed with a thud. Verité growled, but she held his reins tightly with her free hand to keep him in check.

"Stop right there," the order came from her left, but she didn't turn. A sword scraped as it was pulled from its scabbard. A man pointed it up at her.

"Get off your horse slowly."

She narrowed her eyes, waiting. Her opening would come. The rest of the guards began pulling their weapons and Verité reared up, kicking wildly.

Someone made to grab for the reins and the horse snapped his teeth, drawing blood. "Bloody horse," she screamed.

They began to charge and a volley of arrows sailed over her head. Her chance. The crowd broke apart to duck for cover and she kicked her heels into Verité's flanks.

"Come on, boy," she whispered as he leaped forward.

His hooves thundered through the streets, people ducking out of the way to avoid being trampled. Guards and citizens alike ran in pursuit, but they were on foot. An idea occurred to her as she came upon the stables. Most of the horses roamed in the pen.

Pulling Verité to an abrupt stop, she drew her sword and hacked through the rope that kept the pen closed.

Flattening her palm, she pulled at her magic before curling her fingers into a fist. An array of vines and weeds shot from the ground, wrapping around the iron bars of the long door. She jerked her hand, and it yanked open.

Verité ran into the pen and sprinted around the outer edges, agitating the horses and herding them toward the door.

Free of the pen and chased by Verité, the horses ran wildly through the streets.

Etta glanced behind her where two guards had caught a couple of the horses and struck out in pursuit of her.

"Close the gates," people yelled toward the gatehouse at the edge of the outer castle gates. Unlike the humble inner gates, the outer gates were massive wooden structures that couldn't be shut in an instant.

The gap between them began to narrow.

"Come on, Verité," she yelled, exhilaration rushing through her. The wind whipped the hair from her shoulders and she still held her sword aloft as she charged the gates like a wild woman.

A line of guards formed, some staring with a look of disbelief etched across their faces. Others stood in grim determination between her and the gates. She couldn't stop now.

"You can do this, boy," she whispered, gripping the reins in one hand and his mane with the other. "Show them you're more than the temperamental bastard they think you are."

They didn't slow as they neared the guards. Fear developed on their faces as they realized she wasn't going to stop.

"Not yet," she said. "Wait. Wait." Closer and closer still. "Now!"

Verité leaped.

His legs dangled as they flew through the air and Etta held on tighter than she ever had before. It was a moment she'd never forget. Everything seemed to stop. No sound. No movement. Verité's hooves came so close to the guard's heads, they had to duck as he sailed overhead.

He landed with a spine-jarring force and ran through the barely open gates without missing a beat. The gates closed with finality, cutting off possible pursuit until they could open again. Verité exploded down the grassy hill and over the road, not slowing until they were crossing the path that would take them to the forest.

Etta leaned forward against Verité's neck and laughed as she tried to catch her breath. "Well, that was something, my friend."

They made it to the cover of the trees and she slid from the horse's back, falling to her knees as the rest of her body vibrated with adrenaline.

She rubbed a hand across her face and gaped at her horse in wonder. "I didn't know you could do that."

He snorted and she used her magic to pull grass from the earth for him to eat.

She leaned back against a tree, letting the sounds of the forest calm her frantic heart as she waited for Edmund to arrive.

The woods darkened before she heard the unmistakable sound of footsteps.

"Etta," a voice called.

She jerked upright, taking a moment to recognize the soft timber of the words.

"Edmund." Standing, she brushed the dirt from her pants before calling, "Over here."

A few moments later, he appeared in front of her. She threw her arms around Edmund's shoulders and he stumbled back. "I was worried you hadn't made it." Even she hadn't realized how scared she'd been. Going into Bela alone struck fear in her heart.

He squeezed her and let her go. "Me? What about you? How'd it go?" His eyes flicked to Verité.

She patted the horse's rump. "He got me out of there." She didn't elaborate as the day's events played in her mind. Exhaustion warred for supremacy, but there was too much yet to do.

"I've been searching for you along the edge of the woods for the past hour," he said.

Her body had needed the rest she'd taken, but no way did she admit that. She shrugged and walked by him. "We need to get to the village and collect Maiya so we can be gone before the sun rises."

As much as they each wanted to drop where they stood, they couldn't give in. They had to push. For Alex. For Bela. Even for Gaule.

Maiya launched herself at Etta when they barreled through the door into the relative safety of the old healer's residence.

Etta sagged against the younger girl, too tired to protest, as her pain worsened once again. Pressing her lips together, she pushed Maiya subtly and held her at arm's length, trying to hide the way each movement hurt.

She was too anxious to get moving again to stop for a moment to heal. Maiya's magic had lasted less than a full day before the curse returned in force.

Releasing Maiya, Etta stepped back.

"Did you get what I asked for?" Edmund ran a hand over his tired face and through his bright hair.

"Sort of." Maiya walked to the door. "I could only get one horse, but I did manage something else."

She took a candle from its place on the wall and led them to the alleyway. Edmund sighed. "A cart? How are we to travel swiftly with this?"

A scrawny horse was tied up next to it and Edmund glared at it.

"There is nothing in the village to be bought," Maiya claimed defensively. "It wasn't for lack of trying. At least with Verité, we can tie them both to the wagon and pass as ordinary travelers on the road."

Etta snorted and they both turned to look at her. "Sorry, I'm just imagining the look Verité will give me when I tell him I'm tying him to this broken-down heap." She suppressed the laughter attempting to break through. "But, honestly, Edmund and I are some of the most recognizable faces in Gaule."

"I've thought of that too." Maiya led them back toward her old shop. "Come with me."

Back inside, she picked up a blade from the table and handed it to Etta. Etta studied the engraved steel and lifted her eyes to her friend. "What am I supposed to do?"

"Make yourself invisible."

As the meaning sank in, Etta's eyes widened. She pulled her braid over her shoulder and ran her hand over the intricate loops and twists. Her hair was who she was. When she was killing, it made her feel human. When all she felt was the curse, it grounded her.

"No," she said, walking past Maiya to sit in front of the looking glass. She dropped the knife on the table.

"You can't ask her to do this," Edmund whispered.

"Not just her, Edmund. People know you for your looks as well. We don't have much time."

Etta unraveled her braid, letting her fingers sink in to the silky strands she knew so well. Her eyes drifted shut as she pictured Alex stroking each lock. It'd made her feel like a woman when little else had.

Edmund appeared behind her, brush in hand, and dragged it through her hair. Her eyes met his in the looking glass. Could she still be Persinette Basile without the well-known golden mane?

He rested his chin on her head. "For Alex."

She nodded. "For Bela."

He reached out and took the knife she'd dropped. After gathering her hair, he sawed through the strong fibers. When he was finished, her choppy hair rested at her ears.

She stood and gestured for him to sit. "Now you."

In silence, she took from him the last vestiges of youth. Maybe neither of them had ever had the chance to be young.

An hour later, the horses were hooked to the wagon with only a little argument from Verité. In the night, they rumbled down the road, a band of weary travelers with no end to their journey in sight.

CHAPTER 12

Relief had come in waves for days. Alexandre would fall asleep with the suffering growing strong within him and wake up as if it'd never existed at all. The freedom lasted for hours before slipping away as he sank into the agony once again.

He'd been unconscious when they arrived at the palace of Bela. They'd heard rumors of it being rebuilt, but how? La Dame had only been in Bela for a few months as far as they knew.

A wrongness hung in the air as he sat up and rubbed his eyes. Sunlight streamed through a window across the room. It stood open, with no glass separating the room from the outside world. Had they given him a means of escape? Nothing could be that simple.

He pushed back the heavy blankets and noted his bare legs. They'd removed his clothes. A blast of chilly wind roared through the window, causing the hairs on his legs to stand on end.

Wrapping a blanket around himself, Alex stood from the wood-carved canopy bed. A wardrobe stood tall in the corner—well, not corner exactly. The walls curved in a continuous circle. As he passed the table near the window, his fingers brushed the edge of a silver tray laden with food.

It was more than he fed his own prisoners.

A wide sill lined the bottom of the window. Alex stopped, his eyes rounding. The sky dropped outside the tower, connecting with the ground far below. A breath wheezed in his chest as he gripped the edge and leaned out. He wouldn't be able to make it down without breaking his neck.

Trees stretched as far as he could see without another structure in sight.

Leaning back in, he stumbled and crashed into the corner of the table. He wasn't in the palace of Bela. His prison cell was a tower in the middle of the woods.

His eyes darted around the room in search of a door.

The curse chose that moment to stab into him and he bent at the waist, trying to breathe. Why had he been put there?

A voice sounded outside. Maybe he wasn't alone after all. It was a sweet melody, and it drifted up through his window. He leaned against the wall, allowing it to soothe his frayed nerves. She sang of simple things—a villager's magic and her love of a fisherman.

A scraping broke through her voice, coming from the bottom of the tower. He peered out the window, trying not to be seen and reeled back. It was her.

He'd been a boy when he'd first met La Dame, but she hadn't changed. She continued to sing as she raised her face to him, her blackened tresses curling down her back. Her dark eyes locked onto his and he couldn't move. Her bright red lips curved up into a smile as she raised her hands. The outer stones of the tower wall shook and shifted, and still, Alex couldn't look away even as fear smashed into him.

The stones continued to move until they formed a narrow staircase from the ground to the edge of the window. She climbed it with slow, methodical steps, holding up the hem of her low-cut black dress.

As if released from a spell, he broke eye contact and stepped back, pulling the blanket tighter around himself. She climbed through the window with a tremendous amount of grace.

He stood tall, refusing to cower in her presence.

"Alexandre," she said cheerfully. "It has been far too long." She reached up to kiss his cheek familiarly, and he froze. "Oh, don't be like that, young king. We've been friends for too long." Her eyes scanned the room, and she clucked her tongue. "I left you quite the feast and you haven't touched it." She planted her hands on her hips. "That is rude."

When he didn't move, she frowned. "Sit."

His legs moved with jerky, uncoordinated steps out of his control. His teeth clenched as he tried to stop himself.

"Don't fight it," she said, taking her own seat. "You won't win."

His butt crashed into the chair.

"What's happening to me?" he gasped. "Why—" His voice cut off when she snapped her fingers.

"No talking. Eat." She pushed the tray toward him and he had no choice but to obey.

She steepled her fingers. "I came to extend an invitation to my ball tonight."

He swallowed noisily.

"You can speak now." She sighed.

"Invitation implies I have a choice."

"Ah." She smiled. "You're to be the honored guest. The clothing I'd like you to wear is in the wardrobe. I hope you like to sing."

"Why?"

"I can't give away all my surprises, now, can I?"

"Why am I here?"

"Hmmm, an inevitable question. Although, I am feeling a bit slighted you act as if you'd rather be elsewhere."

"I am your prisoner."

"I don't like that term." She pursed her lips in thought. "Be patient, your Highness. All will be revealed." She stood. "As much as I'd love to stay and chat with you all day, I have a ball to prepare for. Before I go, I brought you a bath."

She walked to the window and gave some sort of signal to a servant waiting below. Heavy footsteps sounded on the stairs and a man who barely fit through the window shoved a wooden tub through and climbed in. A second man followed, dragging someone behind him.

A mop of inky hair covered the boy's face, but Alex would recognize his brother anywhere.

"Tyson," he breathed.

Tyson's head snapped up at the sound of his brother's voice. "Alex?"

"Reunions are lovely, aren't they?" La Dame's voice was wistful.

Tyson was jerked forward, and he fell to his knees in front of the tub.

"Fill it," the man behind him ordered.

Alex glanced from La Dame to his brother in confusion, but Tyson seemed to understand what they meant. He leaned forward and put both hands down into the tub. La Dame poured a pitcher of water over his hands and the water expanded until it filled the tub halfway.

Alex collapsed onto the corner of his bed. He'd been told his brother had magic, but his mind couldn't grasp onto that fact.

La Dame clapped her hands together, the sound jarring him from his thoughts. "Tyson will stay here until the ball. I wouldn't want to break up such a happy reunion."

Without another word, she exited the window with the two men behind her. Once they were down, the stones shifted back into place forming the smooth wall.

Alex stared at his brother for a long moment. Tyson met his eyes.

"You hate me now, don't you?" He gestured to the water he'd created with a defeated sigh.

Opening his mouth, Alex was suddenly lost for words. He stood from the bed and dropped to his knees in front of his brother who still sat by the tub. Releasing one of his arms from the blanket, Alex pulled Tyson into a firm hug that said everything he couldn't.

They sat there for a moment longer, before Tyson chuckled. "I'd feel much more comfortable if you had some clothes on right now."

Alex smiled. When was the last time he'd done that? Pulling away, he climbed to his feet. "I don't want to take anything from La Dame, but my desire for clothes overrides that."

"She'll want you to bathe before the ball." Tyson rose and went to sit in a chair at the table.

"I don't care what she wants."

"You will, brother. Don't be placated by her niceties. I've seen what she does to people who disobey her." He sighed. "I knew they'd gone to kidnap you. When Matteo told me, I feared what kind of shape you'd arrive in."

A grimace flashed across Alex's face. "It would have been worse, but the pain lessens each night. It must be Etta."

Tyson shifted his eyes away. "You've released her then?"

"Of course." He paused. "Tyson, look at me."

A beat of silence passed before Tyson raised his eyes.

"I am not our father." He scratched the back of his neck. "Maybe I was like him, but it's different now. I don't hate you for your magic and I will never forgive myself for what I did to Etta."

"She'll probably never forgive you either."

Alex snorted. "I imagine not."

"But she's coming for you," he went on.

Alex tried to refute that, but Tyson shook his head. "Even if there wasn't a curse tying you two together, she'd come. It isn't in her not to fight. That's what La Dame is counting on."

"What do you mean?" Alex pulled on the clothes that had been left for him and dropped into the chair opposite his brother, wincing from the agony that grew worse by the minute.

"This isn't about you. Matteo says she's playing with us."

Alex raised one finger. "First, who is Matteo. And who do you mean by us?"

"Matteo Basile. His father is Viktor's brother." His eyes darkened as his next confession poured forth. "La Dame isn't after the Durands. She wants her revenge on the entire Basile line. On Matteo. On Persinette. And on me."

CHAPTER 13

In an instant, everything made sense.

Tyson's magic.

His father's disdain for the youngest prince.

His mother's cleaving to one child over the others.

Alex knew his mother loved him. There was never any doubt of that. But with Tyson, she was different. Her mothering bordered on obsession. Even as a child, he'd been stunned when she took Tyson to her own breast despite the arguments from the wet nurse.

A queen didn't serve her children. It was beneath her. But not Catrine Durand.

Alex rubbed his eyes. The days following his father's death now had meaning. It'd struck him odd how deep into mourning she'd gone when she'd never appeared beholden to her husband at all.

Viktor Basile. The kingslayer. His mother had loved the man. He was sure of it now.

His fists clenched at his sides and he glanced at his brother who stood beside him. They'd barely spoken since Tyson's confession hours before.

When La Dame came back to retrieve them, Alex tried to resist, but it was useless. He was her prisoner. Physically. Mentally.

For the first time in his life, he felt powerless. Unclenching his fist, he placed a hand on Tyson's shoulder. His brother's body shook as he stared at the ornate mahogany doors in front of them.

A guard had come to wrap heavy chains around Tyson's ankles, but Alex was left unfettered.

The witch couldn't control the Basiles with her magic so she used other means.

Both princes were dressed in the finest clothes. What better way for La Dame to show off her prizes?

"Alex," Tyson whispered. "I'm sorry."

The words caused more suffering than the curse ever could. "You have nothing to be sorry for."

"But my ... father." The boy swallowed. "I know how you feel about the Basiles."

"I think we can agree, Ty, that if the Basiles can resist La Dame's magic, they're an ally of the Durands."

Tyson smiled tentatively. "Thanks for saying it at least."

"I mean it."

"I know where things stand." Tyson's gaze drifted up to the tall doors. "I'm just not sure I know where I do."

"You're my brother."

He nodded. "Do you get what this means?"

Alex shook his head.

Tyson's smile stretched into a grin. "I have to kill my brother for imprisoning my sister."

A laugh burst from Alex's mouth and echoed off the high ceiling. "And apparently, I'm in love with my brother's sister."

"I'm glad you love her. It gives me hope for all of us."

Hope. It was a foreign concept in one's prison cell. Even if that cell was currently a castle of the likes he'd never seen. It was opulence on its grandest stage. But it was still a prison just as much as the tower out in the middle of the woods.

Even there, his brother had more faith than he'd ever possessed and he was envious. If only he could feel one tiny piece of that.

The doors opened slowly to reveal a ballroom larger than any they'd ever seen.

A trumpet blared, and the ringing sounded in Alex's ears long after the trumpeter was out of breath. The string quartet let their music fade into silence and every ornately dressed person in the room turned to face them.

Alex's eyes drifted over the pillars wrapped in gold, to the twinkling lights made to look like the stars in the night sky. The beauty of it all slammed into him. Who were these people?

Some of their faces held a hint of fear they did their best to cover up. Others looked indifferent. None seemed happy to be there.

"My boys!" La Dame's voice covered the room in a thick wariness. She stood on a balcony leaning against a silver balustrade. Her gold dress shimmered with every movement. Straightening up, she regarded her gathered people with a false joy in her eyes. "Let us welcome Alexandre Durand, King of Gaule." A smattering of claps made its way around the room. "And we are also graced by the presence of Tyson Basile."

Alex started at the name. Tyson was as surprised as he was, judging by his raised eyebrows and clenched jaw. Who cared who his father was? He would always be Tyson Durand.

"Please, make my honored guests welcome." La Dame stepped back, and the music began again.

As if compelled by her words, a line of people began welcoming them to the ball. When they finally broke away, Tyson leaned in. "There's someone you should meet while we have a chance."

He led him toward a table laden with food. The men and women sitting nearby stood immediately and bowed, issuing a quick welcome, but Tyson bypassed them to walk to the servant filling wine goblets.

The servant stopped and his eyes darted around to look for eavesdroppers.

"Alex," Tyson began. "Meet Matteo. He's... well, I guess he's my cousin."

Matteo stepped closer, the chains about his ankles rattling. His eyes narrowed. "So you're the one killing my people?"

Tyson gave Matteo a hard look. "We don't have time for that. She's going to fetch us soon." He didn't need to say who he meant. "She won't want us speaking to you."

His eyes flicked toward the balcony, but she was no longer there.

Tyson turned to Alex. "I've been coming to these balls every night since I arrived. They never change."

"Because La Dame doesn't change," Matteo cut in. "I've been with her my entire life and she has always been as she is now. Seemingly harmless and completely destructive in the same breath. Are you scared, King?"

Alex had barely even admitted it to himself, but he was.

Matteo took his silence as confirmation. "At least you aren't as big a fool as I thought." He studied him. "I don't like you."

"Matteo," Tyson started.

"No." Alex held up a hand. "It's okay."

Matteo sighed. "But in this place, we're allies. What do you see when you look around the room?"

Alex did a quick scan of the crowded dance floor, anger bubbling to the surface. "They're enjoying themselves."

Matteo rubbed his face in exasperation. "I see people who tried to escape the tyranny of the Durands only to walk into another prison." He picked up his pitcher to return to work and glanced at something over Alex's shoulder. "They are no more free than you. But you're the king of Gaule. When you look at us, all you see are enemies."

"Matteo," La Dame snapped from nearby. "Back to work or you will pay for it later."

Matteo resumed his task and Alex turned to face La Dame.

"Are you enjoying my party?" she asked.

Alex didn't respond, and she scowled.

"Obey your most gracious host. Say you are having a pleasant time."

Alex tried to press his lips shut, but they parted on their own and his voice sounded foreign to his ears. "I'm having a pleasant time."

She nodded, pleased, and gestured to one of the men standing close behind her. "Take the young prince to his seat."

Tyson's chains clanked loudly as he walked away, but not a single person in the sea that parted before him took notice.

Matteo was right. They were all under La Dame's power.

She grinned at him with perfect, bright teeth. "My people are in need of a song. Come."

As her magic pulled him along, pain tugged at him and he welcomed the familiar sting of the curse. It kept him tied to a time when he was free. It was a silly thought, because perhaps with the curse he'd never been free.

His life had never fully belonged to him.

And it was because of the woman walking in front of him cheerily as if evil was not a word she knew. She stopped at the edge of the stage.

"Stand on the stage," she ordered.

He did.

"Sing."

"What?" He wasn't a singer. Drawing he could do. Shooting an arrow was easy. But lifting his voice in song? His fingers tapped against his leg as he fought to hold back the music threatening to spill forth from him.

"Sing," she commanded again.

And he did. A folk song his mother used to sing for him flowed naturally.

He sang of power and magic. Of hope and love.

A calmness settled over him and his eyes found Esme sitting alone in the corner of the room working her magic over the crowd. Over him.

He closed his eyes and focused on the words allowing Etta's face, her long golden hair, to eat away at the misery.

No one stopped to watch him, the unwilling entertainment. His heart beat frantically in his chest as he began another song and humiliation reddened his cheeks. Maybe that was her plan. Bring him low. Erode all of his self-respect. And it was working.

Many songs later, La Dame allowed Alex to stop.

Tyson joined him as they prepared to leave for their confinements once again. He leaned in. "I'll get you out of here, brother."

Alex met his gaze with confusion swirling in his own.

"Tonight, I'm going to escape."

"Tyson..."

"Don't try to stop me." Tyson's eyes hardened and he no longer looked like the teenage boy he was. "Etta has to be on her way. I'll find her and we will come for you."

"How do you know she's coming?"

Tyson stared at him. "Do you even know who she is?"

"Persinette Basile."

"That's not what I meant." He turned away to face the doors as they opened. "It doesn't matter if she was born to be queen or if she was a pauper. She is Etta and always will be. There is no doubt in my mind she would risk everything for you. It doesn't matter what you do to each other. She lies. You imprison. Etta is the noblest of all of us. She will come. It's why you're here. La Dame is counting on that too."

A guard ripped Tyson away and shoved him through the door.

La Dame joined Alex, escorting him through the darkened woods to the tower. He didn't sleep that night and when morning came, his freedom was no closer than it had been before.

CHAPTER 14

Edmund froze beside Etta, his hand clamping like a vice around her arm as footsteps approached them across the courtyard.

She placed her hand over his for a moment before busying herself unhooking Verité from the wagon. After days of hard traveling, she wanted nothing more than to collapse into bed and sleep. Guilt gnawed at her for the thought. Alex and Tyson were still captives and she could barely keep her eyes open.

"Edmund," Anders' harsh voice cut through the night air.

"What are you doing here?" Edmund turned his back on his father to unhook the second horse. Two stable lads took the horses toward the stables, but Edmund still hadn't turned back to face Anders.

"I am commander of his Majesty's forces." He scowled. "You do not demand answers from me."

Edmund turned, but Etta put a hand on his chest to stop him. He stared at the father who disavowed him for the magic that ran through his veins. A magic he should have known about as it came from his mother.

"Captain," Etta began. "There are more important things to discuss. We did not expect to see you until we reached the border tomorrow so it comes as a bit of a shock."

Edmund glared at her as a woman walked into the courtyard, dressed in a servant's smock.

"Edmund." She smiled. "We did not expect you back."

"Orenna." His voice went from angry to charming in a matter of moments. "I will always come back to see you."

One eyebrow arched. "Don't flirt with me, sir. It isn't nice when we both have duties to attend to."

He laughed and Anders grunted beside him.

To Etta's surprise, the girl faced her and dipped into a curtsy. "Persinette Basile, if we'd had word of your coming, there would have been more of a welcome than this."

Etta pushed back her hood. "How do you know me?"

Orenna smiled as if it was the greatest jest. "These are the borderlands. Everyone knows you. Once the villagers hear of your arrival, they will rejoice."

Fear snapped into her. "They must not."

"I agree," Anders said, much to her surprise. He cocked his head. "Their presence will stir up unrest and they would not be here if the matter was not urgent. Come, we will discuss it inside."

Maiya had been silent until now and Orenna regarded her with a curious expression. "You can come with me. I'll show you to the guest wing."

Duchess Moreau's estate was unlike anything Etta had ever seen before. It stood in stark contrast to the imposing palace.

Their steps clicked across sky blue tiled floors, past walls of limestone adorned with bright murals.

Anders led them through the halls to a circular room. As soon as Etta stepped through, she stopped, her eyes drifting to the glass ceiling that showed off the night sky. Starlight danced across the shadows, giving the space an ethereal glow.

Edmund nudged her shoulder. "When I first arrived here, I was in bad shape. Guilt and pity ate away at me. I'd come to this room every night and stare into the heavens. The stars healed me."

Anders lit a torch on the wall and sat at the single table in the room. "Now, tell me why you have returned with the kingslayer's daughter."

Edmund glared. "I don't trust you."

"I am—"

"The king's commander. Yeah, I know. But you are also a man who wants to destroy magic. Does your loyalty stretch past the bonds of hate?"

"My loyalty is to the king of Gaule. He sends me to the border and here I am. I arrived at the Duchess' estate this morning. It's a day's ride from the garrison. We have captured some of the folk who've been terrorizing the countryside and I need instruction. The king is too far to receive a messenger in time so the Duchess holds authority over the matter."

"He's closer than you think," Edmund grumbled.

Etta collapsed into a chair. "He's in Bela."

Ander's head snapped up.

They told him everything from the kidnapping to the battle beginning in the streets of Gaule castle. He listened intently as he stood and began to pace. "We can't leave the border unprotected. Not while La Dame is in Bela."

"You can't let the traitors take Gaule either." Etta was losing her patience.

"I know that," he snapped. "We must call in the Moreau forces, but I don't have the authority to do that."

Etta reached into a pouch at her waist and produced Duchess Moreau's ring. "You do if the Duchess has ordered it." She set the ring on the table and pushed it toward him.

He snatched it up to examine it. A long moment passed before he spoke. "I'll get this to the duchess' commander, giving him the power to call them in. Moreau's people can man the Garrison. I can have my men ready to march in two days. Can they hold out that long in the palace?"

"We think so." She paused. "Tomorrow we'll cross the border and reach Alex two days after that."

"I'm sending some of my men with you."

"No." Edmund crossed his arms.

"Boy, you can't go after the king with only two women to help you."

Etta tilted her chin up. "Do you wish to fight me to see if I'm worthy?"

Edmund hid a grin. "Go ahead, father."

He grunted and made for the door, pausing with his hand on the handle. "Bring our king home."

"Make sure he still has a kingdom to come home to."

Etta tossed and turned in her bed until finally giving up on sleep altogether. She dressed hastily and tucked a knife into the sheath on her leg. Closing her door quietly, she padded from the guest wing and backtracked to the room that was open to the world.

It was unoccupied when she arrived, save for the stars winking up above.

Ignoring the chairs, she lowered herself to the center of the floor and leaned back on her elbows. Peace enveloped her.

She imagined Alex looking at these same stars and pain snaked up around her arm and down into her heart. Maiya continued to heal her, but each time she did, the effects lasted for a shorter and shorter period.

The only knowledge that gave her comfort was as long as a heart beat within her chest, one did in his as well.

All of them had grown tense on their journey, rarely speaking. They had no comforting words for each other. Even Edmund was morose.

The door creaked open and Etta glanced back at it. Orenna stood there holding a candle.

"I'm sorry," she stuttered. "I didn't know anyone was in here."

"It's okay." Etta sat up. "Some company actually sounds nice."

The girl smiled shyly and walked farther into the room, dropping down beside Etta. "I come here most evenings to talk to the stars." A flush reddened her cheeks. "You probably think that's crazy."

"What do you say to them?"

She started as if she hadn't been expecting the question. "Well, a lot of things I guess. Mostly I ask them to look after my family."

Etta laid back. She wanted to talk of anything that would get her out of her own mind. "Are they in one of the border villages?"

"They were. After one of the attacks, they disappeared."

Etta closed her eyes almost wishing she hadn't asked. She wasn't good with emotion and Orenna's voice thickened.

"There are rumors," she went on, clearing her throat. "So many of our people have gone missing. People say they are taken into Bela to serve La Dame." She stopped for a moment. "That's good, though. Right? It means they're still alive."

"I'm not sure anything about La Dame is good."

Orenna considered her, but Etta kept her eyes trained on the sky.

"Our village protested your arrest," she finally said, a hint of pride in her voice. "Many of us have magic. The duchess protects us from discovery, but after your identity was revealed and you were imprisoned, we decided we were done living in secret. We refused to send our shipments of food to the palace. At first, the guards arrested anyone who disobeyed orders. Then the attacks began, and they thought it was us, so they stayed away. They didn't care if magic folk killed magic folk." She shook her head. "It wasn't us. La Dame sent her people to sow unrest. When the attackers began naming you as the reason for their actions, we were confused. You were our cause, and they twisted it. They turned you into a prop for their war. Made non-magic folk distrust you." She turned to Etta and dipped her head. "I never distrusted you."

Etta closed her eyes and sucked in a deep breath. Orenna wasn't the first to look at her as if she would save them all, but she didn't know if she could be who they wanted her to be. She wasn't a leader. She could barely trust herself, how were these people supposed to count on her?

"I'm not a queen." It was the first time she'd said it out loud, and it was accompanied by a loud rush of air.

"You were born to be queen." Orenna wouldn't give up.

"You're wrong." She got to her feet and brushed her hands down her pants. "I was born to serve. Born to fight. I never had any choice."

"You do now."

Etta shook her head. She'd never have a choice as long as the curse tied her to Alex. She watched the girl who now appeared younger than before. Her parents had been taken from her and she still had hope brightening her eyes.

She was stronger than she knew. When Etta's father died, she lost her brightness. Her youth. She left the room without another word as her last visit with her father played in her mind. Would he be proud of her now? Her charge was in the hands of the enemy. She'd let that happen because she'd fallen in love. It made her weak. It made her drop her guard.

Viktor Basile would be ashamed.

She'd promised him she'd break the curse. He hadn't believed in her, but her promise stood firm. How could she have grown so complacent?

Was she meant to be queen? Queen of what? A people who were scattered among the kingdoms. A land that had been abandoned before being taken by La Dame. Was she queen of ruins and long-forsaken people?

Orenna was wrong. Persinette was queen of no one.

"Father," she whispered. "I'm going to prove you wrong. I may never be queen, but I will be free." If the curse was no more, what would become of her and Alex? He was the king. No path forward existed for them together, but without the curse, they could both embark on their paths alone.

The descendants of Bela believed in her. If La Dame was taking them, she would stop her. How, she didn't know. The legends of the Basiles were wrong. As the first and only of her generation, her magic should be stronger.

But it wasn't.

As she reached her room, a spasm shocked her as it dug into her shoulder. Gritting her teeth to keep from calling out, she stumbled into the hall to pound her fists on Maiya's door.

The tremor intensified, burning down her arm.

Maiya appeared, sleep ruffled and confused.

Before she could speak, Etta fell through the door and crashed onto the floor.

Sweat poured down Alex's face as he cried out once again. La Dame jerked her hand and her magic ripped into his skin like a thousand white-hot pokers.

He'd been forced to attend another ball, but when it was finished, he hadn't been sent back to the tower. He was in a sizable room with high wooden ceilings that trapped his echoing screams.

Biting down on his lip, he tasted blood.

"Is this because of Tyson?" His voice came out with a ragged moan.

La Dame gave a crooked smile and leaned forward. "He is of no consequence." Her power shot forward once again and he screamed.

Tyson, true to his word, had escaped. Alex waited for news of his capture to come and it never had. His brother was truly away from this place. It was an insufficient comfort at the moment.

"Although," she continued. "I am looking forward to his return with my favorite guest of all."

She was distracted for a moment and Alex let himself breathe.

"You let him go?" He leaned his head back against the chair, his chest heaving. "Why?"

She grinned. "Do you really think you're the one I'm after?"

"Etta." Her name on his lips was like a prayer.

Her smiled didn't waver as she nodded. "You're not as stupid as you look, young king." She ran her fingertips down his cheek. "Such a beautiful boy." Straightening up, she hardened her features. "My men were ordered not to pursue Tyson and his cousin. Matteo was always such an insolent boy. Nothing like his father."

She waved a hand, and the door clicked open. A man walked through, still dressed in his ball attire. The collar of his jacket was unbuttoned, but that was the only liberty he'd taken with his clothing. Alex recognized him immediately. He'd just met him that night. Matteo's father. The brother of Viktor Basile.

He had the Basile look about him. High cheekbones and perceptive eyes. But there was a strength Viktor had always exuded that this man lacked.

He walked forward and kneeled. "My queen. I am sorry my son has caused you so much grief."

La Dame ran a hand over the top of his head. "Matteo has a greater purpose now." Her smile turned down. "But you have outlived your usefulness to me."

His eyes widened a moment before La Dame's magic slammed into him. The impact sent a wave through the room and Alex flew back against the wall.

The man's shock froze on his face as he collapsed backward, a black hole in the middle of his chest.

La Dame had never been able to use her power to control what Matteo and Warren did as Basiles, but that had never meant her other powers were useless against them.

Alex tried to push himself from the ground, but his arms failed him and his face hit the cold stone floor. An eternity passed before La Dame's footsteps moved closer, each slap against the ground reverberating through his skull.

He lifted his eyes up over her swishing skirt and the dark lace of her bodice to where her inky hair framed the black pits of her eyes.

"You killed him," he said. "He was loyal to you and you still killed him."

"He was a Basile," she screamed. "They're loyal to none but themselves."

"Do you have no soul?"

"I did. Many years ago. And they took her from me." She marched across the room, throwing the door open without touching it.

Once she was gone, Alex turned over onto his back, each movement an agony. Even as his lungs begged for breath, his chest screamed to lay still. But the worst of it was still his heart, tied by the curse, and beating painfully against his ribs.

He closed his eyes and forced air in through his lips and then out again.

La Dame's final words wouldn't leave him. She'd lost someone and blamed the Basiles. Was that the reason for the curse? Was it more than a king stealing a healing plant generations ago? King Phillip of Bela took his men over the wall of Dracon not to invade, but to save his queen with a rampion weed. And his descendants paid the price for his folly. It might have taken many years for Bela to be destroyed, but that day was the beginning of the end.

Two guards stomped into the room, the rings of their mail jingling together. Alex barely noticed as he was hauled to his feet. They carried him from the room and into the courtyard where La Dame was waiting with a wagon.

She'd regained her composure, but something was still off.

They dumped him into the wagon and it began to bump along the path through the forest to his tower prison.

As he gazed at the stars above, he wondered if Etta could see them too. Where was she? Wherever she was, she'd have felt every blow he'd taken and he couldn't protect her from any of it.

Delirium took hold and a laugh burst from his lips at the thought of anyone needing to protect Etta. She'd kill him for the thought.

The warmth began in his lower abdomen where the worst of his injuries were and spread from there. He knew the feeling well and sent up a silent thanks to Etta. She must have been with a healer.

The agony abated as comfort enveloped him. He lifted his head for a better look at the stars, counting them until they reached the base of the tower. A guard lifted him from the wagon and La Dame made the stairs appear out of the stone. He let his head loll against the guard's shoulder so as not to let his healed state be revealed.

After the guard dumped him into bed, La Dame left without a word. As soon as she was gone, he scrambled toward the window and sat straddling the sill, bathed in moonlight. Leaning his head back against the stone, he let the silver glow wash over his face.

"I wish you could hear me, Etta. You shouldn't come for me. I'm not worth it. As long as she doesn't kill me, you'll be able to live your life. The only thing that exists here for you is death." A tear slid down his cheek. "Only death."

CHAPTER 15

The minute they crossed into Bela, the band around Etta's heart began to loosen. She hunched forward in her saddle in relief.

"Etta, are you okay?" Maiya asked, riding up beside her.

"We're getting close. I can feel it."

Edmund appeared on her other side. "We're about two day's ride to the palace."

"Let's hope La Dame is really there." Maiya kicked her horse into a gallop and the others followed.

They passed into a sweeping ravine with the greenest forests Etta had ever seen. Bela had lain dormant for so long without people ravaging the land and it thrived as a result. Tall trees stretched as far as they could see in every direction. The paths cut into the forests were long overgrown and hidden.

They slowed to a walk and Etta ducked her head to avoid a branch. She let her magic flow from her fingers to clear the path before them. The trees shrank back, their roots retreating from her power. Vines twisted and slithered like snakes to move from their way.

For a moment, she forgot about the mission or the kidnapped king as she reveled in the feel of the woods. A bird swooped in overhead, its wings stretched out as it glided toward a thickset tree to perch along a high branch.

That's when it hit her. She was home.

Etta didn't know Bela, but in her heart, it was hers. She patted Verité's neck and leaned forward. "The Basiles have returned."

She didn't want to rule. That power frightened her. But she was born to fight and she would fight for Bela until her last breath.

Maiya approached Etta when she slid from Verité's back to begin making camp when the sun began to dip below the horizon. "How's the pain?"

"It won't kill me." Etta set to work removing Verité's saddle.

"Do you want me to..." She waved her hand.

"No." Etta put her hand on the girl's shoulder. "I think I need to feel it right now." She clenched her teeth and hefted the saddle, carrying it toward the base of a tree and setting it down. Verité's blanket was next. He'd ridden hard all day. He deserved to be taken care of first, no matter how deep her weariness went.

He bumped his nose on her shoulder and then walked away to munch on the grass that was plentiful here. Etta was glad she didn't have to use her magic to procure food for the horses because it had been all but depleted during the day.

They tied up the other two horses, but Verité was allowed to roam. He would stick close. He always did.

Satisfied they were okay, Etta, Edmund, and Maiya silently made camp.

Edmund scratched his chin. "I don't think we should make a fire tonight."

Etta's shoulders drooped. The night was already growing colder and the warmth would do them some good. But Edmund was right. "Yeah, I know."

"You think La Dame's people would see the smoke when we're days from her?" Maiya asked.

"She probably has patrols searching the countryside." Edmund spread his blanket on the ground and sat down.

"Are we trying for surprise?"

Etta shook her head. "She knows we're coming." She caught a piece of dried meat Edmund threw toward her and bit down. Venison. She sighed, remembering her own forest in Gaule before life became such a mess. Maybe her life was born a mess.

She leaned back against the rough bark of a wide oak.

Maiya's soft snores began in no time. Edmund glanced at her before meeting Etta's eyes. They both laughed.

"When I first came across Maiya and the group she traveled with, she knew me instantly." He smiled at the memory. "I remembered her from the attack on the village when she helped us." He trailed off for a moment. "She's fiercely loyal to you. When I told her of my mission, she didn't hesitate to join me. Her words were 'I'll get Etta to La Dame if it's the last thing I do.'"

"She's young." Etta studied the girl's handsome dark-skinned face. "She thinks I can win."

"And you don't." Edmund knew her too well.

Etta was quiet for a moment before she spoke again. "I have been training my whole life. My father prepared me to have a place at the king's side. I can kill a man many different ways."

She looked sideways at Edmund but he hadn't flinched. He too was a warrior. "I could have spent my entire life protecting the king and no one could do it better than me."

He raised an eyebrow but remained silent.

"My father didn't prepare me for La Dame. He trained me to do everything in a fight except use my magic. My magic was to be hidden at all times. I'm trying really hard not to be angry at him for that. He should have seen this, should have known the possibility. Instead, he believed I'd just live out the curse as so many Basiles before me have. I'm so utterly unprepared and I don't know if I can do this."

Edmund considered her, staring into the darkness that separated them. "You can," he said simply.

"How do you have so much faith in me?"

"You're meant for this. I knew you'd be great the moment I saw you in the tournament. You won't fail because you refuse to fail."

"So, I'm just stubborn?"

His lip quirked up. "Stubborn doesn't begin to describe you."

They fell into a comfortable silence after that and Etta drifted off to sleep.

She woke with a start as stinging metal pressed against her neck. It took her a moment to come to full awareness and her eyes snapped to the broad-shouldered man hovering over her.

She opened her mouth to scream, but a force slammed into her. Someone was using magic.

The man near her didn't smile and in his eyes, she sensed… regret?

"They're soldiers of Gaule," a woman yelled. "We need to do away with them." Etta twisted hard, catching a glimpse of a petite woman holding up Edmund's sword. On the hilt, was the insignia of the royal guard.

The man removed the knife from her throat as another shock of power slammed into her. "Who are you?" she ground out, panting from the effort.

Another man stepped into view. "People who've been beaten down by Gaule one too many times."

Etta reached out her hand as her eyes shifted to take note of Maiya lying unconscious nearby and Edmund being shoved roughly against a tree. He met her eyes before flicking them to the tree at her back.

Should she tell them who she was? With her shortened hair, she wasn't easily recognizable. Her magic pulsed underneath her skin, begging to be set free.

She let it loose. A branch shot out from a near tree, knocking one of the men over the head. Etta rolled and lurched to her feet as she pulled the grasses from the ground, expanding them and twisting them up around the woman's legs. She slashed Edmund's sword at the grass bands binding her feet.

Etta lunged for her own sword and spun, catching an attacker in the belly. Edmund knocked his man away and twisted him into a headlock. A sickening crack rang through the air and the man slumped to the ground, his neck broken. Two women were left. One raised her hand to use her magic, but Edmund was quick. Etta pulled her knife free and tossed it to him. The first woman dropped as the blade sank into her chest.

The last woman backed away. Etta and Edmund both advanced.

"Please," she whimpered. "I… I didn't want to kill you. That was them." She pointed to her dead companions.

Etta placed a hand on Edmund's arm and he handed her back the blade. After cleaning it on the grass, she sheathed it and regarded the woman with hard eyes. "Why did you attack us?"

"You're soldiers of Gaule. W-we just escaped from there and won't go back."

Etta's heart sank as she turned to Edmund. "They were just scared." Dropping her sword, she turned. "And we killed them."

Edmund was still focused on the woman. "Where were you headed?"

Her face paled, and she diverted her eyes.

"Where?" Etta growled.

"We heard a rumor La Dame was gathering forces to march against Gaule."

A roar ripped from Etta's mouth as she twisted around.

"Why would Belaens fight for her?" Edmund asked.

"Because, Edmund," Etta spat. "This is what happens when you terrorize a people for as long as Gaule has. Eventually, they fight back with whatever means they have." She put her hands on her head and regarded the gray sky. "The only real choice they have is which enemy to serve."

She flicked her hand to the woman who was still struggling against the grass holding her in place. Her bonds loosened, sinking back into the ground. Waving to the two women, she turned away. "Go."

They didn't have to be told twice. Their backs retreated as they ran through the thick forest.

Etta dropped down beside Maiya and felt for a pulse. It throbbed strongly in her neck. She shook the girl's shoulder and Maiya's eyes opened slowly.

"Is it morning already?" Maiya asked.

Etta sat back on her heels. "You were asleep? How could you sleep through that?"

"Sleep through what?"

Before she got a chance to respond, Edmund pulled her to her feet. "Why didn't you tell them who you were?"

"Oh sure, let me just inform them that I am the queen I don't even want to be. I'm sure they'd believe that after the pains we took to change my appearance. I'll tell them that I'm on a mission to save the man they consider to be a greater enemy than even La Dame herself. I'm sure their anger would abate then."

Edmund shook his head and went about checking the bodies for anything they could use. He didn't understand and he never would. The Belaen people were not a singular force. They didn't have a crown uniting them. There was no national pride because most of them were setting foot in Bela for the first time. All they had was anger. Anger and survival.

There was little to be taken from the poor travelers and they were on their way before they'd even eaten breakfast as none of them wanted to stare into the vacant eyes any longer.

Etta killed them without a second thought. Each kill was easier than the one before and that affected her more than the act itself. Was is possible to become immune to guilt? Had her hair really had the power to keep her soul intact? Probably not. That was a silly fantasy. Cutting it hadn't changed who she was.

She'd once told Alex that killing broke apart the soul. What happened when the pieces had been broken so many times it was like they didn't exist at all?

That was when you were no longer a warrior. Warriors had honor. They had a code. When the killing became dishonorable, you were just a murderer.

As if it agreed with her, the sky quaked on their third day in Bela. Verité shook with the vibrations of the thunder as rain pelted down. Etta pulled up her hood and sidled up next to Edmund. "I can feel him. The closer we get, the more I sense Alex."

Edmund gave her a grateful smile. After so long on the road with little hope, it was what he needed to hear.

Maiya grew more withdrawn the closer they got, but Etta let her friend have her peace.

They crested a hill that led down into a wide-open glen dotted with white wildflowers. Even with the angry sky, it was dazzling.

Her eyes scanned the distance, catching on something toward a rocky hillside to the west. "What's that?" She pointed to the swirling mass of water shooting into the sky.

"It looks like the water is..." Edmund shielded his eyes from the rain for a better look. "Going up?"

A thought began in the back of her mind. Did he have that kind of power? She'd only seen the prince perform little tricks.

"Could he?" She didn't need to say his name.

Edmund's face lit up. "Only one way to find out." He kicked his horse into a gallop across the soft ground.

Etta and Maiya raced after him. The cyclone of water continued to rise as they neared the boulders. A narrow path, barely wide enough for a horse, led them through the rocks until they saw him.

Tyson stood in the center of the water as it spun around him and flew toward the sky. His focus was absolute.

Another young man stood at the mouth of a cave yelling at Tyson.

"Ty, you're going to burn out your magic if you keep this up." He stomped toward him, the rain soaking him in seconds. "Cousin." The water cyclone was strong, but the young man managed to reach through and grip Tyson's shoulder. He yanked him back, and the cyclone dissipated.

Etta jumped from her saddle as Tyson glanced up. His eyes widened when he saw her. He stumbled back and his legs folded under him. The other man caught him before he crashed into the ground. He carried him into the cave, laid him down gently, and shook his head.

"I told you not to do it."

"Tyson," Etta breathed, falling to her knees.

The man noticed her for the first time. His eyes scanned their anxious faces.

"You bloody bastard." The man nudged Tyson with his foot. "You win, okay?"

He shook his head and turned. "You must be Etta." He rubbed a hand across his face. "I can't believe it worked. He said if he continued to do that day after day, you'd find us. I wanted to go searching for you, but Bela is a big place. It's probably best we didn't. Not like I think we can save that brother of his. I told him you shouldn't come because, honestly, the king of Gaule isn't worth your life."

Edmund growled.

The man went on. "And that makes you Edmund. Alexandre Durand isn't worth your life either."

Etta was losing patience. She charged the man and pushed him up against the wall of the cave. "I don't know who you think you are, but you're free to be on your way. We are going after Alex."

"You won't win."

Edmund gripped Etta's shoulder and pulled her out of the way before connecting his fist to the man's jaw. His lip cracked and his tongue darted out to find the blood. Edmund kept him pressed up against the hard stone.

The man narrowed his eyes. "Your loyalty makes you blind. Tyson, I understand. It's his brother. The girl is blinded by love. But you…"

Edmund pulled him forward and slammed him back.

"That girl," he growled. "Is Persinette Basile, and you'd do well to show her some respect."

The man stopped fighting, his eyes rounding as they studied her face. Edmund jerked him away from the wall and tossed him to the ground.

Blonde hair flopped into the man's impossibly clear eyes as he rolled to look at her once more. His eyes roamed the contours of her face, her shortened hair, the leather armor she wore.

Tyson coughed and opened his eyes. Maiya helped him sit up slowly and take in the surrounding cave. Edmund still stood in a defensive stance. Etta scowled. The man panted on the ground.

"What's going on?" Tyson asked. "Why is Matteo bleeding?" His eyes narrowed to slits. "Etta, what did you do?"

"Why do you immediately assume it was me?" She crossed her arms.

"Punch first, questions later should be your nickname."

"That's not true," she huffed.

Edmund's shoulders shook with laughter. "If it had been Etta, there'd be a sword protruding from his chest."

"That would be a shame." Tyson's eyes darted around the room nervously. "Because he's our cousin."

Our cousin. *Our cousin.*

Etta didn't understand, but some missing part of her clicked into place as the knowledge permeated every cell. Our cousin.

Forget the blonde still sitting on the floor looking every bit like a Basile. That was something she'd deal with when her mind quit running through scenarios, looking for the things she'd missed.

"Our cousin," she breathed, giving the tiniest shake of her head. *My brother.* That was the more pressing revelation.

Her mother's face appeared, smiling kindly. Had she known? Because as soon as Tyson even hinted, Etta knew it was true. It made too much sense. Catrine's sadness. The secrets. The lies. The vehemence with which the king ran her father from the palace.

Should she have seen it? Even as a child, maybe she missed things. Had her father been in love with the queen?

The anger that'd begun to build in the pit of her stomach now threatened to boil over. Not only had her father failed in her preparations, he'd betrayed her mother. For what? Had he even loved her?

She pulled her rage back from the edge bit by bit, remembering her father's tears. Once they'd escaped the palace after her mother's death, he'd broken down. It was the one time she'd ever seen him cry, but it had been real. She knew it had.

"Etta." Edmund's voice was cautious as he reached out to grip her arm.

Only then did she realize she was shaking.

She brought her hand up to her shoulder to wrap it in the end of her braid. A nervous tick. But like everything else in her life, her hair was no longer there. She turned on her heel and ran back out into the rain. Leaning against a worn boulder, she hunched forward trying to catch her breath.

Did she know her father at all?

"Etta," Tyson called, running after her.

"You shouldn't be out here, Ty." She sucked in a breath. "I'm okay. I'll be back in a moment."

"I'm not a kid anymore, Etta. You can't order me to go back in. Not after everything I've gone through. And what gives you and Edmund the right to be rough with Matteo? He helped me when you weren't there."

"I'm sorry." She wrapped her arms around herself as the chill clung to her sopping clothes. "I should have been there."

"That's not what I meant." He sighed in exasperation and moved closer. In an instant, the rain stopped slapping her in the face.

She looked up to see it coming directly for them, but then it bent out, giving them a small, dry circle. Her mouth dropped open.

"Tyson, since when do you have this much power?"

He waved the words away. "Don't change the subject. We're talking about this."

She closed her eyes briefly. "The first time I met you, I felt this connection."

He snorted. "No, you didn't. When I met you at the tournament, the only thing on your mind was glaring at Alex."

Her lips curved up into the barest of smiles. "After that. At the palace."

He nodded. "You're my sister."

"And you're my brother."

A disgusted look crossed her face. "That means I've been sleeping with my brother's brother."

He held up a hand. "First of all, ew. Don't ever say that again. And second of all, Alex said the exact same thing. Weird."

"You've seen him?" She grabbed the young prince by the shoulders.

He nodded. "If you come back in the cave, we can all talk and you can meet our cousin officially."

He turned to head back in but she turned him back around and pulled him into a hug. In his surprise, he released his magic, and the rain pelted them mercilessly.

He hugged her back just as hard. "Do you think we can get him back?"

"I do, Etta." He paused, resting his chin on her shoulder. "But it isn't going to come without a cost."

She leaned back. "Then it's a good thing the only life I've ever known is sacrifice."

His lips pressed into a thin line, not quite a grimace, and he walked back into the cave.

Maiya was healing Matteo's split lip and Edmund glared at them from across the cave where he sat spinning a knife on its blade.

Etta pushed back her hood and removed her dripping cloak. A fire struggled to stay lit in the corner near Edmund and she dropped down as close as she could without being burnt.

Her clothes began to dry so suddenly she startled. The water was pushed down her shirt, leaving it looking as though it hadn't rained at all. Her hair lightened as it too was drained. She touched the short golden tresses and met Tyson's eye. He shrugged, a satisfied smile spreading across his lips.

"What the hell?" Edmund jumped to his feet, looking around. "Dammit, Tyson, I'm never going to get used to that." He breathed out heavily.

Tyson's shoulders shook with laughter. "Because your whole wind thing is the epitome of normal."

"You two are messed up," Matteo groaned. "We're about to go against everything that is evil and you're making jokes."

"What would you know about it?" Etta snapped. "You may be a Basile, but only one of us carries the curse of our family."

"Etta," Tyson warned.

She brushed him off. "Where have you been while I've been living out our family's curse? Hiding? Living your life?"

"Etta, stop." Tyson's voice was strained.

"No." Matteo got to his feet and walked over to look down on her. "She doesn't have to stop. Go on. Tell me what it's been like for you in Gaule serving a king you love so much you're risking everything. Tell me how much better it was for me as a puppet of La Dame's since the day I was born. With a father who is more beholden to her than his own people. You think you've lived your life in chains, but have you felt the manacles cut into your wrists? Have you been beaten and starved? Has anyone ever owned you so completely you had no identity?"

Etta's eyes softened as her head bobbed up and down. "I have." She flashed back to her time in the dungeons. "But only for a short time and it was my choice. We've both been prisoners, cousin. I've come to set us free."

"By getting us killed?" He sighed. "Death isn't freedom, Etta. It is only death." He went back to his spot beside Maiya and sat against the wall. "Let me tell you a story of a king. When the Basile line was cursed, Phillip was not without power. His magic fought against La Dame's creating unintended consequences for her curse."

Each word he spoke had a bite like he was chastising a child, but Etta let him continue because she knew so little about her family's history.

"La Dame cannot just take you. That's why she has taken the Gaulean king. It's why she didn't just kill every member of the Basile line when they took up the curse."

"What are you saying?"

"The cursed must come to La Dame of their own free will." His eyes pinned her to her spot. "Alexandre Durand is the bait and you're giving her everything she wants."

Tyson scooted next to her and put his arm around her still form.

She couldn't abandon Alex to that fate. He was imprisoned because of her.

"I don't think you're going to get us killed," Tyson whispered.

"What would he have me do?" she asked. "Go into hiding?"

"He doesn't think we should be saving Alex at all because he's a Durand and the purge still weighs heavy on the minds of all magic folk."

"I know. It weighs heavy on me as well. If this was your ..." She stopped herself.

"My father?" Tyson asked. "That's what you were going to say, right? I guess he still is my father. I did grow up in his household." A grim smile flash across his face. "I never did want to be a prince."

She laughed softly. "Ty, technically you're still a prince. Just of Bela, not Gaule."

His face fell. "Right."

She hesitated for a moment, wondering how much she should tell Tyson of what was happening in Gaule. He had a right to know.

"There's something I need to tell you." She leaned her head back against the wall and began to recount the siege and events leading up to it. They had no way of getting information. Had the palace fallen to the traitorous nobles?

Tyson was silent as she talked, but his eyes widened as the story went on.

When Etta finished, he swallowed hard. "Amalie. My mother. Are they okay?"

"When we left, they were as good as could be expected."

He nodded slowly. "My mother will win this." His statement held such a faith that Etta had never felt about anything and she envied him. Tyson found it easy to believe in the people he loved.

She was trained to question everything. To trust nothing. It wasn't the way anyone should live.

Tyson was quiet for so long, she thought he'd fallen asleep. His voice made her jump when he spoke again. "Can you tell me about him? Our father. I remember little from when you lived in the palace as a kid."

Tyson's eyes latched onto hers and she could have sworn it was her father staring back at her. But it probably wasn't real. People see what they wanted to see and in that moment, she imagined a piece of her father was sitting beside her. He wasn't perfect, but he'd crafted the warrior she'd become.

Tyson didn't even have that.

She took his hand and leaned into him to rest her head on his shoulder. Her father wasn't what mattered at the moment. Alex was counting on them.

"Let's get our Alex back first and then I'll tell you what you want to know."

"Everything," he whispered. "I'll want to know everything."

Gray light illuminated the gloomy clouds in the darkening sky as Alex swung his leg over the sill of the tower's lone window. He sat, gazing out over the forest surrounding his secluded tower. Parts of the castle could be seen above the treetops, glittering like a diamond in the distance.

The white stone palace perched precariously at the edge of a high cliff. Even in the growing darkness, he could see the sheer drop down to the sea.

He'd never seen the sea. It both terrified and excited him to be this close.

Back when Bela was a thriving kingdom, they'd welcomed ships from across the sea, bringing wares that were then transported to the markets of Gaule. Without the ports of Bela or Dracon, Gaule had become isolated from the world many years before the wards were in place, cutting them off further.

What would it be like for people to return to Bela? For trade to begin anew?

But nothing was that simple. For while Bela thrived, conflict brewed. The history books were filled with wars. Bela was an enemy of both Gaule and Dracon.

People had begun to return. He didn't know how or why, but each ball was more extensive than the one before and he couldn't figure out where those people were living. There wasn't supposed to be anything for them in Bela.

After the beating he took many nights ago, he hadn't heard another word about Tyson. He listened at every opportunity, but it was like his escape had never happened at all.

He'd been given a sketchpad and charcoal and he didn't understand that bit of kindness. Even as his hands itched to draw, he refused. It was the one rebellion he had.

The stone below him began to shake, and he scrambled from his perch before peering down at La Dame. The steps formed, but she didn't come up. Instead, she gestured to her dark-haired companion. His kidnapper.

Esme ascended the narrow steps carefully before climbing through the window. The steps molded back into the wall.

Alex crossed his arms over his chest, waiting as she dusted off her skirt. Finally, she looked at him.

"I'm here to talk."

His aggravation rose. "I'm not telling you anything."

His anger began to unravel. His mind tried to hold onto it, but it was no use. A calmness settled in his chest.

"That's better," Esme said with a smile.

He sat on the edge of the bed. "That's how you got me out of the palace."

She nodded. "I showed you only part of what I could do when I saved you from your attacker. You know, some would say you're now in my debt."

Irritation was a fleeting feeling, replaced immediately by acceptance. "You were kind to me."

She smiled at his words but they sounded wrong to his ears. Why had he said them?

"I see that you have healed fully from your ordeal with La Dame." Her smiled didn't reach her eyes. "Your Basile witch's doing?"

He slammed his lips shut to prevent her magic from making him spill his secrets.

"You don't need to say it, Alexandre." Her voice softened as she moved toward him and dipped her head to whisper in his ear. "I already know."

Her fingers trailed the length of his arm while the other hand landed on his thigh. "Can I tell you a secret?" she asked.

He nodded, enjoying the feel of her touch despite something niggling at the back of his mind.

"Healing power is not found in the blood of a descendant of Bela. Only a select few Draconians have that ability."

Alarm flashed through his mind even as Esme pushed him back and crawled onto the bed next to him.

She continued. "My daughter has such an ability, but I have not seen her for many years. La Dame sent my husband on a mission fifteen years ago and he took her with him."

She pressed up against him as her words bounced around in his skull, unable to find a place to land.

Etta.

Etta.

Etta.

He held onto the word as if his life depended on it.

Esme's hand crept up his thigh. "You'll tell me all your secrets."

He shook his head violently, weakening the calming effect of her magic. "No," he groaned.

"No." It was more forceful that time.

Her magic shifted. Instead of gliding over him to coax his words, it pulled at him, demanding answers.

He pushed her away so suddenly she fell from the bed with a squeak. Getting to her feet, she growled and stomped her foot.

She cast her magic out again, but he pictured Etta and it failed to take root.

"How are you doing that?" she asked, more curious than angry.

"No matter what kind of power you have, I will never betray Etta or Tyson."

Something flashed in her eyes and he would have sworn it was respect, but then it was gone.

"Your loyalty will be your end."

He sat up and rested his arms on his legs. "It isn't loyalty. It's love."

She studied him for a moment and shook her head sadly. "It was love that destroyed Bela."

"No, it was an evil woman with a vendetta and a king who wanted the weed to cure his queen."

She tilted her head to the side. "You think Rapunzel was a weed?"

"That's what the legends tell us."

She shifted her eyes to the window where La Dame was no doubt waiting down below. "Because the legends were told by the Belaens. The truth would change everything you think you know."

"What's the truth?"

Her eyes flicked to his once more. "I've said too much. Just know La Dame will destroy you. She will take the ones you love. She will force you to follow her. No matter how much you fight, in the end, she wins."

When Esme looked to him once more, it was not the hard eyes of the woman who'd kidnapped him, nor the calculating tool of La Dame. There was fear swirling in her depths. She had the power to control the emotions around her, but not her own.

She could force others to do her bidding, but something was still not right.

"What have you lost?" His voice was soft. "Is it your daughter?"

She shifted her eyes away. "You cannot take what someone does not have. My family never belonged to me. Their hearts, their very souls were always hers. You aren't the only one with no control over how your story goes."

"You could have control. Persinette Basile is coming for me. Soon, everyone will have to choose a side. Soon, your choice will be freedom or death."

Her hair swung as she shook her head. "Only the young can have such faith. The rest of us must live in reality and my reality is shaped by La Dame's power."

She leaned out the window as the steps formed once again.

Stepping out the window, Esme didn't turn back.

Had she wanted him to be able to resist her magic? He focused on each word she'd said. Each secret she'd revealed.

One stuck out above all else.

Etta traveled with a traitor. Everything had been planned from the start. Her friendship with the healer. The healer's betrayal that got Etta thrown in the dungeons. Her aid in freeing other magic folk so her father could bring them to La Dame.

Etta was coming for him, but it was a trap and there was nothing he could do to help her. He pounded his fist against the bedpost and threw the pillow across the room as hard as he could, never feeling more helpless than he did right then.

A hand covered Etta's mouth and her eyes snapped open to find Matteo hovering over her. Instinct had her reaching for her knife. Matteo held a finger to his lips and released her, motioning her to follow him to the mouth of the cave. She rolled to her feet and silently padded past the still-sleeping forms of Edmund, Tyson, and Maiya.

"Where are we going?"

Matteo jerked his head around. "Quiet."

Narrowing her eyes, she trailed him out into the early morning light. A chill hung in the air as they clambered over a boulder. Etta's feet slammed into the dirt as she dropped from the rounded rock and prepared to climb the next. Matteo stopped at the top and crouched low as his eyes focused on the valley down below.

Was he going to kill her? She didn't know her cousin. He could be in league with La Dame. She opened her mouth to speak and then she saw them.

Four soldiers urged their horses across the flowering fields, toward the pass where their cave sat.

"How much time do we have?" Etta whispered.

"Not much."

"And yet you wasted some of it by bringing me out here?"

He slid down from the rock. "I didn't think you'd believe me."

As they sprinted back, she veered toward the horses while Matteo went to wake the rest of their friends. Verité reared up excitedly as she neared.

"We need to get on the move, boy." She patted his neck as she began to saddle the others.

Tyson appeared to help her and they'd managed to saddle every horse except Verité when Edmund, Maiya, and Matteo came running. "They're coming," Edmund yelled.

His words were punctuated by the sounds of their pursuers entering the rocky outcropping. Etta flicked her eyes from

Verité's saddle on the ground to the round brown eyes boring into her. Shaking her head, she gripped the ragged mane and Edmund gave her a boost before getting into his own saddle.

They took off, wanting to put distance between them and the soldiers behind them. Squeezing her thighs together, Etta lifted her rear higher and bent forward.

Quickly prying one hand from Verité, she flung it back. Roots erupted from the ground behind them, splitting rock and dirt alike. It slowed their pursuers, but they kept coming. The path widened as they rode in the shadow of the great hills. Forested hillsides rose up around them, stretching all the way to the base of the mountains bordering Dracon.

"Come on, Verité." The horse sped up and led the others onto a path that veered off the main road and wound up higher.

A creek ran down from the hill, blocking their way. Verité leaped easily, landing with a jarring impact on the other side. As soon as they all made it, Tyson pulled up on his steed and concentrated.

The water began to bubble and rise, spilling over edges of the creek. Etta pushed Verité up beside Tyson and closed her eyes, feeling every branch, every root, every bit of living earth in the ground. She jerked her hand and it shifted, cracking open the land, sucking the water back in.

The creek became a lake, too wide to jump, too long to go around. Their pursuers appeared on the other side, pulling their horses to abrupt stops.

Etta slumped back. She'd never attempted magic of that size. It'd drained every bit of energy from her bones.

Tyson let out a whoop beside her. "That was cool."

Giving him a weak smile, she nudged Verité and continued moving along the path. As they reached the hill's apex, the trees gave way to an open glen. Etta slid from Verité's back and fell to her knees.

Maiya scrambled from her horse and dropped down next to Etta. "Are you okay?"

"How am I supposed to face La Dame if my magic drains me so completely?"

"Oh, Etta. No one expects your magic to be able to beat her." Maiya's eyes widened as the words left her and she clapped a hand over her mouth. "I'm so sorry. I shouldn't have said that."

Etta collapsed onto her side. "It's the truth and the truth should always be spoken."

"But it's not the truth." Edmund shot daggers at Maiya.

She started to protest, but a crash sounded behind her as Tyson fell from his horse.

"Looks like you aren't the only one who can't handle their magic." Matteo checked Tyson's pulse. "He'll be okay. You both lack stamina."

"Stamina?" Edmund asked.

Matteo put his head in his hands and groaned. "Have any of you been trained in magic?"

Once again, the thought of her father leaving her so ill-prepared stabbed at Etta.

Matteo studied each of them in turn. "I'm the only one here without magic and the only one who knows anything about it. How's that for irony?"

"Stop being a dick and tell us," Edmund growled.

Matteo leveled him with a glare. "Magic is not an infinite source. Like physical prowess, it must be trained. The more you practice, the more you will be able to use it."

Etta half-listened because something rose up among the dense trees below. She raised a hand to shield her eyes and look closer. A stone tower stood as tall as the trees surrounding it. Spikes lined the top of it and a single open window was cut into the face.

Her heart squeezed, the curse pulling tighter.

All talk ceased behind her. Maiya was on the ground pouring her healing power into Tyson. He woke slowly and Maiya moved to grip Etta's hand. Strength flowed into her and for a moment, she forgot the mysterious tower.

Until Tyson got to his feet and followed her line of sight. His eyes lit up and she knew. Alex was near.

"We have to go to him." She turned back to focus on the stone prison.

Tyson's voice was cautious. "Etta, that tower doesn't even have stairs. We can't just show up and get him out."

"Alex is there?" Edmund's voice held every ounce of hope she now felt. "What are we waiting for?" He swung up onto his horse and took off.

Matteo grimaced. "I guess we're doing this with a death wish instead of a plan?"

"No one is asking you to come." Etta climbed onto Verité and went after Edmund. Alex was right there, so close, and she'd be damned if they were going to waste another moment.

The sun was high in the sky by the time they reached the base of the tower. Still hidden in the trees, they trotted in a wide circle to scout the surrounding areas.

"You think La Dame is here?" Edmund asked.

Etta scanned the area around them. "We'd see some sign."

"There aren't any guards."

"Edmund, there isn't even a door, why would she need guards?"

Her heart pounded as she slid from Verité. Edmund stopped next to her and gripped her shoulder.

Every day had been leading to this moment.

Every shock of pain the curse sent through her held purpose.

It was all meant to bring her to Alex. He was more than her charge, more than the king she was cursed to protect.

He was everything.

And she'd found him.

She closed her eyes for a brief moment. The pounding of hooves echoed among the stillness in her heart as Matteo, Tyson, and Maiya appeared. She didn't wait for them.

The risk no longer mattered. It was in that moment she realized, she'd sacrifice everything for the man in the tower.

She reached the base and lifted her eyes.

Edmund nodded as he prepared to use his magic to push her voice into the tower and she spoke. "Alex. Are you up there?"

For a few torturous moments, all she heard was the thundering of her own heart.

CHAPTER 16

Alex. Are you up there? Alex. Alex. Alex.

The sound of his own name ricocheted through his aching head as he lay in bed. All morning, he'd felt an exhaustion unlike anything he'd experienced before. It had faded away, but he still couldn't bring himself to rise.

Etta had been hurt this morning. Hurt and then healed. He was sure of it. That was what caused his current state. She was out there and there was nothing he could do to protect her.

Etta. Etta?

His time of imprisonment was beginning to scatter his brain. No. He didn't hear Etta's voice. His mind was playing tricks, giving him what he wanted most.

Alex.

He covered his ears and shook his head violently. Was La Dame playing a cruel joke? She was nothing but cruel. But he would not give in. He would not give her the satisfaction of breaking him. She seemed to take pleasure in his love for Etta. It gave her power.

"No," he grumbled, stumbling from the bed. He lurched toward the chamber pot and lifted it. If La Dame was on the ground taunting him, he'd get back at her. It was petty and childish, but it was all he could do. He carried the pot to the window and prepared to turn it on an unsuspecting sorcerer as she created the stairs she'd climb to torment him.

It slipped from his grasp when he looked to the ground, hitting the edge of the window on its way out. Urine flew through the air, but all he could do was stare at the two people scrambling back away from the falling waste.

Edmund grinned up at him once the pot landed with a thud. The other person had their hood up, but there was no mistaking the set of her shoulders or short movements of her gait. He sucked in a breath.

They were here.

"Etta." His voice was too quiet the first time he spoke so he cleared his throat. "Etta."

She snapped her head back to peer up at him, her hood slipping from short golden hair. His fierce protector looked even more dangerous than before.

She turned away from him to say something to Edmund and Tyson appeared at the tree line. Alex leaned against the side of the window. His brother was safe.

But he was here.

Panic clawed at him. They had to go. La Dame could return at any moment. Before he got another word out, Etta had placed her palms on the stone. He watched in amazement as vines slithered up the tower, crossing and wrapping around the structure. He touched one as it whipped past the window.

Glancing down at Etta, he shook his head. Edmund tried to hold her back, but she pushed him away and started to climb. Her sword was strapped across her back and gleamed in the sun as she ascended the vines she'd created, showing no fear.

The moment she reached him, he grabbed her arm and pulled her in through the window before crushing her to him. His pulse hammered in his ears as she pressed her face into his chest.

"You shouldn't be here," he whispered into her hair.

She shook her head. "I had no choice."

"Because of the curse." He nodded in understanding.

She pushed away from him. "Because..." Her voice wavered, and she turned away to hide her face. When she faced him once again, her look broke him in two. "Because I haven't fought for you. I've lied to you and hated you. I've protected you and loved you. But I didn't fight. When you imprisoned me, I let you despise me. When you wanted to let me go, I said the reason I couldn't was the curse." She stepped forward and fisted his shirt. "I know you won't agree, but I need to fight. For you. For me. For us. It's probably going to kill me, but how could I live knowing I didn't fight?"

When she lifted her face once more, he claimed her lips with his. Possessing. Demanding. Hello. Thank you. I'm scared.

I love you.

She deepened the kiss with a moan low in her throat and he wanted nothing more than for it to last forever.

His mind finally caught up. His Etta had come. As scared as he was for her, he loved her all the more for it.

"I'm going to tear it all down." Her voice vibrated against his lips. "If I'm going down, I'll take her with me."

The tower shook and Alex broke away with a frantic look to the window. "She's here."

"Etta!" Edmund's voice was cut off abruptly.

La Dame's steps were slow, each slap of her shoes against the stairs, sending a jolt through them.

There was nowhere to hide. She knew Etta was there.

"I love you," Alex breathed, tightening his grip on her.

A tear shone in the corner of her eye. "I never thought I'd love you."

"Etta, there's something you need to know. Maiya–"

He suddenly couldn't speak as La Dame's magic stole his words. He pulled Etta to his side as he tried once again to speak. To tell Etta she had a traitor in her midst. La Dame climbed through the window and righted herself. A bright smile stretched across her deceptively beautiful face.

"Persinette," she said pleasantly.

Etta shook beside him as she straightened her spine.

"La Dame." Her voice was cold, strong.

La Dame stepped forward. "It is a pleasure meeting someone I feel such a connection to."

Etta cocked her head. "Is connection another term for curse?"

"Ah, but it isn't a curse for you at all, is it, my dear?" She walked forward and patted Alex's cheek. "He's such a handsome boy. I can see why you'd forsake your family's long enmity for his family."

Alex flinched away from her.

La Dame lowered her hand and quirked her lip. "I'm in the mood to make a deal."

"I'm listening." Etta grit her teeth.

"A trade. You take your young king's place and I will release him. Simple as that."

"No," Alex tried to cry.

Etta stepped away from him. "Done."

Alex shot her a pleading look.

La Dame laughed. "I'm afraid you don't know the Basiles, Alexandre. I wouldn't try to tell her what to do."

Etta advanced on La Dame. "You destroyed my family. What are you waiting for? Kill me. As long as Alex is released."

"Your love for him is endearing, but I'm afraid today is not the day we make the trade. I throw balls for my townsfolk every night. You will be there two nights hence. Only then will you save your precious prince. Until then, we have no need of you."

La Dame shot a blast of power toward Etta before Alex could shove her out of the way. Her arms flung out to the sides as she sailed backward through the window, a scream dead on her lips.

Alex ran to the window as her lifeless body crashed toward the ground. "Etta," he called, his words finally breaking free as he collapsed against the sill.

Helplessness settled over him as he could do nothing but watch the woman he loved falling. The impact sent a shock through his system and he fell back, gasping for breath as if every bone in his body broke. Pain spread out from one localized spot in his abdomen. He didn't hear his own scream as everything faded away.

Voices surrounded Etta, but she couldn't make them out through the heavy hammer crashing inside of her skull. Each word spoken sent another sharp pain against her temple.

A groan worked its way up to escape her lips. "Stop," she murmured.

They didn't hear her.

"Stop talking so loudly."

The voices ceased abruptly, and she opened her heavy eyelids. Dark curls swam before her as Maiya leaned over.

"Etta." She placed her hands on Etta's head and the pulse of her magic sent the pain on its way. "I'm glad you're awake."

Darkness covered the room they were in and her friends stood out like shadows in the night.

"What happened?" She pushed herself up on her elbows.

"That bitch pushed you from the tower," Edmund growled.

It all came back to her. The tower. Alex. Her eyes snapped to Edmund, but he shook his head. Alex was still a prisoner.

Leaning back, she breathed heavily. She'd failed him. For a moment, she'd gotten lost in his arms and she'd let her guard down. How was she supposed to save Alex now?

"I've been out all afternoon?" A candle burned nearby illuminating the bare wooden walls and dirt floor. A stack of crates stood in the corner. Where were they?

Tyson sat down beside her. "You've been unconscious for a night and a day, even after Maiya healed you."

Alarm bells rang in her head. "We have one day until the ball."

When they regarded her quizzically, she explained everything that transpired in the tower. Finding Alex. Their invitation.

Tyson shot Matteo a look and her cousin sighed. "She holds these balls every night. She enjoys the show of fidelity from the villagers and it solidifies her power in Bela."

"Villagers?" Etta tried to climb to her feet, but Maiya put a hand on her arm. "There isn't a village in Bela."

"There is now." Edmund glanced toward the door. "People have been disappearing from Gaule in droves and this is where they've ended up."

"None of this makes any sense." Etta shrugged Maiya away and climbed to her feet.

Matteo followed her. "The first thing you need to understand about La Dame is you may never have answers to your questions. Her reasons are never known. Her magic is infinite."

Etta stopped when she stepped outside. A village sat before her, not unlike the one near the palace of Gaule. Darkness covered the street, but the cobblestones beneath her feet were plain. Wooden, flat-roofed buildings stretched out on each side of her, each one connected to the next. Wind blew her sticky hair from her forehead as her mind tried to grasp the truths before her. She'd thought it was all gone. Her kingdom. But here it was, come to life again.

A door opened nearby, spilling candlelight onto the street. Boisterous voices poured out until they were abruptly cut off by the closing door. A tavern. Those people sounded... happy? Did they know they were controlled by La Dame?

Edmund stepped up beside her and bumped her shoulder. "Are you okay?"

"How is any of this here?"

"Tyson and I came through here soon after leaving Gaule and it was nothing but overgrown forests and the ruins of a castle."

"You mean this is magic?" She sucked in a breath. None of this should be real. Her heart thundered in her ears. La Dame was more powerful than she'd imagined.

He draped an arm over her shoulders and pulled her into his side as if reading her mind. "This doesn't mean we can't beat her."

Etta dropped her head onto his shoulder. "I had him, Edmund. He was in my arms."

"We still have a chance."

She didn't tell him how much she doubted his words. It wouldn't do any good. Whether they had a chance or not, they weren't going to quit.

"Where's Verité?"

Edmund grinned. "You and that damn horse."

"Tell me."

"He's fine. When La Dame showed up, she shot out a blast of magic that sent us flying toward the woods. With the exception of Maiya, we were all knocked unconscious. But the horses were out of her range of power, hidden back in the trees. They're in the village stables."

Something about his story didn't sit right with her. She glanced behind her but the others were lost in discussion.

Leaning closer to Edmund, she dropped her voice. "If you were all knocked out, why wasn't Maiya?"

"She said she was near the horses."

Etta ran a hand through her hair, a nervous habit from having long hair most of her life. "She wasn't. I saw her from the window. She was right behind you."

Blonde brows drew up over clear blue eyes.

"How did you find the village?" she asked. "Was it Matteo?"

"No." He frowned. "Matteo was as surprised as us. He said he knew the people coming to the balls had to live somewhere, but he hadn't been allowed outside the palace until his escape." He scratched the back of his neck and met her gaze. "Maiya chose our road. You were draped across my saddle and the only thing I could think of was how her healing couldn't wake you. Matteo and Tyson had grown quiet. She rode at the front and none of us questioned her direction. When we came upon the village, she acted as if it were a shock to her as well."

"We can't—"

They were interrupted by the appearance of the girl in question.

She smiled shyly. "Are you two going to stand out here all night? You'll freeze."

Etta opened her mouth to speak, but she didn't know what to say to the girl. Maiya, the first friend Etta had ever made, was a traitor. The burn of betrayal caught the words in her throat. What about Pierre? Her father's closest friend. Had it all been orchestrated from the beginning?

Etta brushed past her into the room and took up residence in the far corner. Drawing her hood and pulling her knees to her chest, she rested her chin on her arm and held back the angry tears. La Dame owned her. She'd owned her father. Everything was controlled by the woman who wanted nothing more than to destroy her family.

Maiya and Pierre proved she could reach them even in the warded Gaule. La Dame could enter any part of her life and now she sat with a traitor a few feet away. The wide, innocent eyes were a trick.

Edmund positioned himself near Maiya, watching her every move.

It was only when he spoke that Etta realized Matteo was next to her. "Did you know I'm a few weeks younger than you?"

Weeks? That meant… she scrubbed at her face. Too much information. Maiya's betrayal and now Matteo. She'd come so close to avoiding the fate of the Basiles. If she'd been born only a few weeks later – after Matteo – the curse would have fallen to him instead of her.

When she didn't respond, he continued. "I waited to take up the curse for my entire life. My father didn't know about you. He didn't even tell me about his brother. But La Dame knew. I've been in her household since I was a child, but you know why she didn't tell me? Control. As long as I believed her curse would be my life, I was beholden to her."

"I'm not beholden to her," Etta snapped.

"As long as you need something from her, that's exactly what you are. It's why she's doing this. We are not her enemies. To be such, would give us a power in her mind she refuses. No, we are merely her playthings. It's why she kept me and my father instead of killing us. In her eyes, death is too easy."

"Didn't you tell me there is no freedom in death? How is it too easy?"

"That's true. There is no freedom. But there is finality. An end. Maybe a little peace. Peace. As long as we're alive, she can at least make sure we have no peace."

"She can try." Etta's voice hardened. "But what she didn't count on was the curse providing the peace we seek. I don't need her to break it anymore. I could live my entire life connected to Alexandre Durand, and it would be a good one."

"Don't underestimate her. She will use your love against you."

Etta's eyes drifted to where Maiya had fallen asleep. "Maybe she already has."

"You've found the traitor in your midst." He nodded in understanding.

"You knew?" As if his words confirmed Maiya's allegiance in her mind, the anger she'd felt returned in force.

"She's a healer, of course I knew. The healing magic is a Draconian one."

"I'm such a fool." She buried her face in her hands. "Why didn't you tell me?"

One of his shoulders lifted in a shrug. "I didn't think it mattered. She wouldn't try to kill you. La Dame wants you alive. It seems her job is to guide you to the palace. Make sure you get there. That's where we want to go anyway, so what's the harm?"

"We? I thought you were against us going."

He tilted his head back against the wall, blonde hair falling into his eyes. He looked every bit the Basile. Every bit her family.

Family. It was a foreign concept to her. Matteo. Tyson. She didn't know how to be family.

When Matteo answered her, his voice was barely above a whisper. "If I thought I could stop you, I would. But I will go where you go. I know I can be harsh, but I've never had anyone in my life I could care about."

"What about your father?"

He shook his head. "No. You need to know... my father is a Basile, but he's loyal to La Dame. He won't be on our side."

Etta hesitated before taking his hand in hers. Her cousin had lived his life in solitude similar to hers, both in their own kind of prison. He'd been alone. At least she'd had her father when he wasn't off trailing the king across Gaule. Matteo gave her hand a grateful squeeze, and it tugged at her heart. Her connection to him had nothing to do with a curse, it was blood, pure and simple. Their blood bonded them and in Bela, blood was the most important thing of all. It held their power.

She thought over every interaction with Matteo, coming to one conclusion. "You don't have any magic, do you?"

He hung his head in shame.

"How is that possible?"

"I don't know." He took his hand from hers. "I waited my entire life for the legendary Basile power. The kind that hadn't been seen in generations. The kind that the stories told could defeat La Dame. I thought maybe that was the reason I didn't even have small-scale magic, because it would come. Then I found out about you and knew it never would."

"But I don't have it either." She held out her hand, palm up. "All I can do is grow plants. And Ty… he hasn't shown anything other than a water ability."

"And so it passed another generation." He shook his head. "And we're no closer to taking her down for good."

CHAPTER 17

A cart rumbled by and Etta jumped back to avoid being hit, colliding with an older man behind her. She peered up into his drawn face.

"I'm sorry."

He grumbled something unintelligible and went on his way.

A hand gripped her elbow. Edmund. He led her past the bustling marketplace where a young boy sold loaves of bread outside a bakery and the line at the dressmakers wrapped around the side of the building.

At the center of the village was an open space. When Etta rounded the corner, she stopped dead in her tracks. A stand had been erected in the center of the square and a man's body was held upright by two pikes. Flies buzzed about his face. The villagers avoided coming near, but Etta couldn't stop herself. She recognized his bloated face immediately. She'd probably never forget one of the men who'd abused her in Gaule's dungeons.

"Lance." Edmund covered his mouth.

Etta didn't realize she was shaking until Edmund pulled her away from the horrid sight and into a narrow alleyway.

"He…" Etta put her hands on her hips and heaved in a breath. "I'd heard Alex sent him into Gaule."

Edmund watched her carefully. "Am I missing something?"

She refused to bring the memories from the dungeons back to the surface so she swallowed past the bile threatening to rise and shook her head to explore the alley.

It turned into a narrow passageway that led to the docks where fishing boats unloaded the day's catch. An acrid smell hung in the air and Etta covered her nose with her hand. She'd never been near the sea before. Brilliant blue water stretched across the horizon. The docks themselves were made of narrow wooden slats that the fisherman navigated with ease as they yelled to each other above the flapping of the sails. It was such a stark difference to the square they'd come from.

Bela was an ocean kingdom, serving as the trading connection to the rest of the world. Its ports were once busy with vessels of all sizes from Madra and the other kingdoms across the sea. Gaule and Dracon once sent their goods along Belaen roads to be sold.

But that was before.

Etta's eyes scanned the coastline to the white cliffs looming over the sea. There, atop the cliffs, sat the palace. The breath caught in Etta's throat.

Edmund followed her line of sight. "Matteo says La Dame recreated it to the exact specifications of the palace that was there before."

"Why?"

"She's obsessed. Whatever Phillip and Aurora did to her, it must have destroyed any sense of humanity she had left."

"All they did was take a weed. Rapunzel saved Aurora."

He regarded her without expression. "Do you still believe the legends? That she's doing all of this because of a weed?"

"I guess not." She deflated instantly. But then why was she doing it? Power? Did she really hate the Basiles that much? Or did she want to revive Bela, to bring its riches back to the world?

Another boat docked and began unloading buckets of fish with stiff, almost mechanical movements.

"Do you notice something off about these people?" Edmund asked.

"I've seen the look in their eyes before." She turned away from the docks. "They're prisoners just like we will be tonight."

When Maiya brought them to the place they were staying, Pierre was there. Etta's first instinct was to go to him. He'd been like a father after her own died. He'd helped Alex. He'd led their freed people from the dungeons. But had he just brought them here? To be prisoners once again?

He smiled when he saw her, but it fell when he took in her hard eyes. Matteo and Edmund formed up on either side of her. Tyson shook his head in confusion.

Maiya had tears in her eyes. "You know?"

"Know what?" Etta rounded on her. "That my friend has betrayed me. Again. But then, maybe you weren't my friend at all. Deception is all there's ever been between us."

Maiya covered her face as her back shook with tears.

Pierre's face reddened. "Do not speak to my daughter like that."

"I will damn well do what I like." She tried to advance on him, but Edmund held her back. "Did you convince my father to kill the king? To sacrifice himself?"

A sneer curled his lips. "That was entirely his doing. La Dame was pleased."

"Bastard." She ripped her arm from Edmund's grasp and swung at Pierre. A blast of air sent her flying against the wall. He crumpled to the floor and her memory sparked. She'd assumed he was magicless but that couldn't have been more wrong. "The attack in the village when I first became protector. You were part of it."

"Who do you think orchestrated it? My orders were to kill you. But then you fell in love with your charge and all of that changed."

Picking herself up, she advanced forward once again, but this time, not to attack. "Why are you here?"

He smiled, and it was reminiscent of the man she thought she'd known. "To prepare you for the ball, of course."

Maiya wouldn't look at any of them as she followed her father down the street. The people in front of the dressmaker's shop parted for them to enter, an air of fear surrounding them. Pierre must have been well known in the village as one of La Dame's men.

The dressmaker was an older, plump lady who was continuously pushing her spectacles up her long nose. Silver hair was tied into a bun with multiple ribbons. She looked up when they entered, the lines of her face deepening as she saw Pierre.

"Agnus," he barked. "This is Persinette Basile. Dress her to suit her station."

When Pierre rushed out, forcing Edmund, Tyson, and Matteo to follow him, Etta was left wondering what station an enemy queen who was no queen had in La Dame's court.

Agnus tsked and tutted as she took Etta's measurements, but there was otherwise no speaking. At one point, she disappeared into the back room, returning with deep pink gown in her arms.

"It will need a few adjustments." Agnus shook it out and Etta gasped.

She'd never see anything so fine. Even Catrine and Camille's dresses in Gaule were understated compared to this. Gold embroidery stretched down the corseted bodice in a flowered design. The skirts were layered with various shades of pink.

"Strip," Agnus ordered.

Etta obeyed and stepped into the dress, pulling it up over her hips. The neckline dipped low, showing off the tops of her breasts. She swallowed heavily as Agnus pulled her laces so tight she could barely breathe.

With the exception of the length, it fit like a glove. Agnus sat heavily on her stool and went to work shortening the hem as Etta ran her hands down the corset.

When Agnus was finished, she moved to a wooden box on the table and opened the lid. Lifting out a necklace, she turned. "La Dame has ordered you to wear this."

Even as she bristled at the command, she couldn't take her eyes from the ruby hanging on the end of a thick golden chain. As soon as Agnus dropped it around her neck, something clicked inside her.

Agnus handed her a pair of glass shoes and she shrank back. "Glass? How am I supposed to wear these?"

"With grace, my queen."

Etta snapped her eyes to the elderly women who seemed to be following La Dame's orders so completely. A twinkle lit her eyes.

"Remember, Persinette, most of us have had no choice but to help her. Please don't forget us."

"I promise," Etta whispered. "You have never been forgotten. Bela's time is coming."

Agnus nodded, a small smile coming to her lips.

Etta stepped out onto the street, expecting the others to be waiting, but they were nowhere to be found. The village had begun to empty as people made their way to the palace for the ball. Each night, this was their life. They knew their will had been stolen, but their minds couldn't overcome their bodies actions.

Etta didn't know what would have been worse. Having your awareness stolen and becoming a mindless follower or knowing exactly what you did and being unable to stop it.

She heaved a sigh and began walking slowly. The glass shoes sat heavy on her feet and she worried they'd break with each step.

The stables weren't far and when she made it there with her shoes intact, she considered it a success. Taking them off, she padded on bare feet to the second to last stall where she could see Verité hanging his head over the short swinging door of his stall.

She smiled when she saw him, finally believing he was okay after the events at the tower. Meeting his immense brown eyes, she twirled. "How do I look, boy?"

He snorted, and she rubbed a palm along the ridge of his nose. The smell of horses hit her, and she hoped, just for a moment, that the stench clung to her dress. Any rebellion against La Dame. She wanted Etta to be the perfect guest. That would never happen.

Etta sucked in a constricted breath. "How did we get here, Verité? Do you remember when it was just you and me in our forest? Wild and free. Now we know nothing but cages."

"Knew I'd find you here." Edmund's voice snapped her out of her thoughts. "It's time to go."

She turned to face him. He'd been scrubbed and dressed in fitted trousers, a silk blouse, and a jacket that looked like it belonged on him and no one else.

"You're very handsome, Edmund." The words slipped out before she could stop them.

He grinned. "I don't think now is the time or place to woo me, Etta."

"I wasn't—"

"Even if it were." He leaned close. "You're not my type."

She punched his arm. "I'm trying to tell you I'm glad you're with me."

"Because I'm handsome? You don't have high standards going into a fight."

"Shut up."

He chuckled. Were they supposed to laugh before a night such as this?

Wrapping an arm around her waist, he rested his chin on the top of her head. "No one is going to be able to look at you tonight and not want to follow you no matter where it leads. You look like a queen."

"I'm worried that's what I'm meant to look like. Make me a queen and then destroy me."

Matteo walked through the door in a more ornate outfit than Edmund's and stopped in his tracks, mouth hanging open. He shook off his momentary shock.

"Why are you looking at me like that?" She eyed him skeptically.

"I'll show you when we get to the ball. Come. We must leave."

A carriage awaited them. Pierre and Maiya sat on the driver's bench. Matteo opened the door to reveal Tyson in an identical outfit.

"Seems she's putting the Basiles on display." Tyson helped her into the carriage and she slipped the glass shoes onto her feet.

"Glass?" He raised an eyebrow.

She shrugged and leaned back as the carriage jerked to a start and rumbled along the road that would take them to the palace.

There was no more waiting.

No sneaking.

No plotting.

La Dame was bringing them to her and Etta couldn't even fathom what she was planning. They rumbled past the square, each watching the dead man as they passed. Tyson shot Matteo a knowing look but stayed quiet.

Matteo averted his eyes and leaned forward. "Okay, the great hall is in the center of the palace. It will be crowded with people, many of whom are there because they have no other choice. They've been taken from Gaule. Others escaped from Gaule only to walk into La Dame's trap. Her people will be there as well. Many of them don't have magic."

"What?" That surprised Etta.

Matteo went on. "Like the patrol that chased us. Draconian magic has been weakening, diluted, and many are being born without it. Even La Dame doesn't know why. She also has mercenaries from across the sea in her employ. They will have no mercy and their loyalty is probably the strongest of all because it's based on gold."

"What can we expect from La Dame?"

Matteo shook his head. "That I can't say. She is an unpredictable force."

They rode the rest of the way in silence and when the carriage finally stopped, Etta opened the door.

Towering above was the most magnificent sight she'd ever seen.

It was the castle that had once been her family's home. Destroyed and remade, but still the same.

And she would take it back. La Dame didn't belong here. Bela was the Basiles' realm and it would be until there were no Basiles left to claim it.

The palace sat on a strip of land with a river separating it from the main road. The river carried water from the mountains before narrowing as it reached the cliffs and tumbled over, sending a brilliant waterfall into the sea below. It was almost magical in quality and Etta had to tear her eyes from the sight to look up at the white-faced building that held both her wildest dreams and her greatest fears.

If she somehow survived the night and took up her birthright, would such a place ever feel like home to her? Pierre urged them over the wooden bridge. It creaked underneath her feet. Two massive doors hung open, revealing a long marble adorned hallway. Silk drapes fluttered as a light breeze rushed into the palace.

Each surface was gleaming white and untouched. It was breathtaking. The palace of Gaule was a harsh place in comparison. Tyson caught her eye as if he too had been thinking about the stone fortress across the border.

Their steps echoed along the vacant corridor.

"Where is everyone?" Edmund whispered.

Matteo was the one who answered. "Attendance at the ball is mandatory. Even for servants. They aren't allowed to leave until La Dame gives them permission. Her magic would stop them even if they tried." He gripped Etta's elbow and held her back. "Are you sure about this? The door is right there. We can still try to make an escape."

"I can't." She flattened a hand against the waist of her dress. "La Dame dressed me as a queen tonight. You see that plain as I do. So, I will be a queen. These are our people, Matteo. Yours and mine. After seeing that village, how could you want to forsake them?"

He rubbed his chin and gave a single short nod. "You're right."

She patted his arm. "One thing you'll get used to, Cousin, is that I'm usually right."

Edmund snorted beside her.

Matteo hastened his steps before stopping in front of a row of portraits hanging along the wall. The first was of a handsome man in battle uniform. His blonde hair shone underneath a cap and his eyes held an untold knowledge. But something about the smug set of his lips didn't sit well with her.

"That's Phillip." Matteo pointed to the man.

Edmund gasped in front of the next portrait and when Etta saw what he did, her heart stopped beating. A beautiful woman looked down on them with joy on her face as she danced. That wasn't what stopped Etta. It was the dress. She glanced down over the rose-colored gown she now wore. It had the same embroidered pink design and flowing skirts.

Etta fingered the necklace resting against her skin, an identical match.

She knew who it was without asking. "Aurora," she breathed.

The woman's long, golden hair sat in an ornate style atop her head. No doubt Etta would be wearing the same style if she hadn't shorn off her tresses.

"She's made you into her." Tyson stared with a mix of wonder and fear.

"Aurora and Phillip were the Basiles she cursed. But Aurora died before the true weight of La Dame's vengeance could be felt." Matteo turned away from the portraits.

Etta wasn't prepared for this. Was she supposed to follow in her ancestors footsteps? She knew little of Aurora, but was connected to her. If it hadn't been for them, Bela may not have been destroyed. They betrayed La Dame by crossing into Dracon and stealing from her. They condemned their people, their family to this fate.

Would Etta do the same for Alex? If he were dying, would she choose him over her people?

She hated that she didn't know the answer to that. And in that moment, she knew without a doubt, she loved Alex like Phillip had loved Aurora. She'd protect him always.

She was no different than the king and queen she hated because of the curse that had fallen to her.

Pierre appeared behind them, snapping her from the realizations that shook her to her core. "Come. Now."

In silence, they followed Pierre and Maiya who hadn't said a word since the village. Their betrayal would always burn within her, but this wasn't about them. Not anymore. La Dame was putting her into a role for the grandest act yet. She would play her part well.

If Etta had to become Aurora, she would.

Her glass slippers clacked against the floor in time with her heart. When they reached the wide mahogany doors, they stopped. Music drifted from the hall and Etta steeled herself.

Beckoning Tyson and Matteo forward, she offered them her arms. Edmund would go first and then the Basiles. Together.

The people beyond those doors didn't belong to La Dame. It was time the Basiles claimed their kingdom once more.

The doors opened with a low grown and the music stopped abruptly. The chatter died off as the people turned to stare. A fork clattered against a plate as the rightful queen and princes of Bela stepped forward as one.

CHAPTER 18

"Wonderful," La Dame's voice boomed. "You have arrived." She turned to the crowd. "May I introduce Queen Persinette Basile?"

Gasps rang out in the crowd.

"Here in Bela, Persinette translates into another name. An ancient one." Her lip curled and Etta held her breath. "Join me in welcoming Rapunzel Basile."

An excited chatter wound through the room.

Etta leaned into Matteo. "Did you know?"

He shook his head.

La Dame raised a hand to silence the assembly. "You have all met the princes Matteo and Tyson Basile. Join me in welcoming them back into our fold."

Edmund was ignored as he melted in with the crowd to find any information they could use.

Etta fought for her breath and squeezed Tyson's hand as he shook beside her.

La Dame descended the marble staircase from the balcony and made her way past tables of onlookers and a full orchestra.

When she reached them, she curtsied low. "Your Majesty." She rose with a gleam in her eye. "Not going to curtsy for me? I am Queen of Dracon after all. And almost Queen of Bela too."

Etta gritted her teeth. The only way she'd ever cede Bela was if she was dead, which was a real possibility.

"I have a throne prepared for you." La Dame waved her hand in an arc toward a golden throne.

The crowd parted for Etta to walk through and examine it. "It's identical to the throne in Gaule." It's high back rose up with a line of sapphire jewels stretching across the top. The wide seat lay between two curved arms that had a pattern carved into them. She'd never noticed the details in the chair in Gaule that made the chair look as if it was encircled in golden hair, the jewels at the top acting as the crown.

A grin stretched La Dame's thin lips. "I crafted that one as well. Gaule, Bela, and Dracon have always been connected. They will always be connected."

The cold of the hard throne permeated the fabric of Etta's dress as she sat cautiously, perched on the edge as if she didn't belong.

It was her kingdom. The place where her family's palace had stood. Her ancestors' portraits were even hanging in the hall. But it felt wrong. La Dame flashed her another smile and sat on the smaller throne beside her. The boys were left to stand.

Etta scanned the room, looking for any sign of Alex, just needing to know he was okay. Had the blast of magic in the tower hit him as well? He was nowhere to be seen, but she didn't stop watching for his handsome face.

The dancing began again. Skirts swishing. Feet stomping in time with the beat. Bright smiles plastered across the faces of the revelers. Was anything here real?

Her people looked as if they were enjoying themselves, but something was off. They were prisoners, weren't they?

"I don't see my father." Matteo clasped his arms in front of him, his eyes sweeping the area in front of him.

La Dame's smile didn't waver as she dropped her voice. "Warren was useful to me for a great many years. But with Persinette on the way, I found I had one too many Basiles. Plus, I needed someone to help me make a point to young Alexandre."

A crease formed in Matteo's brow. "He's..."

"Dead, yes. I thought I made that quite clear, Matty boy."

Etta reached out to squeeze his hand and La Dame scowled.

"Sorrow is a useless emotion, Matteo. I'd hate to think you were so weak as to mourn a man who never loved you. I mean, how could he when you killed your mother on the day you were born. Once he learned of Persinette's existence, you meant even less to him because you were not the heir." She regarded him closely. "Cheer up, my boy. I did you a great favor."

Someone walked forward and whispered in La Dame's ear. She got to her feet. "I'll be back."

Etta rubbed her hands up and down her arms, avoiding the eyes that kept flicking toward her throughout the room. No one approached, but they were all aware of her presence.

"Are you okay?" She squeezed Matteo's hand again.

He breathed heavily. "She wasn't wrong. There was little love between my father and me. But for so long, he was the only family I had."

"You've got us now." Tyson clapped him on the shoulder.

"I don't like this." Edmund changed the subject as he leaned against the side of her throne, a clear threat to anyone who even considered coming near. "She didn't bring us here to dance and eat."

"Of course she didn't." Matteo scowled. "She brought us here to destroy a queen."

Someone began to sing and his voice wrapped the room in its warmth. Etta lurched to her feet as Alex came onto center stage. His eyes found her immediately and he gave his head a tiny shake. She couldn't help him.

The song he sang was a mournful melody of loss, but his voice was rich with a deep raspy tone.

A laugh burst from Tyson's mouth and Etta couldn't fault him. In their desperation, what else could they do?

"Did you know he could sing?" Etta asked.

Edmund and Tyson's silence was answer enough. But why was he singing? As soon as the question entered her mind, an answer struck her. It was another of La Dame's humiliations. The king of Gaule had been turned into nothing more than a court performer.

His eyes burned into her as his words made the hair on her arms stand on end.

It was wrong. This was wrong.

She'd come prepared for a fight. Not this.

Where was her sword when she needed it? Oh, right. They'd taken that too. La Dame stood to the side of the stage talking to a few well-dressed attendees, but her eyes never left Etta and one corner of her mouth tilted up into a smirk.

"Etta." Matteo took hold of her arm. "You need to calm down."

"Why?" Etta and Edmund asked at the same time.

Matteo sighed as if he was talking to children. "You two are too impulsive. We're going to take her down, but to do it here would mean putting these people in danger."

It all clicked. Every action. Every word. And Etta understood. La Dame was scared of the legends. Only the ancient power of the Basiles could destroy her. She didn't know Etta possessed little more than parlor tricks.

"She fears me."

Matteo nodded. "And she's counting on your family's history of protecting their people to give her more time."

Etta's jaw clenched, but Edmund pulled her away. "Let's dance."

She tried to stop him. "I don't dance."

"I seem to remember you dancing with a certain king from Gaule. Come on. I need to talk to you."

Pairs parted to give them an ample amount of space and Edmund held out his hand in front of him with a bow. A few ladies nearby sighed. Etta rolled her eyes and took his hand while he put the other on her waist.

"Just playing to the crowd, my dear." He flashed her a dimpled grin, and all sound faded away. Even Alex's words disappeared in the zone of Edmund's magic.

"We want the people here on our side," he explained.

"They will be. I'm their heir."

He spun her around, the glass slippers causing her to stumble. Catching her around the waist, he leaned close. "We need to do something. Matteo wants to let this play out, but we can't sit around while she's within reach."

They danced, and they planned. Everything they'd discussed before the ball, every plot, had dissolved as soon as they arrived. After a few more dances, Alex stepped from the stage and disappeared behind it.

"Go time." Edmund released her and they hurried over to their seats.

"Tyson." Etta grabbed his arm. "I need you to come with me. Matteo, you're with Edmund. It's time we play by our own rules." She turned to Edmund. "I'm counting on you."

Matteo tried to argue, but Etta didn't stay to hear. Instead, she gripped Tyson's hands and pulled him into a dance. "Smile. Act like we're doing nothing but enjoying the ball."

"She'd have to be delusional to believe that," Tyson said.

Her heart slowed dangerously as every one of her muscles waited, praying Edmund wouldn't let her down. He never had before.

The screams began after a few minutes from the far end of the long room. The curtains framing a tall window overlooking the dark, fathomless sea caught fire. Her eyes found Edmund using his magic to fan the flames as Matteo touched a torch to another piece of fabric.

"Come on." Etta started to run. She didn't know where La Dame was, but Edmund would get the people out of the room.

Her feet pounded against marble as she rounded the stage to find Alex sitting on the steps behind it with his head in his hands.

"Alex."

At the sound of her voice, he looked up.

"Come on." Etta reached him, panting. "We have to go."

"You should get out of here, Etta." His voice was bland, emotionless.

"Not without you."

"You can't save me."

She latched onto his arm and started to pull. "Why won't you come? You have to come now. Please, Alex."

He stared through her to his brother. "I can't do that."

She dropped down in front of him and yelled, "Why not?" Tears clogged in her throat. She had him right in front of her and he'd never felt so far away.

"Go. Get out before she traps you."

Etta looked back at Tyson frantically needing some backup, but the torture she saw in his eyes tore at her.

"He can't come." Tyson's voice was quiet.

"What do you mean?" Etta screamed at both of them.

Tyson met his brother's eye. "She told you to sit there, didn't she?"

Alex's shoulders dropped. "Please. Go."

More screams reverberated around the room. "This place is going to go up in flames. You have to come!"

"Persinette." The voice sent a chill down her spine as La Dame found them. "It's no use. I'm quite vexed at you for ruining my ballroom, but it was all for nothing it seems. Your pretty little king is mine and will remain until I release him." She turned. "Alexandre, come."

Alex rose to his feet and followed her without even an argument. Etta ran after them, Tyson close behind.

With a wave of La Dame's hand, the doors to the room slammed shut with a startling finality.

La Dame raised her voice. "Stop screaming." The mob obeyed. "Sit where you are." As one, they dropped to the floor as the flames lit the final curtain, spurred on by Edmund's remaining magic.

"Edmund, come."

Edmund stopped what he was doing and walked mechanically to where they stood. La Dame shoved Alex toward him and ordered them to sit.

Two meaty hands wrapped around Etta's arms and she was forced to her knees, her magic useless when there were no living plants nearby.

Tyson picked up a wine goblet and tossed it into the air, using his magic to expand the wine as it shot like a dagger toward La Dame's chest.

She held up a palm, and it stopped mid-air before dropping to the floor. Her heels clicked as she stepped over the burgundy puddle to face Tyson. "I may not be able to force you to bend to my will, Basile, but I won't have you soiling this room any more than your friends already have. A guard crept up behind Tyson and Etta's scream died in her throat as he knocked him over the head. The prince crumpled as if he had no bones in his body.

Tendrils of smoke wound through the room and the people of Bela began to cough and choke.

"See what you've done?" La Dame asked. "I could put the fire out but I believe in actions having consequences."

"Let them go." Etta ground her teeth together.

"Their fate is of your own making." She turned to the crowd. "The woman you proclaim as queen has betrayed you and sentenced you all to die. Just like Aurora and Phillip."

Etta's eyes drifted down to her dress, realizing for the first time why she was dressed as Aurora. Her ancestors starting the destruction of Bela. La Dame was showing them Etta was no better than them.

La Dame smirked down at her as if she'd won.

"Matty boy," she cooed. "Come to your mother."

"You are not my mother," he spat, not moving an inch.

"Ah, but I raised you. I know you enough to know you hold no power in your blood. It's Persinette who surprises me. I'd assumed a daughter of Viktor would have stronger magic than yours." She paused. "There is one thing she has that you lack, Matty." Her eyes narrowed as she stopped in front of Alex.

"Alexandre, stand." He did.

One of her guards held out a knife to him hilt first.

"Take it."

Once again, Alex obeyed.

Etta watched in horror, her heart pounding painfully against her ribs.

"Good boy." La Dame traced a line on her own arm with her finger and Alex pressed the knife against his skin. Blood beaded around the blade and his hands shook as he tried to fight it.

"Alex," Etta cried. "Please. You can fight her. Don't let her win."

His lips pressed together and sweat broke out across his forehead. His chest heaved with the effort. The blade moved and didn't stop until a design was carved into Alex's arm.

Etta bit back the pain as red lines appeared on her own skin, glowing beneath the surface.

Guilt pooled in the depths of Alex's eyes . Crimson blood ran the length of his arm.

"It's okay." Etta sucked in a breath. Tears pricked the corners of her eyes. "It's okay. I trust you, Alex. I love you. It's okay."

"You shouldn't have come for me."

His words shattered something inside her. She tried to crawl toward him, but La Dame's guards held her in place.

Edmund thrashed beside him on the floor, wanting to break free of La Dame's magic.

"Your concern is touching." Magic shot from La Dame's hand and struck Alex at full force. He flew into the air before slamming back to the ground. Etta felt it all. She screamed as his bones broke.

"Stop!"

Matteo dropped down beside where Etta was now curled in on herself. He pulled her into his arms. "Don't forget who you are," he whispered.

Who she was? She was nothing. A girl who'd failed at the one thing she'd trained her entire life for. Protecting the king. Saving Alex.

Matteo helped her sit up again as pain radiated through every inch of her body. Alex barely moved, but a groan rumbled in his chest.

Edmund balled his hands into fists, but there was nothing he could do while under La Dame's power.

"Why?" Etta screamed. "Why do you want to destroy us? Do you have no soul?"

La Dame laughed, and it angered Etta more. "Your king asked me the same question as I marred every inch of his skin. The Basiles stole everything from me." Her crazed eyes darted between them.

"Everything? Generations ago, Phillip stole a weed to heal his wife and now you're still bent on vengeance. Why don't you kill us off once and for all?"

"Death is too good for those of the Basile line," she sneered. "A weed? You call her a weed? I know the stories. They name the healing weed rampion. But to me, she was Rapunzel."

"She?" Matteo asked desperately.

"Rapunzel was no weed. She was a healer. Phillip Basile stole my daughter and so I have stolen every child of his line."

Tears clung to Etta's lashes. "You lie." As she said the words, she knew how false they were. The truth was written across La Dame's face. Healing magic only existed in Dracon. Phillip doomed Bela by betraying the most powerful woman in the world in the worst possible way.

La Dame's face reddened. "Rapunzel was her name, but it has been translated from Draconian. Persinette."

"No." Etta shook as realization crashed in on her, drowning out everything she thought she knew. Truth always came at a price. She raised her eyes to the powerful woman standing over her as the smoke slithered down her throat. Why would her father name her after the cause of all their family's pain? There had to have been a reason. Had she known the man at all?

Her voice rasped on its way out. "It wasn't us." She covered her mouth with her arm and coughed. "That happened a long time ago."

"Oh, but dear, I made a promise to Phillip Basile. I would see to the torment of his line."

She motioned behind her and Pierre and Maiya came forward. Pierre handed her a bundle Etta recognized instantly.

"Persinette's own sword." La Dame raised an eyebrow. "Fitting." She unwrapped the sword Etta knew well. Every nick. Every imperfection. It was a part of her.

La Dame held up her palm, and the sword rose into the air.

Smoke swirled around the blade and Etta pushed away from Matteo to rise on her knees.

"A curse," La Dame began, her voice dangerous. "Is not supposed to bring happiness. Comfort. The Basile curse is my greatest accomplishment."

Her hand twisted the sword to Alex.

"Take it." The knife he'd been holding clattered to the ground and his fingers closed around Etta's sword.

La Dame no longer smiled. "We are at the end of our game, I'm afraid. Stab the sword through your abdomen."

Etta and Edmund screamed in unison as they could do nothing but watch Alex push the blade through his skin.

The burning began low in Etta's gut and she fell over sideways. "Alex," she cried. Matteo pulled her into his lap and rocked back and forth.

She was still alive. He couldn't be dead. She raised her head to see Alex lying in a pool of his own blood beside Edmund with Tyson barely stirring behind them.

La Dame shrugged. "I don't want him to die yet." She nodded to a woman who stood beside Maiya with the same caramel skin and corkscrew curls. "Esme, keep him alive."

The woman rushed forward and all Etta could do was watch as she went to work healing Alex just enough to keep him alive.

"Why don't you just kill us?" Etta cried.

La Dame's eyes darted around to the flames encroaching on the room. "I don't think I'll need to be the one doing the killing. We're running out of time thanks to your little fire trick. You're going to die, dearest Persinette. But before you do, I'm going to take everything." She scanned the crowd of people who'd begun to pass out from the smoke. "Who knew that in the end, breaking the curse would finally give me vengeance?"

Dark dots swam before Etta's eyes and she could barely breathe, but there was no escape.

A guard yanked her up, and she cried out in pain, wishing they'd let her die. He carried her to Alex's heavily breathing form and dropped her into the sticky path of his blood. She touched him gently, and he opened his eyes.

Bending over him, she leaned her forehead against his. "I love you," she whispered, her tears dripping onto his face. "I will always love you."

He smiled weakly but couldn't speak so she pressed her burning lips to his colder ones as if it was the last thing she'd ever do. It probably was.

"Touching." La Dame's voice made her jerk back. "Before you die, I will take even your love from you."

Etta shook her head violently. "Not even you have that power."

A wall of magic slammed into her from behind, sucking the remaining air from her lungs and pushing her forward. She collapsed onto Alex's chest and everything disappeared.

Etta was out for a moment, but it felt like years. When she opened her eyes, the first thing she saw was flames. Everywhere flames and smoke were killing her people.

The pain was gone.

Alex's eyes drifted shut, but she couldn't bring herself to care. Scrambling from his chest, she turned to face La Dame.

"How does freedom feel?" La Dame leaned forward in anticipation. "You have a few moments of it left."

How did it feel? Etta no longer felt Alex's pain. In fact, she felt nothing at all. No ties to the King of Gaule, no tug on her heart. Instead, she felt… empty.

The emptiness began to fill as a power she'd never known flooded her veins. It buzzed through her, strengthening her resolve. Hatred. Anger. Vengeance. Her mind turned to darkness as the Basile magic took hold.

"Etta." Matteo's voice was awed as he pointed to her arms. Her veins glowed through her skin for a few moments before fading entirely. But the power she felt remained.

Hair brushed her shoulders, and she raised a hand to feel the golden locks as they grew out from where she'd shorn them off. The strands drifted through her fingers and down over her back, light emanating from each.

La Dame's mouth hung open, and she backed up a step.

"The Basile power." Matteo rushed to her side, covering his mouth with his jacket.

Behind them, Tyson woke and got to his feet, slightly disoriented as he positioned himself at Etta's other flank.

Etta's gaze flashed over the crowd almost separated from her by the fire and two familiar faces stood out. Analise lay on her side as Henry swayed where he stood before collapsing amongst the smoke. She was right. Pierre had brought them here. Anger unlike anything she'd ever felt surged through her and red tinged the sight before her.

With a quirk of her lip, power shot from her fingertips and the flames were extinguished in an instant. Etta cocked her head, regarding the woman who'd destroyed her family. Destroyed, yet here they stood. The three remaining Basiles.

She punched her hand forward, throwing La Dame through the air.

La Dame landed on her feet and skidded to a halt with a growl. She sent bolts of magic to each Basile, but Etta blocked them, instinct taking over.

Tyson met Etta's eyes and she nodded. She flicked her finger and a cup of wine flew into the air. Tyson expanded the liquid and Etta set it aflame as it rushed toward the guards who were running to La Dame's defense.

Etta made the flames grow, engulfing the guards in the inferno and it didn't faze her. Her magic whipped around her uncontrollably as adrenaline flooded her veins.

A crack boomed through the room and the floor split open. Etta leaped to avoid getting sucked into the darkness. La Dame threw a bolt of lightning at her and she dodged it.

They stayed, locked in their duel as their magic weakened with each use.

"I can't hold her off forever," Etta yelled to Tyson. She strained to get control, but that dominance seemed just out of reach.

Tyson filled the floor gap with water, pulling it from the ground to keep any of the villagers from being lost. He slumped over from the effort.

Matteo picked up Etta's sword and tilted his head. Etta nodded, and he tossed it into the air for Etta to send it sailing toward La Dame. It hit one of her guards with such force the hilt went straight through him, leaving a hole in the middle of his chest.

"Etta," Edmund yelled. "She's weakening. I can see it."

The villagers started to stir, their screams proof La Dame was losing control.

Matteo wheezed beside her. "She's trying to hold the illusion of the palace while both keeping the villagers under her control and fighting you. It's too much for her."

La Dame stared at them from across the room, her guards closing in around her.

Edmund ran toward them. "I say we take care of her for good."

A steady beat painfully drummed in Etta's head and she leaned over to catch her breath. She could barely feel her magic anymore as weak as it was making her.

The ballroom around them flickered, showing a crumbling ruin—before the ornate, but slightly charred room was back.

Before she could stop it, a spear sailed through the air aiming for Matteo. Everything happened in slow motion. He didn't see it until Edmund lunged for him, tackling him to the ground as the spear embedded in the soft flesh of Edmund's stomach.

He screamed and Etta turned from La Dame to check if Edmund was breathing. Blood dribbled from his lips but his eyes told her to continue the fight.

She pulled on every ounce of magic she had left and twisted around to find the guards disappeared and La Dame with them. Not even Pierre and Maiya were still present.

Her eyes darted around as the room descended into darkness and the palace disappeared altogether, leaving behind the ruins of what had once been the Basile home.

The magic snapped back into her and Etta stumbled forward, dropping to her knees as exhaustion took hold of her body. Around her, people ran. Some screamed. Others didn't know what to do.

"Etta," Tyson called through his tears. "You need to come now."

Alex struggled to keep his eyes open, and each breath was weaker than the one before. He met her emotionless eyes with a similar look. She couldn't decipher what she was feeling. Every memory of her and Alex remained, but all she felt was rage. No other emotion could permeate that red-hot wall of fire inside her. It was as if along with the curse, her love for him had been ripped away. The Durands and Basiles would always be enemies. Her magic hated the Gaulean king. But she couldn't turn away.

"Etta!" Tyson's voice turned frantic. "He's dying, Etta." He wiped his face on his sleeve.

Etta looked from Alex to Edmund, a struggle brewing in her heart. Unable to resist any longer, she knelt down beside Alex. How had something that had made her so happy suddenly fill her with despair? Alexandre Durand was an enemy of her magic. He would always be her enemy. The curse had fooled her into thinking differently.

But she couldn't let him die. Not after everything they'd been through.

"Is anyone a healer?" she screamed to the magic folk who remained.

None came forward. She knew now that healing was a Draconian magic. Her people couldn't help her. A tear fell from her lashes and she met Tyson's swimming eyes with a shake of her head. "I can't help him. I'm so sorry."

Pushing to her feet, she went to check on Edmund.

Her friendship with him remained and when she saw him with his eyes closed, tears rolled down her cheeks.

"Is he…?" She couldn't get the words out.

"Not yet," Matteo answered as he cradled Edmund's head.

Etta sank down beside him and put her head in her hands. Her back heaved.

"So the curse was keeping the Basiles from their magic." Matteo nudged her.

"Matteo, I've never felt that kind of power. It… It was like I could tear the whole world apart." She observed her shaking hands, curling them into tight fists. "Yet, I can't save Edmund or Alex."

"Maybe I can help with that," a soft voice said.

The woman who'd been ordered to help Alex before lowered herself beside Edmund.

"Who are you?" Etta loomed over her.

"My name is Esme. I believe you knew my daughter, Maiya."

"She betrayed us." Etta crossed her arms, but allowed Esme to place her palms against Edmund's abdomen. She couldn't do anything to make it any worse.

"Let me help and then I will explain."

Edmund's wound closed up and before long, he opened his eyes. Etta choked out a relieved laugh and lunged to hug him.

"Take it easy there," Edmund wheezed.

Esme moved to Alex next and then went out among the villagers treating burns and other wounds.

Tyson helped Alex to his feet and steadied him before leading him toward the others. Edmund wrapped Alex in a long hug. Etta kicked a rock on the ground and her glass shoe cracked.

"I can fight La Dame with no problem, but the minute I kick a stupid rock, these damn things break." She shook her head and removed both her shoes. She wrapped an arm around Edmund's waist and another around Matteo as she led them from the ruins, creating a torch to light their way. They stopped at the cliffs and looked to the east where the village should sit, but it was hidden in the night.

Something was missing. There was a hole in Etta's chest. A gap where her heart should be. All she felt was a void, black as the night, and her power.

Without a word to any of them, she turned and walked away, past the ruins and crowds of people who were moving toward the village. Past the unconscious forms of the two friends she'd made promises to in the dungeons. Past the woman who claimed to be the mother of Etta's once-friend. Maiya's betrayal no longer hurt. She felt nothing.

For the first time in her life, she was free, and it weighed down on her, crushing her. She began to run, knowing she could only flee for so long. By the time she reached the tree line, her breath wheezed in her chest. She wiped at her face furiously but the tears were relentless. She stopped running and put a hand on a nearby tree to steady herself as she hiccupped back a sob.

She'd been fully prepared to die. A willing sacrifice. No one considers what happens after the battle. How was she supposed to help her people recover when she was utterly destroyed herself? She'd never imagined breaking the curse would break her as well.

La Dame was still out there. Would she'd return to the mountains of Dracon and resume her duties as La Dame Dracon? Always waiting. The only thing Etta knew was the fight wasn't over. It had only begun.

Etta sank down to the forest floor, the woods more a home to her than any palace could ever be. Drawing on the smallest amount of power she had left, she pulled budding flowers through the pine needles that covered the ground. Only three grew at her bidding, but it was enough to remind her who she was and who she could become.

This power that had belonged to her ancestors before her, it churned and boiled. She held it down, but the ire it evoked could not be so easily kept away.

Supplies were consolidated and moved to the only structures still standing in Bela. The small village. It was a quiet night with most people still stunned from events of the day.

Etta and Edmund stood on guard most of the night, despite their exhaustion. They didn't trust that La Dame had taken all of her men with her.

Etta's long sword hung at her waist and as she fingered the hilt, she pictured it sliding into Alexandre's stomach. The memory was tainted now. La Dame's magic had forced the action upon him, but her own magic wished for it as well. Why had she been so adamant to save him?

No. She couldn't let herself think that. It wasn't her. The damn power would not control her. None of her memories were gone, they were just altered. The magic twisted everything. She'd been sleeping with her charge, nothing more. Despite her position in his palace, he was not a friend to her family. He'd persecuted her people, killed and imprisoned them. Hell, she'd experienced his dungeons for herself.

The Basile in her wanted to hate him, but as hard as she tried, she couldn't. Still, she couldn't pick out the love between waves of confusion and resentment. Maybe it had only been effects of the curse after all.

A Gaulean king didn't belong in Bela, her magic pleaded.

Why couldn't she despise him?

She scanned the darkness, still searching for a single face. Vérité wouldn't have found his way to the village stables without seeking her first. He'd find her. He always did.

A voice cleared behind them and she turned abruptly, preparing to draw her sword.

"King Alexandre," she barked. "Do not sneak up on a soldier in the dark."

Dark brows drew together. "Etta…"

Edmund put a hand on her shoulder. "I'm going to give you two a few minutes." He walked away before she could stop him.

Alexandre inclined his head formally, and she did the same before an uncomfortable silence stretched between them.

He studied her for a long moment before grabbing her roughly and kissing her. She hit him but he didn't stop. Sliding her hand down to his waist, she pulled the knife he had stuck there and held it to his neck.

He pushed her away. "Etta..." He closed his eyes with a sigh. "It's me."

"I know very well who you are, Alexandre Durand."

"You would kill a king?" Amusement flashed across his face. Did he think they were playing a game?

"One who kisses me against my will? Yeah, I think I would." She pulled back the knife but didn't give it to him. "Why did you kiss me, Durand?" Did his feelings change as the curse broke?

He ran a hand through his thick hair. "I don't feel it anymore." He clutched at his chest.

"Feel what? Love?" Her magic curled in disgust.

His eyes widened, and he grabbed her shoulders. "Etta, I will love you for as long as I live. It's the curse. I... we aren't connected anymore, are we?"

She pushed away from him. "No." Sheathing her knife, she couldn't meet his eyes. Everything inside of her screamed that she should take her chance and cut him down where he stood. It was a new feeling and the strength of the power, it's ability to turn her thoughts, scared her.

"Etta." Alex brushed her hair back over her shoulder. "Your hair... it glowed."

She brushed off his hand. "Don't touch me." The words were not her own. "A Gaulean king is not welcome on this side of the border. I am a Basile, I could not love you."

His face pinched in sadness and he shook his head. "You don't mean that."

Did she? Her magic reveled in the words, but the rest of her didn't know. Yet she couldn't stop them from spilling forth. "Do not question my words. I am Persinette Basile. I have more power than you could ever imagine. Everything I felt for you was just the curse masking my real feelings. Your kingdom is on the brink of a civil war. You will leave in the morning to return to Gaule."

"Why are you doing this?"

She narrowed her eyes. "I never speak just to hear my own voice, King. This discussion is over." She turned away from him, afraid to see any emotion in his eyes.

Alex was silent for a long moment before the low timber of his voice rumbled through the air. "I have no choice but to return to Gaule. In that, you are correct, but this isn't you, Etta." His voice thickened. "We can find our way back. The curse didn't make me love you. I don't want to say goodbye like this, but you give me no other choice. Fight it Etta. Fight whatever is turning you to stone. When you're finished and there is no more will left in you, I will fight for you. I'll never give up. You are more than this." He began walking away and then paused. "This is not the end, Etta."

Edmund returned, clapping Alex on the back as they passed each other. "Have you guys kissed and made up?"

"Leave it alone, Edmund." Etta's eyes scanned the surroundings. She brushed a few errant tears away.

"You came all this way and risked everything to save him. What is going on?"

"He means nothing to me." The magic-tainted words slid out easily. "As with everything La Dame has done, it was an illusion. Magic makes us believe in realities that don't exist."

"I saw how much you loved him. I can't accept that it's all gone."

She hiccupped back a sob, her knees suddenly crumpling beneath her. They hit the soft earth, and she clutched her arms across her chest as if that would hold her together and keep the hate from overwhelming her.

"I can't..." she cried. "Edmund."

He knelt beside her and folded her into his arms.

Alex was leaving. Even as Etta's magic rejoiced, her heart clenched traitorously. For as long as she could remember, she'd wanted to break the curse, never imagining it would free the Basile magic within her.

Power should have meant freedom.

But now she knew it was only a new set of chains.

Alex sprinted across the open field to recover two of the horses that had been in the stables. They didn't run from him, but the second one snapped at his hand as soon as he grabbed his mane.

Verité.

Damn horse.

He gave up and started leading the first one back to the others. Verité followed close behind.

Persinette's eyes lit up when she saw him, the first sign of real life he'd seen in her since her battle with La Dame.

It struck him like a cudgel how beautiful she truly was. No. He rubbed his eyes. If he continued to stare, he'd never be able to leave. His people needed him. Etta didn't. She'd made that very clear. Maybe they'd been doomed from the start.

My fierce Etta. His own words came back to him and he tried to decipher the feeling behind them. Had she truly never loved him? He imagined them together. Her smooth skin under his fingers. The way she'd softened when she was alone with him. With everyone else, she'd been hard, cold.

They'd recovered five horses and a myriad of supplies once the sun had risen

Many of the people had been taken from his own kingdom against their will. Others had fled into Bela to escape the Gaulean people. He'd had a hand in pushing them toward La Dame and for that, he would always be filled with guilt.

The people avoided him. Persinette wouldn't speak to him. He shouldn't want to speak to her either. It would be too hard. Would the Belaens crown her queen? It was her birthright, but he couldn't picture her sitting atop a throne giving orders.

No, she belonged on the front lines.

A place he'd never been allowed to be. There might not even be a throne for him to return home to. Even if there was, the thought of living the rest of his life in that palace chilled him. He wasn't the same man that was drugged and kidnapped. He'd been beaten, thrashed by magic, and ripped from a curse that had all but consumed him.

Edmund chuckled as Verité tried to nip at Alex again. Alex scowled at his friend.

Edmund hid his grin as he patted Verité's neck and the horse leaned into his touch. They'd formed a reluctant friendship since Verité helped Edmund escape from the palace. Escape from the dungeons Alex had put him in.

Alex reached up to rub the back of his neck as the horse he'd been leading was taken from him. "Look, Edmund—"

"Stop, Alex." Edmund put a hand on his arm. "I don't want your apology. I want you to go take back your kingdom."

"I need you by my side."

"No, you don't. Gaule isn't my home. Not anymore. I have to stay with Etta. These are my people."

Alex pulled him into a hug. "I'm your people too. Don't forget that."

"Never."

Alex grunted and pulled back to find Persinette studying him.

"You must get on the road." She jerked her head toward the horses being saddled. "Your escorts are ready. The faster you are out of my kingdom, the better."

She waved her hand and three packs appeared on the ground. "Supplies."

"Thank you." He nodded.

"Don't thank me. As the king of Gaule, if you set foot in Bela again, I won't hold my people back and every single one of them wants you dead."

He swallowed the knot in his throat as Edmund shook his head sadly. Tyson appeared next to him, staring daggers at Persinette.

"What about me?" he asked. "I am a prince of Gaule. Would you have me killed?"

She couldn't meet his eyes. "You are a Basile. Bela is your kingdom."

"So is Gaule."

His spine straightened, and he squared his shoulders, but Alex didn't miss the sadness in his eyes. "I'm going with Alex. He is my king. His duty is to save Gaule from itself and my duty is to stand by his side."

She met his eyes and the look in them struck something in Alex's heart. There was an emptiness inside of her. After everything they'd been through, she was the one who was broken. All the Basile power she now possessed couldn't fix what La Dame had taken from her.

"You're my brother." Her voice was calm, devoid of emotion.

Tyson's was the opposite. Everything he was feeling was infused into his words as he lowered his voice. "And he's my brother."

"Go." Etta turned away. Before leaving, she spoke once more. "Bela has a greater foe than the boys of Gaule."

It was meant to be an insult, but it served as a shock back into reality. There was a long road ahead of them and the fight was far from over.

Alex and Tyson mounted their horses and rode between two guards. In a few days, they'd reach Gaule and none of them knew what they'd find when they got there. He hoped he wasn't too late.

The mountains cast a shadow over every word they spoke. La Dame was there behind the high walls blocking off the mountain paths of Dracon.

Etta crouched in the sand beside the edge of the ocean using her magic to pull the waves in closer. They crashed at her feet, splashing up onto the worn brown trousers she wore.

In the days following the battle, she'd regained her strength, but hadn't begun exploring her new power. She'd tried once and the anger it brought forth frightened her. She refused to let it change her any more than it already had and the only way to prevent that was to keep every bit of magic locked down deep inside her.

Her people looked to her for leadership, knowing once word reached Gaule of their victory, more descendants of Bela would flood their village.

The palace would not be rebuilt. She refused to even think about that after everything that happened there.

A briny breeze lifted her hair, and she closed her eyes. It was time for her to claim her birthright.

Lines of people covered the beach behind her and as she stood, she turned to face them. There were no nerves as she'd expected. No emotions. Only acceptance.

Edmund and Matteo walked forward to each take an arm, leading her to stand in the circle of Belaens. It closed around her.

She focused her magic on the sand, molding and shaping it until a golden crown sat gleaming in the sun. Each point dipped and curved gracefully. It was simple. No jewels. No etchings. Just like her people. They'd suffered and remained strong. They had been loyal to her family for generations.

The crown before her was not a signal that they belonged to her.

It let the world know she belonged to them.

Her knees hit the sand, and she bowed her head. Matteo, one of the three last remaining Basile's, lifted the crown from the sand.

His voice rang out among the crowd. "I once thought freedom didn't exist. What I didn't realize is that it's not something that just happens to you. You must take it. Today we take our freedom. Bela is our kingdom. There will be many dark days ahead, but they cannot take it from us."

He lowered his eyes to Etta. "Persinette Basile, you have always been our queen. You've fought for us. Bled for us. Given your life to the curse that marked our family. Before you faced La Dame, I told you there is no freedom in death. Now, in life, you can have every freedom, every honor. The Basile power has returned to these lands and we believe in you."

He leaned down and set the crown atop her head. Her magic raced beneath her skin, glowing in recognition of her finally accepting the role she was meant to play.

The crowd gasped as the sand flew into the air, spinning around her. Her heart beat slowly, accepting the power rather than fearing it. Her hair tugged and pulled as it flew out behind her wildly.

She stood, and the sand settled back to the earth, revealing queen Persinette Basile with her long glowing golden hair and a determined set to her mouth.

Her eyes flashed as she beheld the mountains once more, feeling her people move in closer.

They were only in the beginning of their fight. For she was Persinette Basile. Daughter of the kingslayer. Ex-cursed. Queen of Bela. Keeper of the Basile magic. And the magic folk always had greater battles to wage.

EPILOGUE

Maiya stared into the face of Rapunzel where her portrait hung in the great entranceway of La Dame's mountain palace. The depth of sadness in the woman's eyes, matched her own.

Dracon was not her home.

She didn't remember her time there as a child and as she wandered the streets of stone, she couldn't help feeling out of place.

She'd betrayed the one person she'd ever truly loved. A woman who was meant to be queen of Bela. A queen she could have followed with her whole heart.

Glancing to the side, she caught her father talking to one of the guards. They'd been called from their cold, ugly one-room home to attend La Dame. A chill swept through her but it didn't dim the fire of regret.

Maiya had never known her mother. She never imagined she'd been born of someone so close to La Dame. But Esme had found a way out. She'd stayed in Bela when Maiya hadn't been given the chance to.

Had her mother even thought of her?

Her shoulders sagged and her curls bounced around her face as she turned.

"Maiya," her father said sternly. He'd never been stern before returning to Dracon. "Come. We can't make La Dame wait."

She followed her father down the long hall. Two uniformed guards stood outside ornate cherry wood double doors. A dragon was carved across them.

The doors were opened, and they entered the torch-lit room. Pillars lined the walls, black as night. Deep red velvet carpeting created a path to the golden throne.

La Dame sat casually twisting her dark hair around a finger. When she caught sight of them, a smile curved her lips.

"Pierre," she said. "Maiya. So good of you to come."

Pierre bowed and jerked Maiya into a curtsy.

"It is our pleasure, your Majesty."

La Dame's eyes latched onto Maiya and she squirmed under the scrutiny.

"Hello," La Dame said sweetly. "I haven't had the chance to speak with the girl who brought me Persinette."

"I didn't bring her to you," she mumbled.

"What was that, dear?"

"She came to save Alex."

"Ah yes. She loved him very much. It was interesting to watch. But she didn't have power then. She didn't know what it was like to feel it inside her, grasping for more." She tapped her chin. "But she will. Persinette Basile will come to me."

"Don't hurt her." The words were out before Maiya could stop them.

"Maiya," her father snapped.

La Dame held up a hand. "It's okay. Rest assured, I do not plan to harm Persinette... much. I simply want to make her see what she can be. Now that the Basile power has returned to this land, we have a chance at greatness."

"We?"

The woman smiled. "Persinette reminds me very much of my Rapunzel. Viktor named her after my girl for reasons I will not share with you. Yet. I never imagined the Basile power would return, but I have waited to find it. I am a patient woman. I will wait a while longer for the power inside her to draw her to our walls." She stood. "Until then, dear Maiya, you will take your mother's place in my household."

Maiya opened her mouth to protest, but La Dame held up a hand and suddenly she couldn't breathe.

"Apparently, your father didn't have time to teach you manners in Gaule."

Pierre hung his head as his daughter choked beside him.

"No mind." La Dame walked toward them. "We have no need of him, anyway." A blast of power shot out of her and Maiya tried to scream as her father collapsed to the ground.

She fell to her knees, and the breath whooshed back into her. Scrambling to her father's side, she knew it was already too late. Tears clogged her throat.

La Dame bent down and lifted Maiya's chin with one long finger. "Don't cry. You didn't need him any longer, dear. There comes a time when a woman must stand on her own. You'll see." She straightened. "Now, we wait."

"For what?" Maiya held back another sob.

"For Persinette to give in to the river of magic inside her. For her to sink under the current and rise as my equal. Our power creates two parts of a whole. Don't worry, dear. She will come to me and together, we will be unstoppable."

ACKNOWLEDGMENTS

We all know magic doesn't exist - at least in this form. Curses are a thing of fantasy.

But chains… those are very real. We all feel them. Whatever is holding us back, controlling us.

But we get little glimpses of freedom brought on by the people in our lives.

Thanks to everyone who helps me break free of my chains. This series is only possible because of you. This life is only possible because of you.

Magic may be a fairytale … but sometimes, it sure feels real.

www.ingramcontent.com/pod-product-compliance
Lightning Source LLC
Chambersburg PA
CBHW030526310726
48979CB00010B/1821/J

* 9 7 8 1 9 7 0 0 5 2 6 7 1 *